**W9-AIA-830**

Dec '14

# DIRTY WINGS

ALSO BY

SARAH McCARRY

ALL OUR PRETTY SONGS

# DIRTY
# WINGS

SARAH McCARRY

ST. MARTIN'S GRIFFIN ⚓ NEW YORK

DIRTY WINGS. Copyright © 2014 by Sarah McCarry. All rights reserved. Printed in the United States of America. For information, address St. Martin's Press, 175 Fifth Avenue, New York, N.Y. 10010.

www.stmartins.com

Designed by Anna Gorovoy

Excerpt from *About a Girl* copyright © 2014 by Sarah McCarry.

The Library of Congress Cataloging-in-Publication Data is available upon request

ISBN 978-1-250-04938-4 (hardcover)
ISBN 978-1-250-02710-8 (e-book)

St. Martin's Griffin books may be purchased for educational, business, or promotional use. For information on bulk purchases, please contact Macmillan Corporate and Premium Sales Department at 1-800-221-7945, extension 5442, or write specialmarkets@macmillan.com.

First Edition: July 2014

10  9  8  7  6  5  4  3  2  1

*for cristina; here's to bad decisions*

*wipe your eyes*    *and be glad you're still among the living*

—CRAIG ARNOLD,
FROM "HYMN TO PERSEPHONE"

*La musique savante manque à notre désir.*

—RIMBAUD

# NOW:
# BIG SUR

*Before any of this,* she thinks, *there was the kind of promise a girl just couldn't keep.* Before the bad decisions, before the night sky right now so big, so big it's big enough to swallow the both of them, before her hands shaking *stop shaking stop shaking stop shaking.* She is standing at the precipice of a cliff, the edges of her vision sparking out into static, the heaving sea below her moving against the rocky shore with a roar. The wind is wild in her ears, singing her down. Not even the work of a jump. Just let yourself tip backward, let it go. Before any of this, was there ever a chance for something else? The lowering moon swollen huge. Her hands ache, longing and more than longing. *If there were chords that said this.* Out there beyond the farthest reach of the world, out at the edge of everything, he is waiting for her. White face and long black coat and the knife-thin beckon of his mouth. His eyes darker than all the dark around her. The promise of him: honey flowing from the cracked earth, a crown of stars at her brow. The wildness of her despair at last made quiet. In her nostrils the heady tang of blood. A dog howls in the dark, three times. She can see the black palace on the white plain, its hundreds of doors open to welcome the night in. She takes a step forward. *You can play again,* he says. *Play for us. You can play for all the years of the long night in my kingdom.*

"Hey, princess," says the familiar voice behind her. "Come on. Come back from there." A hand takes hers, pulling her away from the brink. "What are you doing? You're going to fall." Cass's touch is insistent, bringing her back to her own skin, the solid earth under her bare feet. The madness leaches slowly out of the night. A car door slams somewhere behind her in the campground; a child shouts. "Maia. Come on. Girl. Come away from the edge." She shudders, thinks of leaping free like a deer, plunging into the abyss, and then the spell of Cass's gentle hands on her bare skin brings her back to herself and her twitching limbs still.

*What did I almost just do,* she thinks. *Oh god, no, I don't want to fall,* even as she stumbles backward, her clumsy feet carrying her away from the precipice. Back to the campfire's kind glow, their tent, Cass's arms around her, Cass's soft voice in her ear, murmuring, "Come on, princess, one foot after the other, come on. Nice and slow."

*I will wait for you, child,* he says, his voice deep as stone in the heart of her. *I will wait. You will play for us.*

*No,* she says.

But even in the circle of Cass's arms she can see his smile.

# THEN

Oscar is wearing his white suit today and he's unhappy with her. "Again," he says. "This passage. We will play only this passage, until it is correct."

He doesn't mean "we." He means her. His disappointment is like a rain cloud filling the room, drizzling resignation across his neat features and tiny frame. In the white suit he looks even more like a child: his ageless face unlined, though Maia knows he's at least fifty, his snowy hair still thick and unruly, his eyes bright and alert as an owl's. And as dispassionate.

"Do you see," he says, pointing to the page, in a tone that clearly indicates she does not. "Here is the song, here in the left hand. You bury it. We listen and we ask ourselves, 'Where is the story? Where is the beauty in this piece?' It is like listening to something that is, how do you say. Muddy. You play this and it is a wall of mud, Maia." Oscar's English is perfect; he's lived in the States for decades. But he likes hamming it up when he's displeased.

"No mud," she repeats dutifully.

"The mud is agonizing to me, Maia."

She nods. Sets her hands at the keys. Plays the arpeggios for him again, and again, and again, each time faster, each time more precise, as though by mastering the passage with near-inhuman speed she can somehow open up whatever it is that's closed in her. When she plays it for a tenth time Oscar gestures to her to keep going and she surges forward, borne away by her own momentum, the notes rolling off her fingers, the music pounding through her and tumbling across the keys. When she's played through the étude, Oscar straightens the lapels of his white suit and leans back in his chair.

"You are very good," he says after a long silence. "You know this. You are the most gifted student I have taught in many years. You work. You practice. You are serious. You have the ability to make a career. Even now, if we were not here"—he makes a sweeping gesture that encompasses the entirety of his house, the city, the backward corner of the world in which they have found each other—"if we were not here, and lived in a real place, a place of culture, who knows what would happen for you already. But you know what I am about to tell you. I say this to you always."

"No emotion."

"No emotion. Tell me, what is it you are so afraid of?" She is silent. "You will not tell me. This is unfortunate." His French accent thickens. "*Chérie.* You mustn't think as much as you think. You must breathe it. You must trust it with your own hands. This is why we practice and practice and practice, so that the notes become our own, so that we inhabit them until it is as though we wrote them ourselves. Until we see through to the other side. We are not *draft oxen.* It is not enough to *work.* Anyone can work. If you were only to work it would be better for you to shovel a ditch, do you see? For to only work, it is never to be great, and if you are never to be great there is no point in trying. You pick a profession that is sensible and have little babies and a house." He says "babies" with a tone of utter disgust. "This is all clear to you?"

"I want to be great," Maia says.

"I know this, I know you do. I see it in you. You look at me, here, all alone, I play for children. I do not mean you. For these wretched children with their runny noses, every day they come to me, their parents say, 'Oscar, you make my child a musician,' and I say in my heart, 'I cannot make a peasant into the queen of France.' You must not end up like me. Broken and old. I could also have been great. I will never be great now. I am a sad man with a sad life, which I have ruined for myself, as you know. But you, child, your life is ahead of you."

"I'll try."

He purses his lips. "It is not a matter of *try.* Come, let us end on a pleasant note, if you will forgive me a little pun. Play for me Chopin's Sonata in B-flat Minor. Just a little of the funeral march, if you please, to soothe my sad old heart. Do you know Schumann said that this piece had something repulsive about it? It only goes to show you that there are Philistines in even the most unexpected places. But of course, now we remember Schumann as a man who could have been one of the greatest composers of the nineteenth century if only he had been *coherent,* which is not a criticism we *apply* to Chopin, is it."

"No, I guess we don't," Maia says.

Oscar is placated by the Chopin and releases her at last. She gathers her things and he escorts her to the door, as he always does, though she's spent countless hours of her life in this house, knows the worn path from the piano to the front door so well she could mark it out with her eyes closed. Oscar's creaking old Victorian is nothing like her own beige-carpeted house with its white walls and spotless floors. Even now, the cleaning lady is probably bleaching counters, scrubbing toilets, washing already-clean white sheets. Oscar's house is an oasis of shabby majesty, littered with books and papers and dirty coffee cups, overflowing ashtrays teetering precariously atop stacks of newspapers and notebooks and sheet music. When she was little, he'd let her linger after her lessons in his enormous library—an entire room full of nothing but books, crammed shelves stretching from the floor to the ceiling, books spilling over into piles on the floor. Books in French and English and Spanish and Italian, books about music and history and gardening and cooking. A disintegrating leather-bound set of the complete works of Balzac, translated into English, that she'd devoured in the drowsy afternoons until he sent her home to practice. Biographies of Ravel and Debussy and Chopin and Fauré, Rimbaud and Baudelaire, Oscar's own teacher Nadia Boulanger. (She has seen him mimic her countless times; when someone asks him what he thinks of something Maia knows he finds distasteful, he says, vaguely, "Oh! You know what I think about *that*.") A battered paperback of *Les trois mousquetaires* that she'd struggled through in the original French. If Oscar was happy with her he would read passages aloud in a hilarious, affected baritone.

The rooms in Oscar's house are papered with ancient, hand-painted wallpaper, once grand but now peeling in long strips from the walls. His dusty wooden floors are scattered with threadbare Oriental carpets, piled three or four deep; the windows are hung with velvet drapes, in some places so worn that light drifts through them to stain the dark floors gold. The disorder of Oscar's house is like a sanctuary. No one here to follow after her with a dustcloth, check the soles of her feet for dirt, demand she remake the bed until the spread lies without a single wrinkle, the ruffles falling from the decorative pillows just so. Not that Maia has friends who might see the dust ruffle askew. Oscar can pick a single bad violinist out of a symphony orchestra, but Maia cannot imagine him noticing if she moved a pile of dirt into his kitchen with a bulldozer.

Only Oscar's front room, the piano room, is tidy. Oscar keeps his immense Hamburg Steinway—Maia has no idea how much it cost, or how he'd afforded it—polished mirror-clean. No rugs on the swept floor, no shelves on the walls, no tables littered with teapots and packs of the Gauloises that his cousin sends him from Paris by the carton. No paintings, no chip-eared busts of famous composers, no highball glasses with sticky smears of bourbon at their bottoms. Just the piano and Oscar's armchair, where he has sat and watched her play three times a week for the last fourteen years.

"Listen," he says now, one hand coming to rest lightly on her shoulder. "I wish for you to play something new."

"Okay." She stands the way her mother hates, one foot turned inward, resting her weight on its outside edge. He takes his hand away and disappears into the other room for a moment, returns with a sheaf of sheet music.

"*Gaspard de la nuit?*" She riffles through the pages. Ravel, three movements. She can tell at a glance that it's harder than anything she's ever played.

"It is, how do you call." She resists the urge to roll her eyes. "*Difficile.*"

"*Comme tous les autres.*"

He laughs. "*Bien sûr, chérie.* We will begin with the first movement. '*Ondine,*' you will play for me next week. I wish you to play it for your audition." He means her audition for the music conservatory in New York he has chosen for her, the audition this spring that will decide the course of her future. "It must make you think of demons and that sort of thing."

"What?"

He clicks his tongue against his teeth. "Demons. Demons and ghosts."

She keeps her face neutral, wonders if Oscar's shucked straight off his rocker. "Demons. Okay."

He beams, pats her shoulder. "Demons. Next week."

"Next week." As always, when he holds the front door open for her she almost curtsies.

It must have rained while she was at Oscar's; the sidewalks are slick and slug-streaked, and there's still a faint mist to the world that leaves her cheeks dewy. If she walks home it'll take her an hour and there will probably be hell to pay, but she's restless for no reason, too antsy to wait for the bus that won't come for another twenty minutes at least anyway. She tucks Oscar's music into her shoulder bag. She can walk along the canal and cut over to the university before she reaches the freeway.

The January air has a chilly, damp edge to it, and she pulls her jacket tighter as she walks. The streets are deserted. Her brown loafers make a neat tap on the wet pavement. She's tempted to step deliberately in a puddle, take some of the shine off the polished leather, but even tiny rebellions never go unnoticed in her house. Sit up straight, cross your legs like a lady, chew with your mouth closed, speak when spoken to. The severe line of her mother's unsmiling mouth, immaculately lipsticked in her immaculate white face. Tasteful pearl earrings, silk blouses without a single wrinkle, the delicate gold cross always at her throat. Blond hair pinned back into a neat chignon if she's teaching, spilling down her shoulders in rich honeyed waves if she's going out. The click of her heels—never in the house, never ever on the floors; no one wears shoes in the house. Her cool green eyes. When Maia was little, her mother dressed her like a doll, ruffled pinafores and starched collars and a red wool coat that buttoned all the way to her throat; Maia dreams about that coat sometimes, dreams where she's choking. Her mother dresses her still. It's easier than fighting and anyway, what does she care about clothes. When she sees herself in a mirror, her dark hair sleek and straight, twins of her mother's pearl earrings—a sixteenth-birthday present from her father—dotting her own ears, pressed khakis, the loafers with their tassels falling neatly over her instep, she sometimes fails to recognize herself. And then she sees her brown face and remembers. Her skin makes it hard to forget.

She stops by the canal for longer than she should to watch a yacht make its stately way toward the Sound. Even this early in the year the water's dotted with kayakers, wetsuited against the chill. Their boats flash bright yellow and orange against the grey water, double-bladed paddles dipping with a rhythm like wings. Her father took her kayaking once, when she was small. They'd both been clumsy, splashing more water than they moved through; Maia nearly upended herself in the lake. Shrieking with delight, sun hot on her shoulders, the white sails of a nearby boat crisp against the blue sky. The water so close to her fingers, that far from shore, was disconcerting. If she'd fallen she could have tumbled endlessly through that deep green world to some alien kingdom at the bottom of the lake, where fish-finned women swam with their long hair streaming behind them. A palace she could almost picture, dark turrets rising against the darker depths. But there's no fear in the memory, only joy. When she thinks of darkness, she thinks of sleep, not death. The moments of her life when she was happy are easy for her to catalogue, because there are so few of them that aren't at a piano. She keeps walking.

It takes less time than she thought it would to reach the Ave, and she wonders why she's never walked home from Oscar's before. If she hurries, she might even beat her mother home from her afternoon seminar. Her mother teaches the history of ancient Greece; it's easy to impose order on dead civilizations. Maia's never sat in on one of her classes, but she can imagine the scene. Her mother, starkly beautiful, moving her elegant hands to illustrate the difference between kinds of spears. The front row of desks crowded with admirers writing down her every word.

Despite the chill in the air, the Ave is crowded. Students laden with books hurry to classes; a couple of jocks play Hacky Sack outside a coffee shop; a patch of scraggly street kids trailing hemp ropes and mangy dogs begs for change on a corner. Maia looks away from them, walks faster as she passes. One girl calls out to her. "Hey, princess. Spare a quarter?" Maia pulls her shoulders up to her ears. But the voice gets louder. "Hey, princess. You got somewhere to be?"

Maia stops. The girl's gotten up to follow her. She's about Maia's age, with wild-cropped blond hair dyed red at the ends. She's wearing a dog collar as a necklace, a filthy T-shirt under a cardigan three sizes too big for her, and a pair of camouflage pants tucked into black combat boots. But the most striking thing about her is her eyes—sea-grey pools Maia can't look away from. "You got somewhere to be?" the girl repeats. Maia shakes her head. Then, pan-icked, she nods. "Which one is it?"

"Somewhere," Maia whispers. "Somewhere to be."

The girl looks her up and down. "Tea party? Etiquette lesson? Damn, girl, who put you in those shoes?"

"I don't have any money."

"Someone you know does." The girl's mouth twitches into a smile that's gone so fast Maia wonders if she imagined it. "Come on. Help me out."

"I really don't."

"Then at least do me a tiny favor. Look, I'm not from here. I need directions."

"Directions where?"

"Complicated directions. I need a map. Can you get me a map?"

"A map?" Maia repeats.

"You dressed like a stockbroker *and* deaf? Hello, cruel world. I bet they have some kind of map in that convenience store. Of the area. Or the state. State parks. Like, any kind of map. But listen, you don't know me, right? So don't act like you know me. Because you don't. Come on."

"I told you I don't have any money."

"Then get me a free one."

The girl propels Maia with one hand toward a convenience store across the street. Bemused, Maia lets herself be directed. Once they're inside, the girl whips her hand away and saunters over to the beer aisle, whistling. She pulls bottles out of the refrigerated case, puts them back again.

Maia looks for a rack of maps, doesn't see any. "Excuse me?" she says to the man at the register. He's watching the girl with a wary eye, doesn't notice her. "Excuse me?" she repeats, louder. He looks at her. "Do you have maps?"

"Maps of what?"

"Of, um, the area? Like a tourist map?"

Now he's irritated. "I look like a tourist to you, kid?" The girl is rummaging through bags of chips. "Hey!" he yells at her. "You ain't got money. I know you kids. Come on, get the hell out of here."

"No crime being in the aisle," she snaps back.

"It is if I say it is. Get."

She storms up to the cash register, knocking Maia aside with the full weight of her slight body. Maia can smell her skin. Sweat and underneath it something musky and wild. "I could call the cops on you," she hisses. "Fucking old perv."

The man at the register has gone from cranky to irate. "I mean it! Get the hell out of my store!"

She lifts her chin. Despite the dirt, the ragged clothes, she looks like a queen. "I go where I want," she says softly, and then she walks out the door. The man at the register scowls.

"Goddamn street kids," he mutters. "Someone oughta exterminate the lot of 'em. What kind of map you want, honey? I got a street map."

"You have any free maps?"

"*Free* maps? Go to the goddamn *library*." He stares at her in disgust. For the first time it occurs to her to wonder why the girl didn't ask for her own map.

"Okay," she says. "Thanks anyway." He snorts.

Outside, the girl is waiting for her in an alley down the block, one foot against a brick wall. She's smiling for real this time, a smile that's not going anywhere. Her teeth are fetchingly crooked.

"I didn't get your map."

The girl puts both hands on her knees and hoots. Maia is bewildered by her reaction. "I bet you didn't," she says, still laughing. "It's cool. Let me see your bag."

"No way," Maia says. "Look, I don't know what your deal is, but I'm going to go."

"Sure thing, princess. Just one minute, though." The girl pushes off with her foot and in one swift movement reaches into Maia's shoulder bag before she can protest. To Maia's utter astonishment, she pulls out two bottles of beer.

"Where did those come from?" Maia gasps.

"You stole them."

"I didn't steal anything!"

"What did you think I was doing in there? Coloring? Come on, girl, don't tell me you're that dumb."

"I didn't—"

"You did. That deserves a drink, don't you think? Come on." The girl takes her hand, tugs her down the alley. Maia knows to say no. Maia knows to get the hell out of here, right now, get home, never come back to this corner again as long as she lives. The girl pries the bottles' caps off with a lighter and holds one out to Maia. "It's just a beer," she says gently. "It won't bite you." Maia accepts the bottle gingerly, as if she expects it to detonate in her hand.

"I'm Cass," the girl says. "Short for Cassandra. The bitch who knew everything and no one would listen to."

"I know who Cassandra was. I'm Maia." She takes a sip, nearly spits it out. Beer foams over the lip of the bottle.

"You ever even drink before?" Maia shakes her head mutely, mortified.

"Well then. It's a day of firsts for you." That grin again.

"How did you even—I mean, I didn't even see you. You did it when you bumped into me?"

Cass rolls her eyes. "You live near here?"

"Up by the college."

"Fancy."

Maia shrugs. "My mom's a professor. My dad—" She stops. What is there to say about her dad? "My dad's a writer."

"Fancier and fancier."

"Where do you live?"

"I squat a place with some kids."

"You squat?" Maia imagines a roomful of dirty girls like Cass, crouched down on their haunches.

"You know, like an abandoned building that we moved into?" Maia's face is blank with incomprehension. "Girl, where are you *from*? Do you know anything?"

"I know lots of things," Maia says, indignant.

"Different things than I know, I guess. Anyway, it's an old house that no one was living in. Some people I know took it over, and I live with them."

"Those people back there? With the dogs?"

"Some of them. People come and go."

"You said you weren't from here."

"I lied. You know how it is."

Maia has absolutely no idea how it is, cannot begin to imagine how it is. How does this girl eat? Take baths? What does she do for money? How did she get here? Does she have parents? Where does she sleep? Does she even have a bed? Maia considers which of these questions would be appropriate, decides none of them. "Do you like it?"

Cass shrugs, tilts her head back, finishes her beer. "Come

on, princess, drink up. It'll do you good. We'll find some more and keep drinking."

Maia thinks about what time it must be, and her heart thumps in her chest. "I can't," she says, handing her beer to Cass. "I have to go. Really. I can't. My mom—I can't." Cass looks at her again. Those cool grey eyes.

"Maybe I'll see you again," she says.

Despite herself, Maia smiles. "Sure."

Cass's story is so boring she tells it to no one. Dad dead of a heart attack when she was just a kid, a series of stepdads Cass's mom picked up somewhere between her favorite bar and her second-favorite bar. Maybe her third-favorite bar. That would explain what assholes they were. Bad grades, bad home, bad friends. Pretty soon having to lock her bedroom door at night: Bad stepdad, what a surprise. Not that the lock stopped him.

There was a shelter for a while when she was eleven, in between stepdads one and two; stepdad one had been a hitter. He'd seemed nice enough at first. He had a real job, something at the bank. He wore suits and took her mom out to dinner and bought Cass a doll with white-blond hair and a painted-on red smirk. When he'd gotten transferred to a branch in Portland he'd told them he wanted to move as a family, and so they did. Cass's stuffed dog next to the new doll in her pink plastic backpack, a rented truck, a new apartment with mint-green walls. And then once the both of them were stuck, once they had no place else to go, no friends, no car, and no one to talk to, he went monster. Stopped going to his job, stopped paying for anything, stopped the candy-sweet words and steak dinners. The first time he'd hit Cass's mom was when she told him she didn't have any money left in her savings to pay for groceries. The first time he hit Cass was when they left, in the middle of the night like secret agents, one suitcase between the two of them. Cass's mom couldn't afford a cab, so they walked two miles across town to the shelter, Cass's cheek blooming with a riotous purple bruise that matched the sunrise sky. *If I were in a movie*, Cass thought, *there would be a shot of my face, and then a shot of the clouds.*

The shelter was in a residential neighborhood, an ordinary-looking house with a yard surrounded by other ordinary houses. The neighbors gave them dirty looks when they walked to the corner store for milk. The shelter was supposed to be a secret, but the neighbors weren't stupid. There were other women and kids who lived in the shelter. The women who worked there sat in a little office by the front door. The daytime office women were serious and wore real office clothes. They had meetings with the moms and gave them lists of places to call and appointments to keep. But the women who sat in the office at night wore cutoff shorts and T-shirts and no bras. They chewed gum and ate their dinners, which they brought from home, in the big common room with the women who lived in the shelter. They slept on a bed in the office, and if you needed cold medicine in the middle of the night you could knock softly and they would come to the door, sleepily pushing their tousled hair out of their eyes, and hand it over to you in a tiny cup. All of them were pretty. Some of them were in college and told Cass about their classes. *Anthropology*, Cass said to herself later. *Chemistry. Psychology.* Those were things you could do, if you were a girl like that.

One of the nighttime girls had brown skin, sleek black hair, orchids tattooed across her shoulders, and a ladder of white scars that stretched from her left wrist to her left elbow. Her dinner was always sushi that she had made herself, and once she gave Cass a piece: tofu, avocado, carrot, and brown rice, none of which Cass had ever had before. The orchid girl was Cass's favorite.

Cass did not like the shelter, which smelled bad a lot of the time. The bathrooms were always dirty, no matter how many times they got cleaned. The mattresses had plastic covers on them that rustled when you moved, and at night the sonorous breath of too many people in too small a room kept Cass awake. The other kids went through her clothes. Sometimes the moms got in fights. Her own mom had gotten a job at a gas station half a mile away and was so worn thin with worry and weariness that Cass thought she might disappear altogether. After they had been at the shelter for a week, the orchid girl came out of the office one evening and asked Cass's mother if she could talk to Cass for a little while. Cass had been in the office that first morning, when one of the women had asked her mother a lot of questions about her life and what had happened before they came here, so many questions that Cass had eventually fallen asleep, but not since then.

"Cassandra," the orchid girl said. She sat down on the floor, her back against the bed in the office, and stretched. After a moment Cass sat down next to her. She stretched, too.

"Do you like it here so far?" asked the orchid girl. Cass considered lying; she did not want to get her mom in trouble. One of the other kids had told her that his mom had gotten kicked out of the last shelter and they had had to spend the night in an alley before his mom found a man who would pay for a hotel room. But something about the orchid girl's face was so honest, so friendly, that Cass trusted her immediately.

"No," Cass said.

"That's pretty normal," the orchid girl agreed. "Not the most fun, right? Where would you go if you could go anywhere?"

"I'd live on the beach," Cass said, surprising herself. "I'd live in a little cabin on the beach. And I'd eat tofu and avocado every day. I would have a boat."

"A warm beach?"

"Maybe. Well, no. I mean, the beach where I'm from. My mom took me there when I was really little. We went to the rainforest and then the ocean. It would be that beach, but warmer. So I wouldn't need a coat."

The orchid girl nodded thoughtfully. "I like that. Would your mom live with you?"

"If she wanted," Cass said. "My mom's okay. She's just tired. If we lived on the beach she wouldn't have to work. She could eat tofu and avocado, too."

"You must really like tofu and avocado," the orchid girl said solemnly. Cass shot her a sidelong glance and saw she was making a joke. Cass grinned a little.

"We could eat spaghetti, sometimes," she said.

The orchid girl asked her more questions: What she liked to do for fun, what was best about school, what had happened in their last house. Sometimes she wrote Cass's answers down on a piece of paper. Had the stepdad ever done anything bad to her? What was Cass afraid of? Cass wasn't afraid of anything, but she told the orchid girl about her dreams. She'd always had dreams that were more than dreams. She'd dream of glass breaking, and the next day her mother would drop a bowl in the kitchen, curse as it shattered. She'd dream of a raft of dying animals, floating in a dark sea, and in the morning she'd find a newly dead kitten moldering next to the sidewalk, eyeless, its matted fur crawling with maggots. Sometimes she dreamed things that she knew would not come to pass for a long time to come: herself in a bright kitchen, its shelves lined with mason jars, tendrilly plants hanging from baskets. Herself on a beach, a white-sand beach, not the one she knew. Sun warm on her bare arms, the ocean flat and glassy before her. Herself in a vast apartment, chandeliers filled with candles hanging from the high ceilings, floor-to-ceiling windows showing a view of a dark sea under a darker sky. A dark-skinned man with long dreadlocks sailing a little wooden boat across a whitecapped grey sea. A girl whose blue eyes were startling in her brown skin, looking up at a night sky glowing white with stars.

When Cass was a small child, she'd been out one afternoon in the woods, playing alone in a stand of evergreens. A cloud moved across the sun and a hush fell through the forest. She lifted her head and saw a man standing between two trees a little ways away. Tall and thin, in a long black coat. Death-pale face. The glitter of rubies at his throat. "Hello," she said.

*Hello, Cassandra,* he replied, in a voice like stone. His mouth did not move when he spoke.

"Are you a ghost?" she asked.

*The people of your time do not have a word for what I am.*
"You look like a ghost. Are you sad?"

He had taken a step forward, looking down at her. *I am very old.* And before she could tell him that that wasn't what she had asked, that wasn't an answer at all, he stepped back into the shadow of a tree and vanished. There was a bright fuzz around the edges of her vision and the air tasted of smoke and ashes. She went home and told her mother she'd seen a ghost. Her mother was watching television with all the drapes drawn, her face slack, lit greenish in the flicker of the screen. "I told you not to talk to strangers," her mother said, changing channels. "Go outside and play."

Even then, Cass understood that the world was not quite the same for her as it was for other people, that the lines between the real and the not-real, the present and the past, were sometimes blurred inside her. She tried talking to animals, but they did not understand her any better than they understood other girls. She tried telling the weather to change its patterns, but the sun shone or didn't no matter what kind of morning she'd asked for. But sometimes out of the corner of her eye she saw a group of tall, stern, pale people, battling one another with swords, or sailing ships across a wine-dark sea. She saw an island of one-eyed monsters dotted with sheep. She saw a woman with the face of a goddess and serpents winding out of her skull. She saw these things when she slept, and saw them again in waking, and sometimes if she called after them, if she cried out, "Wait, wait," one of them would half-turn as if listening. "Take me with you," she begged. "Take me with you." But they never did.

———

The orchid girl was quiet for a long time, and Cass wondered if she'd said too much. If they were going to take her away now, make her sleep in an alley. Call the police. Whatever happened to freaky monster-seeing girls who didn't fit the right way in the world.

"I have dreams like that, too," the orchid girl said instead.

"Does everybody?" Cass asked.

"No," she said.

"Is there something wrong with me?"

"Do you think there's something wrong with me?"

Cass looked up at the orchid girl. "You seem fine," she said.

"Well then," said the orchid girl. "There you go."

After a month, Cass's mom saved up enough from the gas station for them to take the bus back to Seattle and get a room in an apartment they shared with another mom and her son, who went into their bedroom and shut the door whenever Cass was in the apartment. Cass went back to school. For a while, things seemed like they might be good. But then came the second stepdad, and another apartment with just him, and Cass having to lock her door at night. She knew better than to tell her mom. It was the stepdad or the shelter again, and anything was better than the shelter. After the second stepdad came the third. The third was a yeller, not a hitter or a toucher. "You little whore," he liked to yell, at either Cass or her mother. Or sometimes "You goddamned whores," at both of them: two birds with one stone. By the third stepfather, Cass's mother's eyes were dead and her shoulders had a permanent slump to them, and though she'd been pretty and chatty and alive when Cass was younger, the stepfathers had wiped anything like beauty from her face. By the third stepfather, Cass's mom had stopped saying anything at all. It was easiest for Cass just to leave, and so she did. Became her own bad news. Cass, catlike, landing feetfirst, teaching herself young to fight her own battles with fists or with wits. Whichever got her clear of trouble she didn't go out seeking herself. She took to drugs like she was born with an addict's sneaky wit, rifling her mom's prescriptions, and then, when her mom caught on to that racket, finding the first of a long stretch of mean-eyed boys way too old for her.

Half the girls Cass knows, all the girls Cass lives with, are living the same after-school special, with minor variations. She loves them, to be sure. They've kept her safe and fed and watched her back. The squat is like a family, riddled with squabbles and bad blood and old grievances, but at the end of the day they take care of each other. They share what they have, split their food stamps, aren't stingy with their drugs or their booze. Cass fell into them, and they caught her. Brought her back to their derelict manor and welcomed her in.

*Squat* is the wrong word, technically. It's somebody's aunt's brother-in-law's cousin's house, more or less condemned, its front yard overgrown with chest-high weeds and pieces of its roof missing. No rent exchanges hands, but there is, somewhere, an actual owner; the only thing, Cass is sure, that keeps the neighbors from being able to get them out. There's no power, though somehow they still have running water. They carry their garbage to a Dumpster outside a minimarket down the block, rather less often than they should. They keep a low profile in exchange for the neighbors' unwilling silence, and this tenuous equilibrium lurches forward toward an indefinite future. Cass has only lived here a year. Their elder statesman, Mayhem, has been here for four. It's better than her mom's house, though that's not a particularly strong recommendation. Cass even has her own room, with windows she edges in duct tape in winter to keep out the cold and throws open in spring to let in the warm new-scented air. The room was carpeted in a filthy shag when she laid claim to it, but she's since torn it out, sanded the floor, and painted it a rich dark brown. (That crisp fall afternoon, Cass and Felony pushing a full-to-the-brim shopping cart of paint and sandpaper and brushes and paint trays out the front door of the hardware store, cool as you please. Felony'd stolen a virulent magenta with which to color her own room's walls, but the color was, not surprisingly, an eyesore. "Goddammit," she'd sighed, gazing at the fluorescent horror she'd created, "now I'm going to have to go *back*.") Cass papered her walls with a collage of show flyers and pictures of faraway cities cut out of magazines pilfered from strangers' garbage, made herself a desk out of milk crates and a board. Mason jars in the windowsills, filled with dried flowers. Candles to keep away the dark. Cass doesn't like to sleep, because sleeping means dreams.

Lately, in her dreams, she's begun to talk to dead people. This, she tells no one at all, but that makes it no less real. Shades slip in, uninvited, to the twilit world she wanders somewhere between waking and sleep. Her father, his eyes pleading, reaches out to her, but when she moves to touch him her hands strike an invisible wall, as though she's trying to push through a window. She sees a man with bloody holes where his eyes should be, tears of blood trickling from the sockets. She sees people she has never met, but knows from newspapers or television: overdosed rock stars, politicians killed by snipers, voiceless legions who died in genocide or war. She sees the tall man in the black coat again, looking down at her as she sleeps, but when she opens her mouth to say hello she finds her lips are sewn together with thread. She dreams about a black river in a dark forest, a palace dotted with a hundred open doors on a dead white plain, a three-headed dog. Sometimes the thought of sleep is so terrifying she stays up for days, doing speed until her eyes feel as though they will come out of her head and the walls crawl with things that aren't there and it's as bad being awake as it is being asleep. Mayhem gets her hands on some Dilaudid and that, for a little while, sends Cass into an intense, dreamless sleep like a coma. She's so grateful for the respite she cries when she wakes up, her body fighting its way out of the abyss of oblivion against her will.

"Do you ever see things?" she asks Felony, the evening of the day she shoplifts beer with the weird preppy girl she met on the street. They're rooting through a grocery-store Dumpster. Felony trains the flashlight on Cass, so that her face disappears behind a blaze of white light. Cass squints.

"See what?"

"Like, things that aren't real."

Felony turns the light back to the Dumpster. "You're doing too many drugs, Cass."

"Not like that. I know the difference."

Felony holds up a plastic package of strawberries. "Look at these, only a couple moldy ones." She tucks it into her backpack. "I don't know, girl, just lay off the speed." Cass knows better, really, than to ask, but she thinks that maybe if she's going crazy someone else will have noticed. Someone will tell her, at least, and then she can go about putting a stop to it. However you put a stop to those sorts of things. Exorcism? Ritalin? She pictures herself in a group-therapy situation. "Do you think I'm going crazy?" she asks Felony, on their walk back to the squat.

Felony shrugs, digs the strawberries back out of her bag, and puts three in her mouth at once. "Crazy is relative," she says through a mouthful of fruit. "Why you going on about this shit, anyway?" Which Cass finds inexplicably comforting.

"I met this girl today," Cass says.

"Huh." Felony is going through the strawberries so briskly there'll be none left by the time they get back to the house.

"Hey, give me one of those. I met her in the street. I got her to steal beer with me."

"Huh," Felony says, again handing Cass the strawberries with visible reluctance.

"I don't think she ever drank beer before."

"Weird," Felony says. "What is she, straight edge?"

"No," Cass says. "I think she's just lost." She eats a strawberry thoughtfully and looks up at the sky. "New moon," she says.

"Does that mean something?" Felony cranes her neck, peering upward, and trips over a pothole.

"It means you should watch where you're going, you dumb bitch," Cass says, and takes off running.

"Give me back my fucking strawberries, you mangy little whore!" Felony yells, and they whoop back and forth, their voices echoing down the deserted street, as they race each other the rest of the way home.

# NOW: NEWPORT BEACH

The best of their days are like this one, waking when the sun on their faces is too bright and insistent to let them slumber any longer, stumbling on coltish girl-legs to the edge of the ocean and falling in, shrieking, letting the salt shock of the water startle them all the way out of sleep. Boiling water and coffee grounds on their little camp stove, the resultant sludge strong enough to make their teeth chatter. If they're lucky, like today, the beach will be abandoned. They'll flop down on a sandy blanket above the high-tide line, let the sun bake them into a stupor, crisp their skins golden. Cass is so unselfconscious about her body that it's contagious, and now both of them are naked half the time, not even bothering to hide behind shirts or cutoffs when a stray family wanders their way, parents quickly steering toddlers back down to the waterline when they realize what nest of scandal they've stumbled across.

On days like this they are both happy in a way neither of them has ever been happy before, so happy they are dumb with it, their lazy fingers intertwined as they bask on the pale sand, or one girl's head pillowed on the other's shoulder, bleached and mad-colored strands mingling. They do pushups in the sand, for fitness, collapsing in laughter at the sight of each other, doze like cats, read magazines Cass steals from the gas station, magazines about movie stars who are sleeping with other movie stars' spouses. Maia has brought along a copy of *War and Peace* but cannot manage more than a page without falling asleep; Cass bought a stack of Stephen King novels in a Salvation Army in Portland and is making her way through *Pet Sematary,* reading the most terrifying bits aloud in a stentorian voice. Maia gives up on Tolstoy and makes off with *The Stand.* Cass accuses her of getting sand between all the pages. Maia drops the book in the ocean, accidentally, and they leave it to dry on a campground picnic table.

When they are hungry, if they are hungry, Maia puts clothes on and drives barefoot to the nearest store—in remote places like this, sometimes it's a trip of nearly an hour—and comes back with Perrier and peaches and bags of chips, suntan lotion that makes them both reek of coconut, Dr Pepper and cheese that melts in the hot sun faster than they can eat it, sweating gently in its plastic wrapping. Fried Jo Jos from the deli case, about which Maia has become fanatical. Cass eats Snickers bars by the handful. They both like CornNuts. Maia never ate food like that before Cass, bright-colored food made nuclear with Yellow #5. The drowsy afternoons stretch into forever, the sun slowly lowering at the western edge of the world until the ocean goes molten and the velvety dark of the sky is pinpricked white with stars. They have nowhere to be and there is no one in the world who knows where they are, no one but each other, and there is no one else they need. Not now, not ever, just the two of them, sun-browned bareskinned salt-haired girls, brimming over with joy.

# THEN

The house is quiet when she lets herself in, and Maia thinks for a moment that she's safe. She drops her bag on the couch, slips the loafers off her feet, pads into the kitchen to ferret out a snack. She doesn't hear her mother's footsteps behind her until it's too late.

"Where were you?"

Maia whips around, hitting the open refrigerator door with one elbow and suppressing a yelp. "I walked home from Oscar's." Her mother smells of Chanel No. 5 and her lipstick is a dark, elegant red. She must have had a lunch date. Or an advisory meeting with one of her favorite students. Her mother's favorite students are all men.

"Don't leave the refrigerator door open. What do you want in there?"

"I was looking for something to eat."

"You don't need anything to eat. Dinner's in an hour. How many times have I asked you to put your bag in your room and not leave it on the couch?"

"I'm sorry. Oscar gave me some new music."

"Then put it by the piano when you come in. Honestly, Maia."

"Oscar likes me to read it first."

"Then you should have put it in your room."

"I know. Is Dad home?"

"How should I know?"

"I thought you were here already."

"I don't keep track of your father. Go pick up your bag."

"Okay."

Maia has no real basis for comparison, but she's fairly sure her life isn't normal. But while her mother is difficult, she's not hard to manage; she operates by tangible rules. No emotion, no dirt, no sass, and no deviation from the careful path she has outlined for Maia. Sometimes Maia thinks her parents should have just adopted a dog: easier to train, fewer impulses toward independence. But then, her mother would never be able to stomach dog hair on the couch. Maia has thought, more than once, of asking them why they wanted her, why they went to such enormous trouble—and, no doubt, expense, though to their credit neither of them has ever mentioned how much her adoption must have cost—for a child neither of them seems to particularly enjoy. Her mother is not someone suited to the role of kindness, or nurture; it's no coincidence she chose the cruel, long-dead world of the ancients, with their quests and wars and bloody-minded people stabbing husbands in their baths, baking children into pies and feeding them to their fathers, putting out their own eyes. Maia's mother herself is something out of another century, ruthless and ambitious and scoured bare of any weakness, like some Amazonian queen.

Maia has good memories of her father, from when she was smaller. He used to take her to the zoo on the weekends, or play catch with her in the park. But that was a long time ago. Sometimes Maia imagines her mother scrubbing him away with a sponge, the way the cleaning lady bleaches the counters and the sinks, until someday he will be erased entirely. As the years pass he grows ever more difficult to see. He's like a ghost permanently haunting the safety of his study, where he's been working on the same novel for as long as she's belonged to the two of them. He would read her chapters when she was little, and she remembers only that they were stories about adults at grown-up parties, the women in pretty dresses and the men sharp and witty. A lot of drinks in winking glasses. The chapters were about things she knew she would understand when she was older, and she'd felt a quick thrill at the idea that someday the world of adults would crystallize with her as a part of it, and she'd know then what it was her father had been telling her. Now writing for him means mostly drinking and looking into space. He hasn't read her chapters in years.

Her parents have money. Not yacht and lakefront money,

but big house and two cars money, trips to Europe, a grand piano for her to practice on. They take her to piano competitions, which she wins. They took her to Rome when she was nine and Paris when she was twelve. She rode the Metro and walked across a bridge and went on a boat on the river and everyone around her was drinking white wine, and she ate a croissant at a round table outside a café. Her parents met in New York, when her mother was getting her doctorate at Columbia and her father was spending his parents' money and beginning the novel he has yet to finish. Maia tries to imagine them young and in love, but love seems like an emotion that is beyond the both of them.

Maia does not have friends. She is homeschooled. The only person she sees regularly is Oscar. Her mother likes to have dinner parties, but her mother's friends are composed chiefly of handsome male graduate students and the occasional guest lecturer or visiting professional intellectual. The dinner guests are generally made uncomfortable by Maia; they often seem startled to find her there, peering at her across the table as though she is some sort of mute, exotic pet. Occasionally they ask her about her schoolwork. "Your English is so good," they will say. She is aware that friends are a thing people possess; she sees other girls her own age, girls in jeans and sweatshirts, girls with bright jangly earrings that dangle from their lobes, girls with lipstick and sneakers and fingernails painted pink or red or blue. Girls walking in packs, hands in one anothers' back pockets, girls eating candy together and laughing. Girls like that seem a different species altogether from the somber, makeup-free face that greets Maia in the mirror. When she can get away with it she buys fashion magazines at the grocery store and leafs through the pages later in the safety of her own room, touching the pictures of long-limbed models in their fairy-tale-princess dresses, leaping for the camera like the white-tailed deer that bound through the woods near her house, as though she can step through the glossy pages and into another life.

Her only door out is the piano. Four hours a day, six hours a day. Some days eight hours, ten, twelve. Her mother had wanted a good daughter, a doll of a daughter, placid and dainty and dressed in ruffles. She'd sent Maia to ballet lessons, dreaming of her daughter a graceful Clara pirouetting around the Nutcracker prince. Instead, tiny Maia fell over when she tried to plié and cried every time she was put into a leotard. But Maia took to piano in a way her mother hadn't dared hope for. She'd chosen Oscar because he was the best teacher. Even when Maia was only four, it was obvious that she'd become his best pupil. His other students weren't always kind to her about it. "Of course the Asian girl is perfect," she'd heard one of the girls mutter to another at a recital. But Oscar had heard it, too, and responded with a devastating contempt that Maia hadn't yet known he had in him.

"Do you think it is because of where she was born that she is better than you?" he'd said coolly, in a voice that carried across the entire room. "It is not the color of her skin that makes her less lazy. You have not got half her gift, but even if you had, you are too stupid to use it." The girl had gotten another piano teacher, but none of Oscar's other students ever bothered her again.

Maia drops her bag in her room. The walls are painted a pale pink she'd picked out years ago and long since outgrown, but she can't imagine what color she'd want them to be now, even if her parents let her choose a new one. Ruffled white eyelet bedspread and matching pillow-cases. A framed watercolor of a unicorn. *The girl in the street wasn't wrong to call me princess,* she thinks. *Cass.* She says the name aloud and then looks around furtively, as though she's been caught out at a lie. But there's no one to hear her, no one to mark the flush the name brings to her cheeks. "Cass," she says again, letting the word drop into the silence of her room like a dare. *Maybe I'll see you again,* the girl said, her grey eyes serious. What would they do? Steal more beer? Go shopping? Watch television? Maia is not allowed to watch television, other than the news when her parents have it on. She racks her brain for samples of teen activities. Board games? Tag? She imagines herself walking up to Cass, surrounded by urchins and dogs, and suggesting a game of tag, and buries her head in her hands in despair.

After dinner she takes the Ravel to the piano and pages through it. Oscar likes her to spend a week reading the music without touching the piano, but sometimes his fussi-ness grows wearisome, and anyway she's itchy to try the piece out.

Her mother comes into the room and watches her prac-tice for a while. Maia is always nervous playing in front of her mother, for no real reason. Her parents aren't like the other parents of the ambitious teens she competes against, most of them failed classical musicians themselves who in-flict their own thwarted ambitions on their children, or else career musicians whose luminous talents outshine their unfortunate offspring, doomed forever to labor in their shadow. Her mother likes her to be good at things, and she is better at the piano than either of her parents are at anything they do—even her mother, respected scholar and tenured professor though she is, does not bring to the study of antiquity the rare gift that Maia has for the piano. But as difficult as Maia's mother is, she is content to let her daughter excel without reproach or undue pressure.

"That's Ravel," she says, as Maia works through the first page. *"Gaspard de la nuit."*

"Yeah," Maia says, surprised. Her mother finds the Romantics lugubrious.

*"Yes,* Maia, not *yeah.* Did Oscar tell you about the piece?"

"No, he just gave me the music at the end of my lesson today."

"Each of the movements is based on a Bertrand poem."

"Bertrand?"

"Aloysius Bertrand. Ravel thought his work encapsulated Romanticism—he meant to satirize it, I think, originally, but then ended up writing these sort of hallucinatorily romantic pieces in spite of himself. The poems themselves were a cult thing; the book didn't come out until Bertrand had already died of tuberculosis. The whole story is sort of ridiculous, really. Tubercular poets and demonically inspired composers. Baudelaire loved him—Bertrand, I mean. *Gaspard de la nuit* is an old French expression for the devil." Her mother has slipped into lecture mode, her elegant hands punctuating her points, her eyes fixed on some point over Maia's head. Maia can see why she's a beloved teacher; she's charismatic and engaging when she's telling people what to think. Maia wishes, not for the first time, that she'd drop the act and just be human.

"How do you know all this?"

Her mother comes back to herself, shrugs. "I used to take piano lessons when I was your age."

"You played this?"

"Oh, good lord, no. I was nowhere near as good as you; that piece would have been impossible for me. And to be honest, I liked to play showier things. My teacher used to say there's no reward for the virtuosity required for a piece like that, because it doesn't sound that difficult to the listener. She loved the Romantics. Oscar reminds me a little of her, actually. I have the poems upstairs somewhere in my library, if you want to read them." Maia follows her mother upstairs. It takes a bit of searching but her mother finds them at last in an anthology of French poetry, tucked behind a copy of Racine's *Phèdre,* and hands her the book. The covers are falling apart and it gives off the dead and faintly mildewy smell of something found abandoned in the fifty-cent box at an estate sale. The poems are illustrated here and there with old-fashioned line drawings, crotchety and crabbed in their execution.

"Ondine" is the story of a bitchy mermaid, trying to charm her human lover underwater even though she knows he'll drown. *Listen to my father whipping the water with the branch of a green alder tree, listen to my sisters caressing water lilies with their arms of foam,* she murmurs. *My palace is at the bottom of the lake, in a triangle of earth and fire and air. Put my ring on your finger and come with me to the depths.* When he tells her he loves a human woman instead, she dissolves into a scatter of weeping and rain, streaking across his window. *Here in a gown of watered silk, the mistress of the castle gazes from her balcony at the lovely night.* It's beautiful, but spooky. The lover is as bad as the mermaid, entranced by the sight of her transformed to tears. Maia wonders if Oscar is trying to tell her something about romance.

"Gloomy," she says, handing the book back to her mother. Of course, her mother is the one who loves Euripides; murderous mermaids don't really register on the bloodbath scale when held up next to Greek tragedy.

"Well," her mother says, "you know how I feel about the Romantics." They both laugh, and for a second the ever-present tension between them lifts a little, and they are just two women, unalike, sharing a joke across the wall. Maia goes back downstairs to practice, leaving her mother staring at the bookshelves.

# NOW:
# ARCATA

Cass's booted feet are propped on the dashboard, one arm dangling out the open window, cigarette between her fingers. Maia takes forever when she's in the grocery store. Reading the ingredients on every box and can. Wandering the bulk aisles, deliberating between long-grain and short-grain brown rice, rolled oats or quick oats, banana chips or roasted almonds. Picking up each apple and turning it over, checking for brown spots, testing for firmness, looking for some secret clue to its goodness beneath the slick pink skin. She's never wrong; you can bite into an apple Maia picks knowing the flesh will be crisp and sweet in your mouth every time.

They must be running out of money, but Cass hasn't asked and Maia hasn't offered. The Mercedes takes cheap diesel, and Cass has lived without money for so long that when she has it around it's more like a friendly surprise guest at a party than someone you need to see. Cass pulls her tarot deck out of the cargo pocket of her pants, shuffles the cards one-handed, flips through them. The Fool, the Lovers, Death. Not bad. One last drag of the cigarette. Tobacco out of her other pocket, rolling another with quick fingers. She doesn't light it, waits instead.

The light's dimming, sunset and another ordinary night in this tiny hippie town. Families cross the parking lot toward their cars: moms in long cotton dresses, bearded dads in overalls. Clean-scrubbed faces, roly-poly kids with haloes of blond fuzz. *Why are hippies always blond,* Cass wonders, *blond and blue-eyed like some distant branch of the Aryan Nations.* She touches her own salt-ratted hair; Maia dyed it blue last night in the bathroom of a campground. Where? Somewhere north of here. She loses track of days and miles. Oregon? They were in Oregon. Things have happened fast. Is it the end of July? Probably. She tugs one blue clump toward her mouth, chews it reflectively. Maia, working the dye in with her strong pianist's fingers, both of them watching each other in the dirty mirror. Not glass but a piece of polished steel. Their reflections were blurred, hard to pinpoint. Maia pushing her head under the faucet, careful not to get the water in her ears and eyes. Maia, always kind. Drops of blue water constellating in Cass's hair.

Unable to stand it, she'd shaken her head like a dog, dye flying, Maia laughing, chasing Cass around the bathroom with handfuls of coarse paper towels. So warm that night they hadn't even put up the tent, just spread their sleeping bags out on the ground. Did they sleep last night? Cass can't remember. As long as they sleep sometimes it doesn't really matter.

Here's Maia at last, walking toward the car with a brown paper bag. Long legs in ragged shorts. Maia's body was Cass's own discovery; she'd suspected that under the pressed khakis and sweater sets lurked an angel waiting to be unearthed, and she'd been right, though it took her a while to prevail. Maia, like a princess imprisoned in a tower, just waiting for someone to come tell her to let her hair down. Cass has stolen plenty in her short life, but Maia is by far the greatest heist she's ever pulled.

"Hey," Maia says, sliding into the driver's seat and twisting around to wedge the groceries in the backseat. There's plenty of room back there. Maia makes them keep the tent and their few clothes in the trunk, for tidiness's sake, and neither of them came to this adventure with much. Cass considers a spare T-shirt and a change of socks verging on excess. Maia wasn't too interested in bringing her loafers. Cass stole the tent before they skipped town. It was her contribution, since Maia stole the car.

"Hey," Cass says. Her voice is rough but steady in her own ears. She's definitely not high, then. Always good to double-check. Maybe it's time to remedy that. She digs around in her cigarette pocket for the bottle of pills.

"I got bread," Maia says. "Peanut butter and jelly. You hungry?"

"All that time for a loaf of bread?"

"They had a bunch of kinds. I got some fruit, too."

"I'm okay."

"You should eat. We should eat." They're silent for a moment, remembering the last time they ate. Which was. Cass frowns. Possibly a while ago.

"True."

"Beach picnic?"

"Sure."

Maia starts the car, drives them to a pullout off the highway that butts up against the ocean. The stars are coming out, one by one. Cass used to know the constellations better. That knowledge was a gift from her dad, the real one. But in trying to forget her own history she's forgotten her memory of the sky as well. Orion she remembers, and the Dippers, and Arcturus glittering bright off the Big Dipper's handle. They bypass a sandy roadside picnic table and take the bag of groceries to the beach proper, sit with their backs against a bleached hunk of driftwood. Cass hands Maia her knife; Maia spreads peanut butter and jam on slices of bread, wipes the knife carefully with a paper napkin before handing it back to Cass. Cass has learned a lot from watching the way Maia takes care of other people's things. The idea is new to her. Maia's not like the people she's used to, the family she was born into or the family she chose. She folds the knife and puts it back in her pocket.

The sandwich is good, better than peanut butter and jelly ought to be. Trust Maia to find the best kind of bread. Nutty and a little sweet, soft in her mouth. Hippie bread. She shifts her leg, hears the rattle of pills in their bottle. They can wait for once. The breeze off the ocean is cool. Breakers roll in, one after the other. The sky at the far end of the world is still molten at the edges, the last of the setting sun staining the night gold and purple. They could try for a sea voyage. If anyone could steal a boat, it's Cass; if anyone could teach herself how to sail, it's Maia.

"Where's this house?" Maia breaks the contemplative silence.

"I don't totally remember. But I think I can find it. This place Felony took me to a bunch of times. We could always ask around. Hang out in the park until we find someone."

"You've spent a lot of time here?"

"Not really. I mean, it's easy here. Lots of kids come through. We stayed here for a few weeks one summer." Last summer? It can't have been that many summers ago. Cass used to have an ordinary life, too, or at least a common one. She thinks, as she often does, of her second stepfather's hands, and then carefully stops thinking about anything at all.

"You okay?" Fucking psychic Maia.

"Just trying to remember where the house was."

"You sure?"

"I'm *fine*."

Even in the growing dark Cass can see Maia's frown, but she resolutely avoids Maia's concerned face until Maia looks away and takes another bite out of her sandwich.

"Anyway," Cass says, "they have shows all the time." Maia nods, her bleached hair swinging. Cass wonders if there's such a thing as glow-in-the-dark dye, if she could mark Maia somehow, so as to be always able to find her, no matter how heavy the night. Maia's soft hand in hers, that first day they'd met. Cass steals touches where she can, shy as a middle-schooler. Passing her drugs, palm to palm. One hand on Maia's bony back when she's sad. Combing her fingers through Maia's hair. Cass takes Maia's hand in the pit at shows, and Maia never lets go until the music stops. Cass finds the cigarette she'd rolled in the parking lot tucked behind her ear, lights it.

"You didn't finish your sandwich."

"Not really hungry."

Maia's sandwich, too, lies half-eaten on the sand. Speed will do that to you. Only Maia would still bother to shop for groceries, as orderly and rational in the midst of a coastal road-trip bender as she probably was practicing the piano twelve hours a day in her parents' house. They toss the sandwiches in the garbage on the way back to the car.

It takes some aimless driving and wrong turns before Cass sees a street that looks familiar. It's not hard to find your way in a town this small, although all things considered she's amazed she recognizes anything at all. Once they're on the right street, the house is hard to miss. Kids congregate on the rickety wooden porch. There's a threadbare couch in the front yard, more kids piled atop it, smoking. Forty-ounce bottles of beer and pint bottles in paper bags, dogs running amok, a few toddlers staggering from one clump of people to another, hoping one of these drunks will turn out to be a parent.

"They have babies here?" Maia still has the capacity to be shocked.

"Everybody has babies," Cass says. Maia parks the car down the street, though there's plenty of space in front of the house. Cass hides a smile.

Inside, the house is a disaster. Even Cass would think twice about sleeping here. Maia wrinkles her nose at the torn and stained carpet, shrinking from the walls in rotting clumps. There's another couch, in worse shape than the tattered wreck on the lawn. Kids everywhere, black leather and torn black denim, dirty patches, Crass shirts, spikes, and filthy black baseball caps. The room smells of pee. Cass raises an eyebrow, grey eyes glinting. "You wanted real, princess," she says, grinning. "This is really real." Cass's palm against Maia's; it's their pill-passing grip. Maia gulps hers down, waits for the kick she knows now is coming.

The show is in the basement, which is at least cement. There's no carpet to hold stink and god knows what else. Cass is ginger on the wooden stairs, risers missing and some listing so badly it seems they'll be pitched headlong into the mass of bodies packed into the windowless room. There's space at the center, just enough for a drum kit and a couple of amps. A girl in torn fishnets and a stained white tank top and nothing else is tuning her guitar. Rings through her bottom lip, Cleopatra eyeliner, chain and padlock at her throat, big black boots. Her bandmates, both boys, are wearing more or less the same thing. Maia wonders if these people can tell, when they look at her, how new she is to these clothes, to this hair, to this life, if her past is like a stain coloring the air around her, the beige house leaving its indelible mark on her skin. People look at her twice most places she goes now, truck stops and punk shows, grocery stores, state parks, gas stations, rest stops. But she doesn't know which piece of her otherness draws their eyes: dirty clothes, wild hair, brown skin, or the color of her mother's house hanging over her.

The fishnetted girl jumps in the air, hits the first chord hard as she lands, and as the bass and drums kick in with a roar the speed fires Maia's heart into overdrive and everything is so fast and so loud and so good and everyone is moving, moving, her sweat and Cass's sweat and their sweat, all these bodies, all this sound, all this skin. She shakes her head and howls and Cass hears her and grins big, crooked white teeth against her tan face, and howls back at her, and this time is bigger and better than the last time, faster, faster, faster. This time she can see joy sparkling at the edges of her vision, a glorious static of light. *More,* she thinks, *more, more, more.* Who was she before, that terrified girl, living through dead composers, living through the dreams of other people, who was she before and who is she now, this girl made alive and wild as the ocean outside, wild as the wind. All the girls she could be lodged in her heart, crying *pick me, pick me, pick me.* But none of it matters in this here, in this now, none of it matters with the speed running hard and sweet in her veins and Cass's hand in hers and blood and teeth and noise. This is what Oscar was telling her to seek, this is the place he wanted her to get to, and maybe she had to leave everything behind to find it but she is alive and on fire and this life is more real than any of her life has ever been until now. Just a little farther now and all the pieces will come together into a her that is something like a whole.

# THEN

Cass's dreams have become unbearable since the day she met Maia. Every night the man in the black coat comes to her. He usually says nothing. He watches her, or sometimes he is walking away from her across the flat white plain, toward the many-doored palace. Sometimes her hands are bound with thorn-covered vines and her blood runs down her knuckles and pools at her feet. Sometimes the man in the black coat is leading an enormous, red-furred man with the head of a bull on a thin gold chain.

They are wandering through a series of tunnels under-ground, lit with torches that flicker and smoke, and Cass is running after them, calling "Wait! Wait!" But they never stop, and though they are not walking quickly Cass can never manage to catch them. Once she sees him with a beautiful girl, a girl her own age, with dark skin and long white hair that hangs down her back. They are standing side by side in an empty apartment with floor-to-ceiling win-dows that look out over a dark sea. His arm is around the strange girl's shoulders. "I wish you would tell me why you keep coming here," Cass says, but he is silent. The air in the room is still and cold. Outside, the dark waves heave under a storm-blackened sky. "Tell me," Cass says again. "Please tell me." The words become dusty moths that flut-ter from her mouth. She puts her hands to her throat and her skin is as cool as death and the moths' wings beat around her, whirling and whirling, and she wakes up trying to scream, but nothing will come out of her open mouth.

Finally, one afternoon she walks to the witch store in the second level of the big open-air market downtown that's built into the side of a hill. The street level is a covered ar-cade of stalls: fruits and vegetables, street food, imports from Tibet and Mexico and China, paintings by artists from the tribes that live out on the peninsula. A stall of fish laid out on chunks of ice, handsome boys in rubber waders tossing salmon back and forth and hollering at each other. A little coffee shop with a painting of a naked mermaid in the window, encircled by her own tail. Cass knows the girls who work at the fruit stalls, some of them, pretty rocker girls with beat-up black motorcycle boots and tattoos from their knuckles to their shoulders. She waves to Valerie, the one she knows best, as she walks by.

"Hey, Cass," Valerie says. She's older, lives in a house on the Hill with a bunch of musicians. Cass went to a Halloween party there once. Valerie and her boyfriend were dressed as sasquatches, and his band played, with Valerie on the drums. Cass can't see her now without remembering her in her fake-fur coat, her hair ratted out even bigger than it usually is, her eyes raccooned with black eyeliner. It had been an interpretive sort of sasquatch costume.

"What's up," Cass says.

"You hungry?"

"Sure." Valerie tosses her an apple and Cass bites in.

"What you been up to?"

"Things," Cass says vaguely. She is not especially interested in discussing her dreams with anyone. But Valerie nods as if she's said something meaningful.

"Things," she agrees. "Hey, you know Elizabeth who works in the health food store?"

"I think so."

"We're starting a band but we need a singer. You know anyone?"

"I don't think so," Cass says.

"What about you?"

"Me?" Cass laughs. "No way."

"Too bad. You're missing your shot at stardom." Cass makes a sorrowful face and Valerie laughs. "Here," she says, "take another apple."

"See you," Cass says, waving, and Valerie waves back merrily as Cass heads for the stairs.

"Barbie's Dream Car!" Valerie yells. "You remember that name, 'cause you're gonna hear it everywhere!"

Beneath the street level of the market, wooden stairways lead to a maze of hallways and funny little shops. No matter how many times Cass goes to the witch store, it's always impossible to find. A window facing the bay lets in a smoky, salty light, and the shelves are full of witch books and herbs, tinctures and oils, incense, silver pendants, tarot decks, stones painted with runes. The girl who works there has long dyed-black dreadlocks that hang down her back and crescent moons tattooed at the corners of her eyes. Her arms are inky with more sigils and her fingers are tattooed with runes between each knuckle.

"I need something to keep away bad dreams," Cass says. The witch-store girl is alone, sitting at the counter, leafing through a handwritten book bound in leather. She looks up.

"What kind of bad dreams?"

"People I don't want to see."

The girl gets up and comes around the counter, looks Cass in the eyes. Cass tries not to flinch. She is not accustomed to being examined so closely. The girl touches her palm to Cass's forehead, whispers something, tilts her head as if listening, takes her hand away.

"It's not dreams you need protection from," she says. "You are like me. Someone who lives in too many places. I can help you, but I can't change what you are."

"Anything," Cass says. "I'm scared to go to sleep."

"You have a gift."

"I don't think I want it."

"You cannot choose to have it or not to have it. You can

choose only how you will live with it." The girl takes down jars of herbs, measures them into bags, piles the bags on the counter. She looks through some books, hums to herself, adds a tiny bottle of oil to the growing stack.

"I don't have much money," Cass says. "Any money," she amends.

"Then you will be in my debt," the girl says. Cass scowls, not sure if she likes the sound of that. The girl laughs at her expression. "You can come back," she says. "Tomorrow, same time?"

"Sure," Cass says.

"Take this now, and come back tomorrow. I'll give you a way to earn your keep." Cass stares at her, stricken, and the girl looks at her deadpan. "You can prepare the infants for sacrifice," she says. "And after that, stock the shelves. I have a big shipment of books coming in tomorrow."

"Okay," Cass says.

"Make this into a tea, and drink it at night before you go to sleep." The girl pats the pile of herbs. "I'm giving you a book to start, and a tarot deck. And if you don't come back tomorrow, I'll hex you."

That night, the tea does not take away the dreams but it lessens the terror of them, weaves a barrier between Cass and the dead. When they reach for her they cannot touch her, and it is harder for her to hear the ghastly, jabbering chorus of their voices. In the morning she feels, if not well-rested, at least as though she's slept, and she walks back downtown to the witch store with a lighter heart.

The witch-store girl is named Raven—Cass doesn't ask whether it's a given name or a chosen one, though privately she finds it a little cheesy—and she knows more about what she knows best than any knowing person Cass has ever met. Every possible permutation of tarot deck. The nature and purpose of an encyclopedia's worth of herbs, how to grow them and where to find them in the wild, how to decoct and decant and tincture and salve them, how to make spells with them and how to make them into tea. Runes in dead languages and living ones, the movements of the stars, the messages behind every pattern of wind and wave, the meanings of numbers and days and saints, the history of witches. It's weeks before Cass can tell when Raven is cracking a joke, and even then she's never really sure. A mean-mouthed tourist comes into the shop one afternoon, disorders the divination books and strews about the sage, asks a thousand pesky questions about all the essential oils, who grew them, where they are from, whether they were of a suitable quality or composed of inferior ingredients, which incenses were most likely to be non-allergenic. Raven responds with a stoic patience Cass finds astounding. When the woman leaves without buying a thing, Raven looks at Cass with a perfectly straight face. "Bring me the wormwood," she says. "I'm going to give that bitch warts so far up her ass she'll wish she could shit out her mouth," and it's long, long minutes before she laughs and Cass realizes she's not serious.

"Could you really do that?" Cass breathes.

"Oh, sure," Raven says, and this time she doesn't laugh.

Cass's days in the witch store blur together, long pleasant winter afternoons that shade into twilight at four and full dark by five-thirty. Outside the shop's windows the wind howls and flings spatters of rain at the glass in torrential gusts, but inside they are warm and cozy. Raven makes them tea and sets Cass to dusting, or sorting her Dead Can Dance records out from her Clan of Xymox, or tidying the tarot decks in their glass case, or filling little glassine bags of herbs and handing them over to Raven to be labeled in her painstaking, beautiful script. Cass watches as Raven makes up tinctures for people who come in with aches and pains or broken hearts or longings for other people's lovers—"Be careful with those," Raven says to Cass, when they can't hear her, "no matter what you give them, it will end badly for someone"—or sorrows large and small, wishes for joys, hopes and dreams and fevers. Raven picks out tarot decks, finds the right sorts of oils to make the right sorts of smells, matches eager customers with the futures they hope for, the small magics that puzzle out into a larger pattern of light and care. For all her smart mouth and wicked tongue, Raven is a good witch, and good at being a witch; she knows without being told who wants to be told they are psychic or special or waiting to blossom into beauty or love, and who wants to be told nothing at all, handed discreetly a little bag of herbs or a spell written on a folded piece of paper. When there is nothing to do in the shop, which is not often, Raven teaches Cass how to make magic of her own. Cass works at the shop every day, except for one day of the week she waits with her friends on the Ave and pretends nonchalance until Maia walks past, improbable Maia, with her sylph's face and yuppie's clothes, Maia who's bewitched Cass as surely as if she's cast a spell herself. Maia stops and says hello, shyly at first and then with more confidence as the weeks progress, until she's squatting on the sidewalk next to Cass, her brown eyes alight as she talks about Chopin or Bach or whatever she happens to be reading. They both love Shakespeare, Rimbaud, and Edith Hamilton, but from there their tastes diverge wildly. Cass insists Maia must read Delany; Maia says she will if Cass tries Proust. Cass counters with Angela Carter. Maia insists on Hugo. In bantering about books, they piece together a friendship. If Raven guesses why Cass doesn't show once a week, regular as a metronome, she doesn't say.

From Raven Cass learns the cycles of the moon, the best days of the month for making people fall in love with you, asking goddesses for favors, sowing crops. The crops are just for reference, though someday she would like to have a house of her own, a garden, a ring of herbs and flowers, vegetables growing in neat lines. She reads about tinctures and teas, cooks salves in a dirty pot on the Coleman camp stove they use at the squat. She steals crystals from the new age store on the Ave, soft leather and thread from the fabric store. Raven does not ask where she has procured her materials, but teaches her without comment to make amulets to ward off bad dreams, bad luck, and bad spirits. When Cass herself is so festooned with talismans she clanks when she walks, she begins to hand them out to her friends. It is not long before she has something of a reputation. She's asked to interpret dreams, suggest prudent courses through difficult problems. She makes love spells and money spells—though even she will admit it'll take a lot more than some herbs and a green candle to bring prosperity to her own house and its ragtag gaggle of urchins—and begins to specialize in astrological predictions. Cass has a lot of free time with which to apprehend her new craft, and she takes to it the same way she took to prescription pills washed down with cheap whisky.

Felony and Mayhem are mostly amused by her new hobby, but Felony will take the bus downtown with her to the island ferry, cross the mountain-ringed Sound, hitch rides with pickup truck–driving loggers and back-to-the-landers out along the winding roads that crisscross the island like veins. Felony and Cass thrash through the wet woods, salal slapping at their knees, dripping branches smacking them in the face, while Cass digs for roots and stubborn winter-growing herbs. Felony is always pleased by adventure in any shape it chooses to take. Cass clambers over fallen trees, her muddy boots sinking through deep piles of moss and loamy soil, one eye out for the gold-brown flash of a startled deer leaping away through the trees, or the black dart of a crow winging between the branches. Cass is no woodswoman, but Felony spent a few years living in tree platforms and shackling herself to logging-road gates to stop timber sales. While her efforts did little to slow the increasing tide of clear-cutting that scars the peninsula, she came away from her brief stint as a forest defender with an unerring sense of direction and an uncanny ability to find the road again no matter how many circles they wander in or how far into the woods they stray. As they tramp about, Felony regales her with tales of running away from federal agents, fornicating in the treetops with her revolutionary compatriots of various genders, and defecating in plastic buckets that had to be lowered daily from their platform homes and emptied by ground teams who kept the platforms supplied with anti-capitalist good cheer, Dumpstered vegetables, and soy protein snacks. The winter's too cold and wet for sleeping out, but Felony promises that when the weather changes they can come out to the woods with a tarp, set up a little camp under the trees.

Cass feels, for the first time in a long time, as though she is doing something useful. Learning a craft, thrashing around in the woods, sweating some of the whisky and pills out of her system. She even quits drinking for a while, which Raven guesses, though Cass hasn't told her. "It's good for you," she says, "to let go of what dulls you and puts a veil between you and the world." *I need that veil,* Cass thinks. There are reasons she and Felony and Mayhem drink like they do, reasons that have as much to do with forgetting as celebrating. She's never told Raven any of the secrets knitted into her skin, but Raven's sharp eyes miss nothing.

"The Hanged Man," she says one slow afternoon, as Cass refills the herb jars. "Beyerl tells us that he has lessons for us about letting go, release. We have already learned through our suffering; the time comes to contemplate the wisdom we have gained. To move from action to inaction. We must learn to be a vessel in order to allow ourselves to be transformed."

"I don't need a lecture," Cass says.

"Sorrow can be a teacher," Raven says, "but it can also be a trap. You're a walking wound, Cass. You've been bleeding all over my floor since the first time you came in here. I can't teach you any more until you learn to live with what you carry."

Cass is still, only the twitch of her jaw betraying her. "I'm fine."

"You're not fine. You're full of poison. You're strong, Cass, stronger than even you know, but it takes a new kind of strength to let yourself heal."

"You think what happened to me is *my* problem? You think I just need to get over it?"

Raven raises one hand, her silver bracelets clinking. "Do not change my words into things they are not, Cassandra. I am not your monster. We all carry pain within us; it is how we bear it that makes us what we are."

Cass sets the bag of dried nettles down, stands up slowly. "I have to go," she says.

Raven sighs. "Oh, Cass. Who will you fight, when there is no one left around you? You are always welcome here."

"I'll see you tomorrow," Cass says, not looking at her. The light in the witch store is watery and grey. *Fuck this,* she thinks, but she cannot tell anymore whether she is furious with Raven or with herself.

"Well met, Cass," Raven says softly. "I will see you again in this life."

That night Cass dreams of the skeleton man. She is standing in front of the black palace, all its doors open to the dead world; he is next to her, his black coat flapping in the breezeless air. His bony hand is on her shoulder, his long fingers curled around her collarbone. *You are keeping something that is precious to me,* he says, his voice the dry flutter of moths' wings in her mind. *I will come for it soon, Cassandra.* He is frightening, but there is something magnetic about those flat black eyes, the thin cruel curve of his mouth. What could she possibly have that he wants? An amulet, a pile of crystals? "Take me with you," she says as he lets go her shoulder, "take me with you," but he does not answer her as he walks away.

She does not go to the witch store anymore, after that.

# NOW:
# BODEGA BAY

Here is her body: long legs, long arms, long bony fingers. The ridge of her knuckles. The teeth of her spine. They got a motel room for twenty dollars, the kind of motel where the door doesn't really lock and the people in the rooms on either side of them live here. Women with faces made desperate by hunger and the grief of watching their own lives leave them. Not all at once but in pieces. Grey-faced children with dark shadows under their eyes. The parking lot full of breaking-down cars stuffed with possessions:

blankets, boxes, toys, groceries. The sheets on the motel-room bed are white and stiff, cheap fabric reeking of bleach. A flickering neon sign advertised FREE CA LE but the television is broken, switches on to channel after channel of static.

This is the longest Maia has ever gone without playing the piano. When she sleeps she dreams of her hands on white keys. She dreams of mermaids drifting in the deep, their songs sweet and faint. She dreams of Rachmaninov's *Elégie in E Flat Minor*, the arpeggiated left hand, the smooth sad chords counterpointing in the right, the melody singing between them both; a piece that makes her think of moors, of wandering in some dreaming misty world smeared with rain and love lost and melancholy. Her hands ache, remembering. The weight of what's unsung threatening to drown her. All her life the only words she has spoken well are those spelled out in notes, black marks on the staves' black lines, the only language she knows as her native tongue. The words are someone else's but the song is hers, the longing, the rhythm of it moving in her body, her blood. For all the years and miles and lifetimes that separate her and those long-dead men, for all their whiteness and their polonaises, for all the ways in which they are nothing like her, what they have written lives in her, is made real in her hands, her heart, the muscles of her back and arms. Her own body, moving, her strong fingers poised above the keys. Sometimes when she plays she imagines them standing over her, a silent ghostly chorus, smiling.

She dreams of Ravel, wandering in the dark world where ghosts speak in human tongues and tell human stories, where demons are real and sirens call to human lovers with no love, only malice. In her dreams the white keys of the piano turn to pale trees in a night forest, their branches reaching overhead into the looming dark, the ground cool beneath her bare feet. Her hair long again, spilling down her back; she is wearing a white dress like a bride's that falls to her ankles and moves around her in drifts although there is no breeze. In front of her the ground splits open, revealing a stairway leading down into the dark, and she knows the man in the black coat is waiting for her at the bottom, patient as death. *I'm coming,* she tells him, *I'm coming. Wait for me. I'm coming.* The darkness knits through her, through and through, black thread on a silver needle flashing between her ribs, stitching silent her tongue, and when she reaches the bottom of the stairs his hands close around her like a cage. But when she wakes up she remembers only the piano, only the feel of her hands on the white keys, only the music in her ears.

What was she thinking? That she could walk away? That speed and freedom would fill the emptiness of her heart, teach her how to love? In Cass she sees herself echoed. What's unmatched in their bodies is twinned in their hearts: that same ache, that sorrow, that vast want. Until she opened her eyes to it Maia had no idea of the immensity of her own hunger. But without the piano she is nothing, no one, not even a girl you would remember. Without the piano she has no way to spell out what she's asking for, no way to name a single thing, to give voice to the loss that follows her wherever she goes. She is her own worst curse. Cass was better off without Maia's dead weight throwing her off course. Before, Maia was a blank slate, a girl with no sense of her own yearning. She channeled the dead in her hands and made their dreams hers, played like she was possessed with a genius no less great for not being her own. But now she is cut adrift, lost between worlds, following Cass from basement show to club to basement show as though she'll find the answer to herself in sweaty skin and the crash of noise, bodies wild against bodies in the dark. It's a release, but it's not the solution to any riddle. If she knew what she wanted, if she could put a name to it, would that set her free? Cass is so sure of herself, so clear, so relentless, but there's nothing about Cass that makes Maia think she is happy, either. Both of them, lost in the loss of each other.

They take turns in the shower. Cass first. Maia can't remember the last time she was clean. Things like that used to matter to her. They'd met some people in Arcata, stayed for a while. Sleeping on floors. Or in beds. Not alone. A couple of nights in a hotel room down the coast some drummer from some band had rented for her and Cass and him and some other people whose names she can't remember. Fat white lines of cocaine on a mirror and Cass's big eyes looking straight at her; later, Cass had said she was sorry, and Maia said, "For what," and Cass said, "I didn't think I was this contagious." A life can change so fast. Where is her mother now, and is she worried? Has she called the cops? Are they swarming the coast, even now, searching out a girl gone astray, or are runaways cheap currency on the I-5 corridor, not even worth the effort of a search until they turn up fish-eyed and clammy in some ditch, their underwear missing and their futures gone? Has Maia's father even noticed she's left? They'd swapped out the license plate on the Mercedes in a grocery-store park-

ing lot in Vancouver, traded it for the plate off a truck festooned with American flag bumper stickers. Both of them
had liked the almost-joke, though the extra step meant
nothing if no one's looking.

But in between there are patches of joy. One night wild
with speed and Cass's hand in hers and this show was
great, this show was brilliant, this show was better than all
the other shows. This show was a woman with long black
hair and a great throaty purr of a voice too big and too
gorgeous for the dirty room, her hands sure on the guitar,
each note true. *I've been waiting for my life to start*, she sang,
and Cass and Maia's eyes went wide, because here they
were, waiting too, and sometimes all it takes is another
voice to call out the words living unspoken in your chest.
The kids around them felt it the same way they did, surging
up against the battered stage with their arms outstretched,
singing along to the chorus as soon as they recognized it
well enough to repeat it. *I've been waiting for my life to start*,
Maia and Cass howled with one voice. After the show
Maia pulled her through a knotted throng to where the
woman and her band were packing up instruments and
amps. "Hi," Maia said, her voice tiny, but the woman heard
her. She was older than they thought, up close. Late twen-
ties, maybe. Lines at the corners of her sad eyes where
hard days had marked her, but her face was kind. "Hi," she
said.

"That was really good," Maia said, a little louder, and
then she said, "How do you play like that? How can I play
like that?"

"Like what?"

"Like how you play," Cass said.

The woman laughed. "It's here, little bird," she said, tapping Maia's chest gently, the knot of bone covering her heart. "It's all here. Don't let anyone tell you otherwise. You play?"

"Piano," Maia said. "But I can't sing."

"People always told me I couldn't sing, too."

"But you're a great singer," Cass said.

She grinned. "That's because I told them to fuck off." She rested her palm on Maia's forehead, a benediction, and then hoisted her guitar and gave them a little wave as she rejoined her band, and the warmth of her touch lingered long after she'd gone.

The high-pitched whine of the pipes ends and Cass comes out of the bathroom wrapped in a shabby towel thin as paper and worn through in places. "Classy," Cass says, poking her thumb through a hole. Her thick dyed hair is standing on end. The road suits her: sun's pinked her cheeks and gilded her shoulders, and her eyes are bright in her tan face. They don't discuss the lives they've slipped as easily as the clothes they shuck at the edge of the ocean. Mermaids. Cass swims like a shark, sure and fearless. Maia's learning in her wake. Cass is the first person she's ever let see her naked. *Was,* she thinks. Cass curls up next to her on the bed, slides one damp arm around her shoulders. "Bony thing," Cass says gently in her ear. "We gotta fatten you up." From Cass, this is almost silly; despite her broad shoulders and solid build, speed's slicked her down to skin and bone, same as Maia. Girls across the country would die for this diet, the wild thrill of their vampire nights. Their new life is like a *Lost Boys* remake.

"I'm homesick," Maia says. Cass chins the top of her

skull and she buries her face in the curve of Cass's neck like a kitten.

"We can take you home."

"Not for that home. I don't ever want to go back to that home."

"For Vietnam?"

"I don't remember Vietnam. I miss the piano."

"I imagine."

"And Oscar. My teacher."

"It must be hard, not being able to play."

"It's like part of me is gone. But I don't know—I don't know what I am without the piano. Without music. I wanted to know that. I wanted to know if it was really something that I loved, or if it's just the only thing I know how to do and I've done it for so long I don't know any better. Oscar wants me to be a musician and my parents want me to be a musician but I don't know what *I* want, I've never even asked myself what I want. I didn't know I could want things until I met you. I thought coming with you would show me what I was without it. But maybe all I am without it is nothing."

Cass strokes Maia's hair, gentling her, murmuring nothings into the whorl of her ear. "I know," she says, over and over. "I know."

"I thought running away would fix it," Maia whispers.

"Running away doesn't fix anything," Cass says. "But it makes you harder to find."

Maia wants to buy bread for sandwiches again. It seems like a good idea. Every idea seems like a good idea with drugs like this twitching through you. Cass jitters and grins. Yes, yes, we'll cook dinner—*With what? Never mind*—we'll clean the car we'll make a plan we'll write everything down for this week and the next week and the next. Girl, we have so many plans we can plan out last week, too. Cass waits for Maia on the sidewalk outside the grocery store, tapping her fingers on the cement curb, watching ordinary shoppers in their ordinary clothes: a mom toting sticky-faced toddlers, a droopy old man with glasses, a teenage girl a few years younger than she is holding the hand of a little boy who is maybe hers or maybe just her brother, a woman in a business suit clop-clopping in heels she has trouble walking in. All these humans. Cass is human, too, look at this, look at her human hands, if she holds her hands to the sun the flesh goes almost translucent, doesn't it, not really translucent but lucid, light shining pinkly through the web of flesh between forefinger and thumb. A woman with thick glasses and a mean squint looks at her, scowling, and then Cass puts her hands on the curb again. Maybe they should eat something besides bread. What do people eat? Cass thinks about it, can't remember. Carrots, people eat carrots. Spaghetti. Bananas. Tofu and avocado. A coffee cup. You don't eat a coffee cup. You put coffee in it. Cass puts her chin on her knees, hugs her legs to her chest. It isn't cold. There's a woman by the door to the grocery store handing out Bibles. She has on a long purple dress—*Ugly*, Cass thinks, *what an ugly dress*—and her face is not young but at the same time strangely age-less; she could be forty, or sixty, or any age in between. She's wearing a scarf over her bushy horse-colored hair. No one wants her Bibles; she's been holding the same one since Cass sat here, offering it with insistent jerks of her outstretched hand, but everyone who passes ignores her, tugs a shopping cart out of its corral, pushes it through the sliding doors. There's a lull in customers, the sidewalk deserted, the glass doors snugged shut and unyielding, and the woman offers Cass the Bible with the same enraged ferocity.

"No, thank you," Cass says.

"Do you know," the woman says. It's the first she's talked. Her voice is surprisingly low and raspy. "Do you know where you will spend eternity?"

"In hell," Cass says. "With all the rest of my friends." By which she means Maia. She doesn't mean to be sarcastic; it's not until the woman snorts in contempt that Cass realizes what she's said.

"God has no place for sinners," the woman says.

"I do," Cass says, but low, to herself. "I do." She does.

# THEN

Maia won't admit to herself how hard she's looking for Cass, but she walks home from Oscar's every day that week. At the piano, she's as focused as ever. The Ravel is enormously difficult; she barely makes it through, the first time she plays for Oscar. He tsk-tsks at her. "We must begin more quietly," he says. "It is as the poem: We enter this world that is made without us already, that beckons us in but does not give us answers. We are part of the water, we are bewitched by the water. Do you see? You must make me believe it. She is trying to bring him in, to sink him. Then here"—he taps the page—"further along, he rejects her, and she is furious. But always you, the story-teller, must be in control. She is angry, but also ruined, do you see? She dissolves without him. All of this you must tell us."

She plays, as always, with a ferocity that belies the tini-ness of her world, the penned-in dollhouse of her life. When she was in school, there was school, but it's been years since she was in school. She studies in her room, now, and takes tests on a paper she mails to an office some-where. Her mother is supposed to be guiding her but her mother is always, forever, too busy; something has come up, a meeting must be gone to, a dinner party attended, a luncheon, you'll be fine on your own, won't you. The truth is, Maia has always been fine on her own. When she's not practicing she opens her books at random—trigonometry, European history, biology. Triangles, the roof of the Sistine chapel, a diagram of fruit fly genes. Sometimes she falls asleep with her cheek against the thin pages, wakes with cheap ink smeared on her skin. Equations transferring from the text to her body, marking her with some language that is far less useful to her than the language she lives in, the language of her hands. The notes that move from the page to her eyes to her fingers, quick as sound, quicker.

This week, Oscar is harder on her than he's ever been; maybe he sees in her some seed that Cass has planted. At the piano he is relentless, making her play the Ravel over and over and over for him until she wants to tear the music into pieces and throw them at his head. "You must prac-tice!" he says Friday afternoon, after he's demanded she play a single measure thirty times in a row. "Have you not practiced? Have you got lazy?"

"I practice," she whispers. He shakes his head, exhales through his moustache.

"You have gone," he says, waving one hand. "You have gone to somewhere else, I don't know where this is. Listen, I have an idea for you."

"What," she says, exhausted.

"You must read when you play."

"Read the music?"

"No, no." He makes a disdainful face. "Books. You must read books. This is the trouble, I think. You become bored when you practice. Over and over again, the same notes, this is the curse of the pianist; we must play until our body knows the notes so well it is as if we are born with them written in our fingers. Only then can we play with spirit, with interpretation. Only then can we make good choices, do you see? Because it is not the notes you are thinking about any longer, but the music, what is behind it, what it is trying to say through you. Where your body will be when you play, the color of the sound. This is how we play, when we play well. So you read while you practice."

"I don't—"

"Always it is *no* with you, Maia. Poetry isn't good, it has got its own rhythm." He frowns. "Unless it is *modern* poetry, which one cannot help but find quite upsetting. But I don't think poetry is the thing. And great fiction, you know, it's not the thing either. If the language is beautiful it is most distracting." He looks out the window, tugging thoughtfully at his moustache. "Detective stories," he says.

"Detective stories."

"Yes, detective stories. Also I find that the newspaper is good for this; of course it's harder to put at the piano. Not the front page, the front page is always *very* distressing, this is a country full of criminals. Criminals and disaster. You will read detective stories, when you practice at home."

Maia gives up. "Sure. I'll read detective stories when I practice."

Oscar beams at her. "Next week, my dear, I promise you, you shall see the most wonderful results!"

"Oscar, I read the poem. The Bertrand. My mom had it."

"Ah, yes. Your mother." Oscar hates her mother.

"Ondine, the mermaid? She's sort of horrible." He raises an eyebrow. "I mean, Oscar, she says she's in love but she doesn't care if she kills her lover. She's selfish. She knows he'll die when she pulls him underwater."

Oscar nods. "Yes, my dear, of course. This is true. But it is also—well, we are not speaking of human beings here, for the one thing. We are speaking of creatures of myth. These people, they do not have morals the way that we have morals. They are quite a bit older than we are, you know." Oscar is discussing mermaids as if they're a slightly eccentric family who lives down the street. Maia opens her mouth to say something, but he continues. "They do not share our views of the world. But of course it is more than this. When we fall in love we desire only to live in the shadow of desire. We don't think of the sensible thing. It is no matter if we are a human being or a little fish in the sea. Or this mermaid."

"But he doesn't say she's in love, not like that. She's try-ing to tempt him underwater even though she knows it'll kill him. When he tells her he's in love with a human woman, she laughs at him. It's not tragic, it's—"

"Who are you, child, to say what tragedy is? Have you loved?"

Maia falters in the face of his sudden outrage. "No," she says. "But that's not what he says about her. *'Boudeuse et dépitée.'* He's saying she's sulky. Selfish. Not tragic."

"Love is always selfish," Oscar snaps. "Always. Love is only interested in taking away all that makes a person what they are, and bringing this person into you. There is no love that does not wish to take and take until there is nothing left of the beloved."

Maia is quiet. Oscar can't be right, but what does she know? She has never been in love. She doesn't know anything about the world except for her own house and her piano and this room where she plays for Oscar. All the years she's come to his house, and he's never even let her see the upstairs. She can feel her heart buzzing inside her chest like a bee trapped in a jar, battering itself against the glass. There is a whole world of secrets outside the walls that keep her. When she was younger, she saw her cage as keeping other people out. Now she's coming to understand that instead it's made to shut her in.

"I don't know," she says.

"I am correct," Oscar says, imperious. But under his pompousness she can sense something massive, an old hurt calcified. He's told her countless times he ruined his own life, and that's why he's stuck here, teaching piano to her and a sea of snot-nosed wealthy children. But he's never told her the story of that ruin, or the shape it came in. What kind of wreckage could leave him like this that's not a broken heart? She may have never been in love, but she's read books. Whatever Oscar says, love is messier and more grand than he's willing to let on. Of that, she's sure.

Oscar doesn't let the silence build. "You will go home now," he tells her. "You will practice and practice, with the detective stories, as I have told you." As far as she knows, there's not a single detective story in the entirety of her mother's library. "When you play there must be no Maia. There is only the music, the hands, the muscle of the back. Here, and here." He pokes her shoulders with one blunt finger. She stifles a yelp. "I have seen you do this before and it is why I am asking you to do it again, because I understand that you are good enough. Even though *you* do not."

His last *you* is almost an accusation. Maia nods. She won't give Oscar the satisfaction of knowing he's made her cry. She gathers up her music and puts it in her bag, keeping her back to Oscar so that he can't see her hands shaking.

"I'll see you next week," she says, her voice as even as she can make it. Oscar shows her to the door. She keeps her back straight as she walks away, long after his door closes behind her, long after his house recedes into the distance and she knows there is no one left to see what's left of her pride carry her home.

But Oscar's sternness has shifted something inside her and that night at the piano the music changes. At first the Ravel is as difficult as ever, as heavy and shapeless in her hands as dough. Her arms are stiff, riddled with their old familiar aches: strained tendons, cramping fingers, the ordinary pains of the pianist who wishes to be extraordinary. *What do I know about love,* Maia thinks, staring dully at the keys. What is a piano but wood and string and ivory, felt hammer, metal pedal. No secrets hidden in its body, no clues to how she might make it sing. Frustrated, she runs a set of scales, and then another, and then another, until her mind is empty and her hands are limber, and then she tries the Ravel again.

She can feel the difference in the first chords and wills herself not to overthink it, to let the music come from her like dancing or breathing. She imagines the low murmur of Oscar's voice, gentling her through the piece. *We know the notes, do we not? We have played them many times. They are in our memory now. We have only to let them go, to give them shape.* She almost laughs out loud with the joy of it, the music rising out of her like the blood flowing through her veins, pumped through her by the rhythm of her heart even as the meter of the piece tolls through it like a bell. Here it is at last, this window to the other side, this feeling that she lives for, this rare elation. And then she misses a note. *What do you know about desire?* sneers a little voice in her heart. *What do you know about darkness? What do you know about the kingdoms underneath the belly of the earth?* She stumbles through a chord. The piece is clunky again and she soldiers through the rest of it without joy.

But for a moment it was there, it was hers.

"That was beautiful, Maia," her mother says behind her. Maia whirls around on the bench. Her mother is leaning in the doorway, her head tilted, her face soft. Maia has no idea how long she's been standing there. She looks down at her hands.

"I haven't nailed it yet," she says. "The last half wasn't right."

Her mother shrugs. "You'll get it. And it still sounds wonderful."

"Thanks," Maia says, unsettled. Her mother is so stern that she forgets, sometimes, that her mother is also human; that, presumably, her mother has emotions like other human beings; that her mother also loves, looks at paintings and finds them pretty, listens to music and is moved. Once Maia walked in on her mother listening to *The Magic Flute* in her office and crying unabashedly. She looked up as Maia came into the room and smiled. They waited together until the end of the aria and then she lifted the needle off the record and sighed. "Your father and I went to the William Kentridge production," she said. "It was the most beautiful thing I've ever seen. The shadow puppets . . ." She trailed off and looked tearily at the wall. "It's really an Orpheus story, you know," she said, her voice distant. "Charming beasts with flute music. There's a kind of underworld throughout, and of course for Kentridge the metaphors of colonialism, exploration—but really, at the heart of it, his vision is so magnificent, his scenery so wonderfully realized."

"You don't need to lecture me," Maia said. "You can just tell me you like something." But though she'd intended the words to be gentle, her mother's eyes snapped back into focus, and Maia saw that instead she'd landed a blow. "I didn't mean—" she said, but her mother cut her off.

"Did you want something?"

"I just needed to borrow some paper," Maia said.

"Oh," her mother said. "Sure." She'd handed Maia a few

sheets. Maia had taken the paper and fled to the safety of her room.

Sometimes she wishes it were easier to simply hate the woman who bought her, but moments like this one, when the expression on her face is so wistful, so full of longing, make it impossible to loathe her altogether.

"Well," her mother says. "Keep practicing."

"Is it okay with you and Dad if I stay up and work on this?" Her parents don't like it when she practices late, but every now and then she asks for the favor, and they let her.

"I suppose that's fine, just for tonight," her mother says. "I can put in earplugs if I can't fall asleep."

"Are you going to bed?"

"Soon."

"Goodnight, then."

"Goodnight, Maia." Maia presents her cheek dutifully, and her mother crosses the room in a few long strides and kisses it. The smell of her perfume lingers long after she leaves.

Maia plays through the Ravel again, and again, and again. The moment she had earlier never returns, but with each repetition the notes come more easily and she makes fewer and fewer mistakes. At last, she is getting somewhere. She tamps down the spark of glee that leaps up in her lest she get cocky, plays the piece again. And again. And again. Imagining as the night passes that she is first the mermaid, then the lover, the seductress and the seduced. And if she were the lover, what would her own answer be? To live in the dark below the surface forever, wandering the lightless, frigid depths in the company of her beloved? There are worse fates. The room grows cool and her attention drifts.

Under her feet she can feel a smooth path; around her, the undulating lines of a kelp forest rising toward a surface too far away to see. *What would Cass do,* she thinks. *Cass would find out where the path goes.* She takes one step forward, and then another, and then she is walking forward in the dark and the path opens up into a fissure in the earth and there is a man standing in front of her, at the place where the descent begins. He is looking somewhere over her shoulder and because he does not seem to notice her she stares at him openly. He is terribly thin and so pale he glows against the velvety dark, and he is dressed in a long coat that moves in the darkness like a deeper darkness, and Maia thinks, *Are we underwater, we can't be underwater, I can't breathe underwater, I'm not a fish,* and then the man looks at her. His eyes are very black.

*Here you are at last,* he says. His voice is dry and so low that she can feel it inside her, somewhere in her chest.

"Who are you?"

*We have a mutual acquaintance,* he says, smiling, a death's-head grin with no real joy behind it. *But it is your music that makes me wish to know you better. It has been a long time since the sound of a gift like yours found its way to us in the deep. Come with me, and I will show you a kingdom the likes of which you have never even dreamed.*

There is something about him that is both sinister and lovely, and his voice is in her ears and her throat and her body, and he is reaching one hand out to her, his lips slightly parted as though he is readying for a kiss. She takes his hand; his cool fingers close around her wrist. *Are you the lover,* she thinks, *or are you the beloved,* and she remembers that the human refused the mermaid not only because he was fickle but because loving her would mean his death, and she pulls her hand from the man's grasp and takes a step backward, shaking her head.

"I can't," she says, "I can't, you know that, I can't come here," and he smiles then and his smile goes all the way through her like a knife splitting open her rib cage and laying bare the pulsing muscle of her heart.

*We will see each other again,* he says. *I am a patient man.* Then the earth swallows him up and Maia comes awake with a jolt where she is slumped against the piano, her hands stiff and cramping. She knows without looking at the clock in the kitchen that it is late. She climbs the stairs to her room, her body aching as though she's run a mile underwater. *Jesus,* she thinks, *what a weird dream.* She washes her face in the bathroom, looks at herself in the mirror. The piano keys have left their imprint across her cheek, and she touches her face and then runs her fingers through her black hair. There are droplets of something silvery caught in the long strands. She touches her tongue to the tip of her finger. There, unmistakable, the salt taste of seawater.

# NOW: SANTA CRUZ

Maia calls Oscar from a pay phone in Santa Cruz. It's a sun-basted college town, peopled with newly minted trustafarians flush with their parents' cash and relics left over from the era of free love and psychedelics shuffling down the main strip in dirty corduroy bell-bottoms. "Someone should tell them Jimi died," Cass says.

"Jimmy who?" Maia asks.

Cass rolls her eyes. "Never mind."

It's a funny place, filled with white students a couple of

years older than them, hair knotted into clumpy dread-locks and stuffed into crocheted Rasta hats. The boys grow scruffy, pubic-looking beards that straggle up their acne-spotted faces. Cass holds hippies in the deepest contempt, grumbling about them as Maia drives past head shops and burrito places with big rainbow-painted signs.

"Let me know if you see a phone," Maia says. Cass doesn't ask who she wants to call.

They find one in a grocery-store parking lot. Cass waits in the car, chewing her thumb and smoking, while Maia picks up the receiver with shaky hands. She makes a fist around the handful of change in one pocket, waits until the coins are sweaty and her hand is hot. What will she say if he answers? What will she do if he doesn't? She feeds nickels and dimes into the phone, dials, holds her breath. He answers on the second ring, as though he's been wait-ing next to the phone all this time.

"'Ello?"

"Hi, Oscar."

"*Maia*," he says, his tone equal parts relief and accusa-tion. "Then you are alive."

"I'm alive."

"You are coming home."

"Not for a while."

"You are practicing, where you are?"

"Oscar. No."

He makes an exasperated noise and she can picture him, pursing his lips and pushing out air. She has tried, herself, to replicate his hilariously French disgust, but it never looks the same on her.

"I needed a break," she says.

"You needed a *break*," he repeats. "What is this, your summer vacation? You think this is how the world works? When we are tired, we run off with our parents' little car and do not tell anyone where we are for weeks, hmm? This is what you think adults do?"

"I don't—no, I don't think that. Are my parents looking for me?"

"I would imagine. I have not spoken to them since they called me asking where you were and I was obliged to tell them I did not know."

"Oh."

"You have made me quite unhappy, Maia."

"I know, Oscar. I'm sorry. Will you—will you tell my parents I'm okay?" His silence on the other end of the phone is deadly. "Just tell them—tell them you heard from me. Tell them I'm fine." No answer. "Oscar?"

"I do not understand why you could not tell me."

"Tell you?"

"That you are so miserable with me."

"Oh, Oscar. It wasn't you. It was—there's something wrong with me. I can't—I have to figure out—" She falters.

"I was like you once," he says abruptly.

"What?"

"When I was young. You know, it is difficult, this life. I am not unaware of this. I have led it also. Sometimes a child has certain ideas. He has grown up certain one set of things is true, yes? He is talented, he practices, he works hard, everything falls into place. It is a simple path if he can follow the rules. But then something comes along to change this. He sees something about himself that he did not see before, and perhaps it frightens him."

"Something like that," Maia says.

"I ruined my own life," he says. "I did this, Maia. Me and no one else. I had a good career ahead of me, and I destroyed it because I looked inside myself and I could not manage what I found there. I do not wish this for you. I have spent every day of my life with this thing. It is not pleasant. Do you know why you are my best student, Maia?"

"No," she whispers.

"It is because you are afraid also. It is this fear that pushes you to work, like an engine in your heart, do you see? But this fear, it will also take you apart. If you can conquer this, you will be a better pianist than I ever could have been. I teach you because you are on the edge of being magnificent. I cannot tell you what you are afraid of; only you can know this. It is not my business. But I see the mistakes I have made when I was not much older than you, and I do not wish you to make them."

"I have to find out," she says, "what it is."

"Maia, I do not believe you," he says. "I think you have already got the answer inside you, and you are running away."

She thinks of her mother's stern, pale face, her father's sad eyes hazy with whisky. She thinks of Cass, waiting for her in the car. She thinks of the last weeks, of how it feels to have no one watching her, nowhere to be, no rules for the first time in her entire life. Free of everything except the trap of her own heart.

"I don't," she says. "I don't know. I'm sorry, Oscar. I can't come back right now."

There's a rustling noise. She can picture Oscar running

his hand across his moustache in exasperation as clearly as if she's standing next to him. "Fine," he says. "I will tell your parents I have spoken to you and you are not dead. Although I imagine they might wish to hear this from you directly."

"Don't be mad at me. Please."

"When you are ready to return to me," he says coolly, "my door will be open to you."

"Thank you," she says. "Oscar, I love you." But the unmistakable click of his hanging up is followed by a dial tone that swallows her words whole.

She replaces the phone in its cradle, leans her head against the glass of the pay phone booth. She stands like that for a long time before she walks back to the car.

Cass is dozing in the passenger seat, but she opens her eyes as soon as Maia gets in. "You don't look so good."

"Probably not," Maia says, wiping her eyes.

"You want to talk about it?"

"Not really."

Cass hands her the tobacco and Maia tries rolling herself a cigarette, but she can barely manage this new skill when her hands aren't trembling. Cass takes the tobacco back without comment, rolls two cigarettes, passes her one. Maia lights it and blows a column of smoke out the open window.

"Let's find some weed," Cass says. "And some surfers. And a nice beach." To her delight, Maia smiles.

"You know what?" she says. "I think that is an excellent plan."

# THEN

"Take me to your house," Cass says one afternoon. They're sitting on the sidewalk, talking about nothing. Cass rolls a cigarette and hands it to Maia, who takes it and then looks at it, uncertain. "I'll get cancer," she says.

"Eventually," Cass agrees. She lights the cigarette. Maia takes a single, cautious puff and doubles over, hacking into her knees and flinging the cigarette away from her into the street.

"Oh my god!" she wheezes. "That's disgusting!"

"It grows on you," Cass says. "Come on, let's go to your house. What are you afraid of?" Maia can't answer with the truth. *You.*

"Nothing," she says, wiping her mouth with the back of her hand and wishing she had something to wash out the cigarette's taste. She has a few hours before her mother will be home. It's safe, she thinks, it has to be safe. It's a bad idea, but if no one finds out no one will know any better. She stands up and tugs Cass to her feet. "Come on."

Cass inside her house is a revelation. Cass stands in the front hallway, silent, looking at the polished floors and the beige carpets and the white walls, and Maia sees the house as if for the first time through Cass's eyes, smells its too-clean chemical tang. Maia's house looks like no one lives in it.

"Well," Cass says. "No wonder." Maia takes her shoes off and wills Cass to notice, to unlace her dirty boots without being asked, but Cass is oblivious or ignoring her and Maia, cringing, says nothing as Cass's big black boots cross the hardwood, the forbidden carpet. She follows Cass from the front hall to the kitchen. Through the kitchen. She watches Cass eye her reflection in the mirror-clean surface of the oven. In the hallway between the kitchen and the living room Cass pauses to take in the wall's sole decoration, a blurry framed photo of Maia as a toddler, bookended by her parents. Her father is holding her hand; her mother is staring at the camera with the haughty, bored expression she always has in pictures.

"Your parents are white," Cass says.

"I'm adopted," Maia says. "From Vietnam." Cass nods and says nothing else, and for that Maia is so inexplicably grateful she wants to hug Cass, take her back to the kitchen and feed her snacks, make sandwiches with the expensive paté her mother buys and leaves untouched in the refrigerator. Maia's mother is not a big eater, but she likes the appearance of fine things.

Cass stops again in the living room, takes in the overstuffed matching furniture, the matching end tables, the matching crystal-based lamps with their matching shades. Matching throw pillows for matching couches. Matching paintings of abstract taupe expanses on the matching walls. The glossy piano dominating the room like an altar. "Who plays this?" she asks.

"I do," Maia says.

"Far *out*," Cass says. She crosses the room to the piano, depresses one ivory key so gently it doesn't make a noise. "I can't play a thing. Used to want guitar lessons so bad when I was little, but I think that was just too much MTV. Will you play me something?"

Maia, who's played for Oscar, for rooms filled with faceless adults, for judges, for her vicious peers, for hundreds and hundreds of people, is suddenly frozen with terror. "I'm not any good," she mumbles. Cass shrugs.

"You have to be better than me," she says. "Come on."

Maia takes her seat at the piano, bewildered by her sudden stage fright. Cass is chewing on a piece of dirty hair, watching her with those solemn grey eyes. *Chaque flot est un ondin qui nage dans le courant.* For this girl, Maia will play the way to the kingdoms of the deep.

She's never played the Ravel so well, and she wishes that Oscar could see her now, her hands moving like light on water, like waves against the shore, like a shipwreck, like drowning. And then she isn't wishing anything at all; she is the water, the deep green roar, the mermaid singing her lover down to darkness, the lover falling. *Come drown with me and be my love.* She stumbles a little in the right hand but keeps going. She plays like the night is moving through her body, plays like a tidal wave. Plays for all the journeys down into the dark she's ever taken, all the lonely nights spent underwater, plays her regrets as salt-stinging as ocean spray, plays to a still deep place where the sunlight cannot filter down. There, in the dark, he is waiting for her, the man who is not the mermaid, not the lover, but something older and wiser and hers alone. The man with the bone-white face and the black coat, the man she saw in her dream, his mouth making the shape of her name: *Maia, Maia, I see you. I see you.* Through the dark water, the white gleam of his hands. *Wait for me,* she thinks, *make me change my mind,* and he smiles.

Cass is silent for a long time after Maia finishes, and then she lets all her breath out in one giant sigh that means she's been holding it in. "Holy shit," she says softly. She touches Maia's shoulder and Maia covers Cass's hand with hers, and they have been standing like that for ten seconds or ten thousand years when Maia hears the front door close and knows the worst has happened, the worst was bound to happen. Her mother is home early. She whips her hand away from Cass's and Cass, startled, takes her hand away from Maia's shoulder, and Maia pushes the bench away from the piano, standing up as fast as she can, wondering if she can get Cass out a window, under the couch, in some closet upstairs where she can be secreted away until it's safe to come out, and then her mother strides into the living room and it's all over.

"Maia, please don't make me tell you again to put your bag—" and then she sees Cass and stops dead. It's the only time in her life Maia has ever seen her mother at a loss.

"Mom," she says. "This is my friend. Cass."

Maia's mother's eyes flicker cold, up and down, taking Cass in. "We don't wear shoes in our house," she says. Cass meets her freezer-burn stare with a wall of ice.

"I was just leaving," Cass says. Cass, dirty and ragged, but she's all queen again now, her back straight, her chin high. Cass, undefeatable. Maia knows how badly she will be in for it later, wishes herself underground, underwater, dead. This was far and away the worst idea she's ever had. But she can't help yearning for Cass's poker-straight spine, her cool grey eyes, the barest hint of a sneer at the corner of her mouth. Cops, adults, teachers, shopkeepers: Cass is immune to the will of authority, made ballistic by any hint of shackle.

"It was nice to meet you, Cass," Maia's mother says, in a tone that conveys the exact opposite sentiment.

"It was nice to meet you, too," Cass says. Maia could swear she's trying not to laugh. She watches Cass walk across the room, her back still straight, waits until they hear the clomp of Cass's boots on the floor, the click of the front door closing behind her.

"What in god's name was that," her mother says.

"A girl I met," Maia says. Then, idiotically: "A friend of Oscar's. I met her at Oscar's." Her mother stares her down until she looks at the floor.

"Don't you ever bring her into this house again," she says. "Get back to practicing."

It's only when her mother has left the room that Maia sees the track of Cass's boot prints, marring the pale carpet all the way to the door.

Somehow Cass has become her friend. Maia is afraid to even think such a thing, terrified lest she jinx this sudden magic; but for weeks Cass has shown up on the same corner, and Maia has to admit to herself there's no other possible reason than that Cass is waiting for her. For her. Maia, loafers and khakis and concert-pianist future and all. The day her mother has her afternoon seminar, Maia has two entire blessed hours of freedom to spend with Cass. They don't steal beer again. Maia is disappointed, but too timid to say so. They have coffee—Maia pays—or Indian buffet if Cass is looking particularly starved, or if the weather is nice they wander around. Cass likes to look in the thrift stores that line the Ave. Sometimes she goes into the dressing room to try things on and emerges looking ten pounds heavier, and when they get outside she giggles and shows Maia her haul: sweaters stuffed under her T-shirt, or jeans pulled on under her army pants. As far as Maia can tell, she gives away most of what she takes. It's the thrill of the theft that brings her back. Once, heart pounding, Maia tries it herself. Nothing special, just a grey thermal that's worn especially soft. In the fluorescent-lit cubicle she puts it on under her shirt, puts her coat on over them both. She's certain someone's noticed, but she walks out the front door without occasioning a second glance from the bored-looking woman at the register, and the shirt is hers.

"See," Cass says, grinning. "I knew you had it in you." Maia smiles, bashful. That afternoon when she gets home she tucks the shirt all the way at the back of her dresser, where her mom's least likely to notice it. The thought of her new secret makes her smile.

After that, grift gets easier, though it always sets her heart to pounding. She pockets lipsticks in drugstores, candy in the checkout line. She eats the candy, leaves the lipsticks unopened in coffee-shop bathrooms. She's nothing like as good as Cass, too clumsy and afraid of getting caught to even begin to try the kinds of tricks Cass gets up to. Return scams, walking out on restaurant bills, palming whole bricks of cheese in the grocery store, helping herself to wool hats on cold days and umbrellas when it rains. Maia can be by Cass's side the entire time and never notice, Cass is so fast and so good.

"Aren't you scared?" Maia asks.

"Scared of what?"

"Getting caught."

Cass shrugs. "I don't think about it," she says. "It's easier that way."

When Maia practices the piano now she thinks of Cass. Cass on the street, Cass on the corner with her dirty friends. Cass asking strangers for change. Cass cutting her own hair. Cass eating meals she hasn't paid for. Where Cass sleeps. Cass won't take her to the squat—"It's dirty there," she'd said—and so Maia can only picture it in her head. She saw a TV movie of *Oliver Twist* once, and she imagines Cass's squat as something like Fagin's lair, cramped and lousy with snaggletoothed waifs. Girls in dirty velvet jackets with tarnished gold buttons, breeches, cravats. Wool caps with brims, fingerless gloves. Cooking porridge over a wood-burning stove. She likes to think of Cass presiding over them, the orphans' queen, demanding they turn out their pockets with the day's loot so she can take her pick of the best of it.

Of course she knows wherever Cass lives is nothing like *Oliver Twist*. Cass has told her as much. Cass doesn't ever bring any of her friends when she spends the afternoon with Maia, but she tells Maia stories about them. Mayhem, who is always getting arrested because she picks fights with cops. Felony, who set her parents' house on fire before she ran away from it. Earth, who's been in and out of foster care and institutions so many times he can't even remember who his parents are supposed to be anymore. Maia doesn't comment on the names of Cass's friends, doesn't ask why all of them decided to be nouns instead of people. It seems obvious, anyway. A name like Felony was a disguise you could step into, along with your torn black clothes and steel-toed boots. Felony, Crowbar, Digger, Chainsaw, Mayhem. With names like those to live up to, you had to be tougher than you actually were until you actually were that tough. Tougher than parents, tougher than teachers, tougher than cops. Tougher than adults and norms and the riptide of your past. Tougher than all your ghosts. Cass herself dropped fey and prissy *andra* for the brevity of Cass, one syllable, sharp and short. Cass could be a thing that cuts or strikes. The hard edge of a stone. Cass is mean where Cassandra is feeble. Cassandra: always predicting trouble and too much of a girl to do anything about it. Cass? Nobody fucks with Cass.

# NOW:
# LOS ANGELES

ater, Cass will think, *I could have stopped it before it even
started.* She could have said *No* or *I'm tired* or *We're almost out of cash and all the way out of speed and let's go rent an
apartment by the beach and find dishwashing jobs and learn to
surf, let's get clean and stay away from trouble and forget about
sad-eyed boys that don't spell us any good.* But she doesn't
know, then, to say any of those things. When they see the
flyer stapled to a telephone pole, their hands still shaky
with the comedown, their veins lonely and aching with

want, when Maia says, "What do you think?" Cass says, "Sure." The band is nobody they've heard of.

"Argo?" Maia says. "What kind of band name is that?"

"A bad one," Cass says.

But surely at this show they will at least be able to forget the loom of their troubles for the space of some angry chords and sweat. Every day Cass wakes with dread in her throat, sure this will be the morning that Maia says, "I'm done," and drives away forever, back to her piano and her shiny house and her normal life and her gleaming future. It's not too late for Maia. She can grow out her hair, wash the dirt from her clothes, shake herself free of road dust and greasy diner food and gas-station coffee and one bad decision piling up on top of another like dominoes in a line waiting for the push that'll bring the whole thing crashing down. Maia's still radiant underneath the patina of sweat and beach sand; Cass, dirty from the heart outward, said goodbye to the bright future a long long time ago.

So now she says yes, yes to everything, yes to every time Maia wants to stop and buy apples they won't eat or pee or brush her teeth in a roadside rest area or look through seaside-town gift shops, tilting snow globes one after the other, laughing at the whirl of white and glitter. Yes to scoring and yes to hotel rooms and yes to rock and roll, and who is Cass kidding, it's not like she ever said no to sex or death or music before now. If Maia wants to get sweaty in California to a badly named boy band, who is Cass to keep her from it. Maia, her eyes bright as a child's, her chin tilted just so, her bleached hair falling in her face. Every time she sticks out her lower lip to blow the strands out of her eyes a thrill goes through Cass, as sharp as a scalpel and as bright. If Cass could memorize Maia, she would; she would hold every piece of this girl in her heart for the long winter the rest of her life will become when Maia leaves her and her world goes dark again.

They ask directions from a couple of sneering punks on the beach who sneer a little less when Cass rolls them a joint. "We're going anyway," says the boy, who's next to bald save a dusting of pink-dyed fuzz and whose spiked dog collar is at odds with his baby face. Underneath the sulk he looks about twelve.

"You can come with us," his girlfriend adds.

"Thanks," Maia says drily, but her sarcasm is lost on Babyface and his paramour.

It's a club the kids take them to, somewhere down in Venice Beach. Maia follows the punks' car, so anxious not to lose them she's almost riding their bumper. Neither Cass nor Maia knows a thing about LA, and they keep getting lost in the tangled maze of freeway. "I just want to find the ocean!" Cass had cried to a man in a gas station. "Pacific or Atlantic?" he'd smart-assed back. "It's rush hour, sweetheart, gonna take you awhile either way."

But Babyface doesn't lead them astray. The show is at a real club. More or less. Maybe less, Cass thinks, as she crosses the threshold, blinking at the sudden dark. At the back of the room she can make out a low-lit stage: a big wooden box painted black, but still. It's something. There's the usual grubby bar, sullen bartender who won't ask questions as long as the girls pay cash, wallpaper of tattered posters gone yellow-grey with cigarette smoke.

"Classy." After all their travel together Maia's still delighted by dark places, the thrill of the true dive. Cass can see the old anew through Maia's eyes and grins, too.

"Only the best for my girl," she says, and she is grateful for the dark that hides her blush. Maia kisses her.

The club is peppered with a sparse crowd, Babyface and more of the same, and a few bored-looking older punks made haggard by drink and hard living. Someone here has drugs to unload, for sure, but for once she's content to set aside the hanker. Her mood must be catching; Maia doesn't say anything about it, either.

The first band is bad, the second worse. The club empties until it's just Cass, Maia, a few stragglers. Cass is bored and tired, but they have nowhere to sleep and nowhere to go and neither of them is particularly eager to go back out into the night. There's a long lag between the second band and Argo, the only name Cass remembers from the poster. Maia sidles up to the bar and charms a free beer out of the stony-faced bartender, a feat so improbable Cass wouldn't have believed it if she hadn't seen it happen. The mood in the room is listless. The eldest of the punks, a decrepit creature near-mummified in fraying band patches and filthy black denim, has fallen asleep standing up, leaning against the wall.

And then Argo comes onstage. They aren't charismatic. Outside of the singer they aren't even notably cute. But there's something about the way they carry themselves, a surety, a grace, that makes Cass stand up straighter and pay attention. They move like they mean business, and they have a confidence about them that makes her wonder for a second if the room hasn't filled with people when she wasn't looking. Maia's noticed it, too, looking up at them like a robin eyeing a spot in the earth she thinks might yield a worm.

When they start to play Cass could swear she's heard this song before, but she hasn't. It's familiar and somehow not, polished smooth but with a rawness behind it that pulls her in. "Are they playing Pixies covers?" Maia murmurs in her ear, but Cass shakes her head.

The singer is skinny and tall, and his bleached hair falls in his face. He's wearing a Misfits shirt and dirty jeans. His voice is the whisky-soaked croon of someone far older and bigger and filled up with sorrows, and it winnows its way into Cass's hard heart in spite of herself. There is a charge in the air around him. Even from where she's standing Cass can tell his eyes are an uncanny shade of blue, and when he looks up, once, from the microphone she feels sheared straight through by his intensity until she realizes he isn't looking at her at all. He's looking at Maia, singing as though he's singing only for her. Out of all the bars in the world they could have come to, all the clubs in this nightmare sprawl of a city, they had to pick this one, this night, where Maia shines alone in the near-empty room like a beacon. You can practically see her fucking halo. The chorus of the song is a lilting refrain that rises clear and incongruous over a wailing thrash of guitar. "I came here to find you," he sings, the anguished rasp suddenly gentle. Cass doesn't have to look to know Maia's mouth is hanging open, her eyes alight.

"Ah, shit," Cass mutters to herself, reaching in her pocket for her tobacco. All this time she's watched Maia, terrified, waiting for the moment when Maia gets tired of being dirty, tired of being cold, tired of sleeping on the ground and spending the last of her parents' money, tired of ragged no-good Cass, the crazy bitch with bad dreams. But for all her vigilance it never occurred to her to keep her eye out for something like this. She wants to grab Maia's hand, drag her out of the club and back to the car, take off in a screech of burning rubber like felons capering out of a fresh-robbed bank. But Maia's unraveling even as Cass hatches escapes, undone by this stupid sky-eyed boy with his stupid stupid guitar. Cass lights her cigarette, chews her thumb between drags, looks at the bartender, the floor, the filthy old punk who's listing to one side with his jaw slack, anywhere but at Maia or at the stage. Now, she knows already, it's too late to run for safety.

Maia can't say what it is that stakes her through the heart. His eyes or his mouth or maybe even the music, which is like all the music Cass has given her but also more so. More something. More than just the promise of each chord. Something bigger, the way that Bach is made up of tiny pieces of order pieced together into a quilt of god far more immense than the sum of its parts. But this music is not god's music, not anything to do with glory. She's not so new to this world that she doesn't recognize with a flicker of delight that he's playing for her and her alone, that Cass is fading into the darkness at her side even as the face in front of her grows more illuminated with the light of their eyes on one another. She imagines a chorus of celestial voices, something ethereal carrying them toward the rafters. His white-blue eyes burn right through her, all the way to the bloody gristle of her heart.

After the show is as easy as breathing. She waits in the parking lot, Cass in tow, as the band loads their equipment into a rusty van with CHURCH OF THE NAZARENE CHRISTIAN ACADEMY painted in fading letters on the side. There's also a drummer and a bassist, a rhymed couplet of torn jeans and patchy facial hair, but they're of no interest to her. The singer's name is Jason, and when he looks at her she can feel all the blood in her body rising to the surface of her skin. She tells him they have nowhere to stay.

"There's a beach near here we can camp at," he says. "All of us. If you want. Half an hour, maybe." Cass is a wall of silence next to her.

"Sure," Maia says. The couplet has finished loading amps and instruments into the back of their battered van, are climbing into their seats, smoking and talking softly among themselves. She looks straight into his eyes. Here she is, out in the world, free as anything. The Maia of six months ago would never in a million years have believed this Maia could exist.

Maia follows the red wink of the van's taillights through the maze of city streets to the freeway north. Cass is quiet in the passenger seat, rummaging through their tapes and putting one in Maia's never heard before. A woman's voice fills the car, big and haunting, singing in a language Maia doesn't recognize against a background of church bells and strings. The music is orchestral and spooky and full of longing, and outside the night is moving past them, filling up with stars as the city slips away and they fly further and further into the dark. Maia can't think of what to say and so she's silent, and the bells ring more and more majestically, tolling down a deep minor progression. To their left the silvered black mass of the ocean heaves liquid and humming against the shore. "Who is this?" Maia asks when the song ends and the tape clicks over to the other side.

"Dead Can Dance," Cass says, looking out her window.

"It's beautiful. What language is that?"

"She made it up."

"Cass, is something wrong?"

Cass pulls her tobacco out of her pocket, rolls a cigarette, lights it. The windows are already open. She blows smoke toward the hills. "No," she says. Ahead of them, the band's van is pulling to the side of the road. Maia parks behind them, touches Cass's shoulder as she reaches for the door handle.

"You're not telling me the truth."

"No." Cass gets out of the car before Maia can say anything else.

They follow the boys through patchy scrub and beach grass to where the sand begins, carrying dirty blankets from the back of the van. The tide is out and there's no moon. The boys range up and down the beach, gathering sticks, until they have enough to start a fire. Cass builds a little pyramid of dried grass and twigs, lights her construction, coaches it into flame. When it's crackling merrily she adds a few pieces of driftwood. The boys arrange themselves around the fire, pull bottles from their pockets and bags. Cass offers a joint. Jason paces to where the breaking waves roll up to the beach, touches his fingers to the water and brings them to his mouth before loping back to join them. He sits next to Maia, close enough that the fabric of his jeans touches her shorts-bared skin. "Communion," he says, explaining, Maia assumes, his brief foray to the water's edge.

He offers her a sip of his pint bottle. "Communion," she agrees, and he laughs. Maia tilts her head back, lets the whisky slide down her throat and turn to courage. Cass is trying to catch her eye; she dodges Cass's unsubtle stare. The joint makes its way around the circle. Cass rolls another. He's asking them questions but instead of answering she takes the bottle back, and so it's Cass who tells him where they're from and how they got here. Cass leaves out the bad parts, leaves in the punk rock and beach sleeping, makes them sound like warriors in the right kind of battle. Maia can't help grinning at the sound of her own story made majestic. They're revolutionaries, storming the gates, piling the paving stones into barricades. *Sous les pavés, la plage.*

"Runaways," he says when she's done, but he's the first of them to bring up the word.

"Not really," Cass says, and then, "I guess a little." Maia can feel the length of his leg pressed against hers. After her third chug of bourbon she lets her weight shift into him and is rewarded by the touch of his hand at the small of her back, his fingers burning through the thin fabric of her T-shirt. It's the drummer who tells Cass and Maia their own saddish story: boys from a little town on the peninsula, cemented by their love of Black Sabbath, Black Flag, and their high school football team's penchant for beating them up each in turn before they gave up the fight and dropped out. Guitars passed down from older friends and older brothers, their first amp, their first drum kit, their first show at somebody's kegger out in the woods. Jason listens to this detailing of his shared history without comment. Kicked out of their parents' houses, sleepless nights curled up with forties in the backseats of cars. Et cetera. And now here they are, doing their best to make a name for themselves. Playing their first tour, basement shows down the coast, passing a hat around to a crowd of filthy punks who reward them mostly in singles and quarters. Cass and Maia have had the privilege of seeing their first real paying gig—fifty dollars, the barkeep handed them, on their way out the door—scored for them by a friend's friend's friend who'd moved to LA and almost made it big some years back.

"It won't be like this for long," Jason says suddenly, cutting off the drummer and the bassist's Greek-chorused narration.

"No?" Cass says, her voice spiraling into arch disbelief.

"I'm going to be the most famous musician in the world."

"And then get rich," offers the drummer, who's clearly heard this all before. "Get rich and die old on a pile of thousand-dollar bills."

"I won't get old," Jason says. "You know that. I'll be the biggest star in the world, and I'll kill myself before I'm thirty."

"Sure, man," says the bass player, yawning. "Spoken like a true rock god." Maia frowns.

"You shouldn't say stuff like that," she says. "Even joking."

"Ah, he's not joking," says the drummer. "But he's still full of shit." The drummer throws an empty beer can at Jason. He catches it, leaps to his feet, shakes his dirty hair, and runs away from them toward the water again. Maia curls her fingers around the secret of his touch, brings her fist to her chin. They are all quiet for a while, save for the occasional whoop from the darkness. Sounds of splashing. Maia can hear a soft buzzing and realizes it's either the drummer or the bass player's snores.

"Goodnight, girl," Cass says from the other side of the fire.

"Goodnight, Cass," she says, her heart full of love that can't find its way to her tongue. How can you ever tell a person all the things you feel for her? Goodnight warrior, goodnight queen, goodnight girl who set me free. Goodnight my best and only friend. Goodnight and here we are, on the edge of something. What edge, Maia doesn't know, but she's sure it's a glorious precipice. She remembers herself at the campground in Big Sur, standing on the cliff, remembers Cass pulling her back to safety. Was she drunk? She can't remember. She'd wanted to jump and she cannot, now, remember why. Something out there in the dark waiting for her. Honey and the sound of wings and a dog howling. *Silly,* she thinks. If she had jumped she would not be here, now, on the brink of whatever magic is about to come her way. She thinks of Jason's hand on her back and thrashes a little, deliciously. Maia rolls herself up in a blanket that smells of pot and cigarette smoke and boy, watches the fire flicker and quiet into reddening coals. She doesn't hear him come back until he's dropping down to the sand next to her, his voice at her ear starting her out of her half-doze.

"You asleep?"

"No."

"Want to go for a walk?" Maia lifts her head. The drummer is canted backward across a log, jaw hanging open, pint bottle still clutched in his right hand. The bassist is sausage-rolled into a blanket, his back to the fire. Cass sleeps pretty as a girl in a painting, one blue wisp of hair falling across her soft cheek, her hands tucked up under her chin.

"Yeah," Maia says, shrugging her way out of the blanket and getting to her feet.

He takes her hand as he leads her down the beach, away from the fire's embers and into the starry dark. The air is clean and cool and salt-heavy, and she opens her mouth wide to gulp it down. All around her the night is listening, the universe waiting, as she is, to find out what happens next.

She's too dizzy with desire to mark the passage of time. His cool hand in hers draws her along. They dawdle at the tideline, dancing away from the edges of the waves, until she yields to the inevitable and water laps over her bare feet. She lets go of his hand long enough to squat down and drift her fingers through the ebbing wave. Sand rushes past her, bits of shell, slick tangles of seaweed. He leads her back away from the water, tugs her down next to him on the sand, and when he kisses her it is, she thinks, the first and only time she has ever been kissed, because all the kisses she has ever kissed before this were nothing like a kiss at all.

*What is this,* she thinks, *oh god, what is this, what the fuck is happening to me.* Like drugs, but bigger than drugs or more necessary or more new, newer even than the flood rush of speed in her veins or the slow sweet daze of pot or the burning glory of whisky in the back of her throat. This is something else again. This is a thing that will erase her and remake her in its own image, this is what she was playing for all those years. *Oh Oscar, this is what you meant.* He is kissing her, kissing her, her mouth, her throat, the fine soft skin of her eyelids, her earlobe between his teeth, his lips at her ear, the hot rough sound of his breath. *Take me with you,* she says with her skin to his skin, her hands to the muscles of his body, *wherever you are going, wherever you are from,* and his hands trace the letters of his answer across her thighs, under her shirt to the place where her shoulder blades fan out like wings. *Anywhere I go with you now is the same place as home.* She kisses him back with all the longing in her body, and when his face grows clearer and clearer she thinks at first it is because she is at last seeing him truly, until he takes his mouth away and says, "Look, it's dawn," and they lie together in the sand, her head on his chest, and watch the sky lighten as the sun comes up into a new world.

"Drive to Mexico with me," he says, and she says, *"What?"* and he says it again. "Drive to Mexico with me. Today."

"I don't even *know* you," she says.

"Love has nothing to do with knowing."

Everyone, it seems, is an authority on this subject, save her. "I just learned your name. Like, twelve hours ago."

"You're the most beautiful girl I've ever seen. Say yes."

She props herself up on one elbow and looks at him. He's shielding his eyes from the rising sun, staring her down with that azure gaze. He is, she realizes, totally serious. She starts to say *of course not* and then she shuts her mouth on the *no.* Isn't this what Oscar told her she lacked?

Passion? Isn't this what Cass has been teaching her these last months? To say yes? To anything, to all of it, the good ideas and the bad ones? Who is she now if she is not someone who's learning to tell her own stories? If she is beautiful, he's more beautiful still: Underneath the stubble and the dirty hair, those eyes, the cut of his cheekbones and the clear line of his jaw, add up to the visage of one of the gods in her mother's books. He's looking up at her, beseeching, and sure she doesn't know him but who knows anything anyway and isn't this the grandest thing that's ever happened to her, and so she opens her mouth, laughing, and says, "Why not. Yes," and then he kisses her again, laughing too, and leaps up, unbuttoning his jeans and scrambling out of them, half tripping, pulling his shirt over his head. He barrels pell-mell into the ocean hollering "Yes! Yes! Yes!" and what else can Maia do but take her clothes off, too, with no more grace than he had, and run after him, shrieking as the wall of turquoise water hits her with the force of a fist. He splashes toward her, picks her up and whirls her around like they're in some old-timey movie and not buck-naked in the Pacific with her only friend in the world just down the beach, and then he falls with a crash into the waves, taking her with him. Salt up her nose and in her face and she's laughing too hard to mind it, staggering to her feet, pulling him with her. Kissing him again and again, and he hoists her up and she wraps her legs around his waist and he stops kissing her long enough to say, "This is some music video," and then she's laughing again, so hard he nearly drops her. "This is crazy," she gasps, but he doesn't hear her.

When they can't stand the cold any longer they scramble

out of the water, run back to the pile of their clothes. He kisses her again, serious now, his hands insistent on her skin, and who is she to say no now that she's said yes. Sex with him is already different than the handful of boys she's slept with this summer, more clumsy but also more real. He is here, with her, present in his skin, and because he is here she stays here, too; this is the first sex she's had sober, she realizes, wondering as she realizes it if that's supposed to make her worry. He's greedy for her, his teeth against her shoulder, his breath ragged in her ear, and she is both startled and pleased by her own power. He pulls out of her, shuddering, and comes in a sticky welter across her stomach, and she holds him and strokes his hair and hums nonsense in his ear while his breathing slows, and when he begins to cry she is somehow not surprised. "You're safe here," she says into his hair, "sshhh, ssshhh," and he weeps without a hint of self-consciousness and she feels, suddenly, very old.

She pushes his wet hair out of his face, kisses his cheeks, curls her fingers in his pale palm, barely bigger than hers. He's fragile as a kitten, this lovely creature, this boy who's hers now. She will have to learn to be strong, to take care of what's been given her.

Afterward she runs back into the ocean again, washing him from her skin, and dries herself off with her shirt as best she can. If she looks half as bedraggled as he does, she looks one hell of a mess. There's sand all through her everything. She touches her hair and a dusting of sand falls into her eyes. He puts his jeans on and tucks the Misfits shirt into his back pocket and leads her back to where his bandmates and her best friend sit yawning by the remains of the fire.

"Well, then," Cass says, looking up at her.

Maia licks her salty, bee-stung lips. "Let's go to Mexico."

Is that resignation she sees cross Cass's face? Whatever it is, it's gone so quick she barely registers it. "No way," Cass says, and starts to laugh. The bass player and the drummer, slower to catch on, stare at her stupidly.

"Way," she says, and she knows she is grinning like an idiot.

"Give me the keys," Cass says. "I'll drive."

"I'll meet you guys up north," Jason says to his gaping bandmates.

"What?" says the drummer.

"Like in a week or something. Maybe a couple of weeks. That cool? I'll call you when I'm back in town."

"Oh, for fuck's sake," the bassist says. He shoots Maia a disgusted look.

"Come on, man," Jason says. "Our tour's over."

"We're supposed to split gas three ways."

"I'll give you money when I come back."

"Sure you will," the drummer says. "Fucking hell, dude, this isn't cool."

"I guess we need a map," Cass says.

"It can't be that hard," Jason says. "I mean, you just go south."

The bass player makes a snorting noise and gets to his feet. "Whatever. Call us when you're back in town and see if you still have a band." He gathers up the blankets, the bottles, the odds and ends they've scattered around the fire. The drummer scowls but gets up, too. "Whatever," he echoes, his voice valley-girling up a plaintive register.

"It was nice to meet you," Cass says. They don't answer

as they trudge away from the beach, backs set in a sulky line, but the drummer flips them off.

"Maybe you should go with them," Maia says. Jason shakes his head.

"They're nothing without me," he says, "and they know it. They'll never find another band like this. They'll get over it."

"If you're sure."

"Baby," he says, grinning at her, "I'm always sure."

"Come on," Cass says, cutting him short. "Help me carry the rest of this stuff back to our car."

When they get to the strip of roadside where the car is parked, they see the band has taken off already, leaving Jason's duffel bag and his acoustic guitar on the trunk of Maia's car. "They'll get over it," Jason says again, still confident.

"What about your other guitar?" Maia asks.

"I had to pawn it," Jason says, "and then Byron got it out of hock, so I guess he thinks it's his."

Cass considers and discards a number of spiteful remarks. There's plenty of time to make him hate her. She climbs into the driver's seat. Maia goes for the passenger door, and Jason makes a noise of protest.

"Come on, baby," he says. "Sit in the back with me." Maia obeys meekly, and Cass does not protest her demotion to chauffeur, though her look is murderous. "Just head south," Jason says. "Until you hit the border. And then head south some more."

"Aye aye, captain," Cass says, and she starts the car.

# THEN

Maia's mother goes out of town for the weekend. For a conference, she says, though Maia suspects the conference is a panel of two. Cass's defiance is catching; the first thing Maia does, when her mother has driven off in her shiny black car, is track Cass down on her corner and invite her over again.

"Come with me," she says. It's a chilly April afternoon, the kind of damp and foggy day that makes you think spring is a foolish delusion. They're huddled up under an awning, watching people walk by. Cass rolls a joint, brazen as daylight. Maia smoked pot with her for the first time a few days ago. She liked the way it made her feel, blurry and loose. She played well that night, her fingers moving smoothly, her thoughts wiped clean.

"To your house? Again? That didn't go so well the last time."

"My mom is out of town."

"Sure, then," Cass says, touching her hand. "Let's go."

Her father is shut away in his study, a dollar-store Fitzgerald lost in his world of cocktail parties and limpid-eyed women in silk dresses gazing sadly into their drinks. As long as they are quiet he'll never even notice. Maia is anxious, at first, to impress upon Cass the necessity of stealth, but Cass seems to understand without prompting and even takes her boots off at the door. "Cool if I take a shower, princess?" Cass asks. Maia gives her soft white towels from the stack in the hall closet and points Cass to the bathroom. "Shit, girl, you got a bathroom of your own?" Cass says. "Plush life." But there's no rancor in her voice. While Cass showers Maia paces her room anxiously, her socked feet silent on the carpet, her pastel walls offering her no answers. Now that Cass is here Maia has no idea what to do with her.

Maia is so engrossed in her thoughts she does not notice the water shut off, and she starts when the door between her room and the bathroom opens. Cass stands on the threshold, wrapped in a towel, her short hair standing on end. "Oh my god," she says. "You don't even know how good it feels to be this clean. You got some fancy soap in there. Can I do laundry, too?"

"The cleaning lady usually does it," Maia says.

"Is that a no?"

"No, I just—" Maia falters, embarrassed. "I don't really know how to use the washer," she admits.

Cass laughs. "Good thing for you I got all kinds of background in domestic servitude. You think I can borrow something while I wash my clothes?"

"Yeah," Maia says. "Yes." She turns to her dresser to hide her consternation. She rummages through neatly folded sweaters, pressed khakis, socks knotted in pairs and smelling of fabric softener. "I think these will fit you. We're about the same size." She offers a pair of pants and a button-down shirt. Cass drops her towel on the floor without a hint of self-consciousness and pulls on the pants and shirt over her still-wet skin. Maia flushes crimson and looks away. "I have underwear, too," she mumbles.

"All good," Cass says, "I'll just wait until mine is clean." She goes back into the bathroom and laughs at her reflection. "Shit, princess," she says through the open door. "It's like Halloween in here. Nobody will believe this is me."

Still blushing, Maia peeks around the doorframe. Cass looks like she is about to apply for a job at the mall. "You're me," Maia says shyly.

"Not much chance of that," Cass says amicably. Maia blinks. "You got some life here," Cass adds. "All boxed up in this pretty house like Sleeping Beauty. Your mom ever let you out?"

"Not really," Maia says. "But I don't know where I would go if she did."

"Oh, come on," Cass says. "All kinds of places. You ever even been to a show?"

"A show of what?"

"Music," Cass says. "You know? A *'rock concert'*?" She makes quotation marks with her fingers.

"I play music," Maia says.

"Not music like that. Like punk music."

"I don't know what that is."

"You *are* like something out of a fairy tale. Let me wash my clothes and I'll see what I can do."

Maia shows Cass the laundry room and watches, fascinated, as Cass piles the contents of her backpack into the washing machine, adds soap, turns the dial. "See?" Cass says. "Easy. You could do your own."

"I never had to," Maia says.

"You wouldn't last five minutes in the wild."

"I would too," Maia says, nettled.

"Oh, there's a streak of trouble in you a mile wide, for sure. But you have no skills. What if the world ended and your house blew up tomorrow? Or if there was, like, a zombie apocalypse? You'd be up shit creek."

"Not if I was with you."

"Well," Cass says, and Maia is astonished to see that it's Cass who's blushing now. "That's probably true. We don't have to watch the washing machine for it to work. You got anything to eat?"

Later, when Cass has eaten six peanut-butter-and-jelly sandwiches and her clothes are tumbling in the dryer, she commandeers Maia's phone and pulls a grubby notebook out of her bag. She dials several numbers in rapid succession, muttering a mysterious series of instructions, and finally hangs up in satisfaction. "Show tonight at the Greenhouse," she says. "It's kind of far, but we can walk there from here."

"The Greenhouse?"

"This punk house over in Ballard. I don't know, some kid had a big garden there for a while and the name stuck. You in?"

"What do I do?"

Cass laughs. "You just go, princess," she says. "You like the music, you can dance around a little. Get drunk. Whatever."

"What do I wear?"

"That, my girl, is a good question. Maybe not your loafers. You have any clothes that don't make you look like the head of the Young Republicans?"

"Not really," Maia says.

"In that case, let's go shopping."

Cass makes Maia reckless. She takes the keys to her dad's Mercedes without asking, drives them to the Ave. Cass reclines in the passenger seat, her booted feet on the dashboard, somehow as ferocious in Maia's clothes as she is in her own uniform of cargo pants and a T-shirt. "Let's go somewhere actually cool," Cass says, and takes her to a vintage store they've never been in. A bored-looking girl with bright-dyed hair and a nose ring leans on the counter, chewing gum. The music is loud, an addictive beat that makes Maia twitch, but the singer's voice is deep and sad. "Joy Division," Cass says.

"What?"

"The band. Joy Division."

"It's good."

"Yep." Cass flips through shirts on hangers, organized

by color, pulls things out and holds them up against Maia, talking to herself. If something meets with her approval she hands it to Maia, until Maia's arms are piled high. Worn-thin T-shirts, jeans ragged and artfully blown out at the knees, even a pair of leather pants. "No way," Maia says, and Cass laughs.

"Come on," she says, "live a little. You have the legs for them." No one has ever in her life told Maia she has the legs for anything. She is not entirely sure she even knows what this means.

"Thanks?" she says. Cass is rummaging through a pile of sweaters on a shelf with the fixed intensity of a blood-hound. The girl at the register watches them with interest.

"What are you, like, her personal shopper?" she calls.

"She's getting a makeover," Cass says.

"You need one," the girl says. "No offense. You look like you fell into the fucking Gap. You guys want help? I'm bored out of my mind. I could show you where the cool stuff is. Some of it is in, like, piles."

Maia nods. The girl emerges from behind the counter. She's wearing tiny plastic shorts and fishnets, and each wrist is sheathed in a jangling cuff of stacked bangles and charm bracelets. Her nails are painted alternating black and bright pink, and a black swoop of eyeliner extends her eyes like a cat's. Maia realizes she is staring, but the girl doesn't seem to mind. "I know you, right?" she says to Cass. "Why are you dressed all weird? I didn't recognize you. I'm Judy. Remember me? We did coke in a bathroom at Camilla Winter's party in like ninth grade. I'm pretty sure. Did you go to Northside? I hated that school. Oh my god, I puked for like *ever* at that party, I swear to god every time I drink tequila I practically puke up my entire small *intestine*."

"Maybe," Cass says, still looking through the sweaters. "I'm around."

"Or wait, that wasn't you. That was Patricia Taylor, and then right after that she got that thing where you don't eat, you know that thing? Like, anorexia. We all thought she was just doing a ton of speed and then she was in the hospital all of a sudden and our first period class had to make her get-well cards and it was so weird because we all thought she was a total bitch but obviously you couldn't, like, put that on the card, like oh hi Patricia sorry you're in the hospital but the whole universe *hates* your guts, can you please stay there for, like, ever. I could never not eat, oh my god, I could probably do that thing where you make yourself barf afterward but not eating would be so hard. I know how I know you, I totally got it. You're Rusty's girlfriend."

"Who's Rusty?" Maia asks.

"Nobody," Cass says. "And not anymore."

"He's fucking crazy."

"Yes," Cass says.

"But good drugs. Oh my god, this one time I got a bunch of speed off Rusty and I was high for, like, a fucking month, it was some crazy rich-lady pharmaceutical shit, like I had never even *heard* of it. Not, like, Dexedrine. Like something *really* good. And I mean, I know my speeds, you know? You have his number?"

"No," Cass says. "You got shoes somewhere? She can't wear loafers."

"Sure." The girl points them to a corner, where combat boots like Cass's lean against scuffed cowboy boots in a rainbow of colors. A shelf displays glittery platform shoes and high heels. "We got some Docs," the girl adds. "New ones. Up by the counter. Fourteen hole. These cool velvet ones, you should see the velvet ones, I totally want a pair but I don't get that great a discount here actually and Docs are totally expensive new, I remember when they were way cheaper but then they got super trendy and now they're practically a million dollars. Soon only yuppies will have Docs, I'm telling you, like you'll open up a fashion magazine or something and there they'll be. But the velvet ones are really great."

"Okay," Cass says. "Thanks."

"You sure you don't have his number?"

"Listen," Cass says, exasperated, "you don't want it. I promise. Can we try this stuff on?"

Judy shrugs and shows Maia the dressing room. Maia piles Cass's selections on a chair. Cass pokes her head through the curtain. "You good to go?"

"I've put clothes on before," Maia says drily.

"Pssshhht," Cass says. "Rich girls like you, never can tell what you know how to do." Maia snaps the curtain shut in her face.

"I was just trying to *help*."

"Uh-huh."

In the clothes Cass has picked for her, she is almost unrecognizable. How could such a tiny thing as someone else's castoffs change her so completely? She looks at herself over her shoulder. Cass sticks her head back in.

"Look at you," she says, pleased. "I knew it. What size shoe do you wear?"

"Eight and a half," Maia says. Cass withdraws and a

minute later hands her a pair of boots through the curtain. Maia laces them up slowly, can't stop the huge smile that spreads across her face. "You can look," she says, and Cass pulls the curtain open.

"Oh, nice," Judy says, leaning in so far that Maia is afraid she will fall over into the dressing room. "You look really good. Wow, do you exercise or something? I mean, wow, you are seriously lucky, you're, like, as skinny as Patricia but not ugly."

Cass ignores Judy's chatter, admiring her handiwork. "We should do something about your hair."

Judy puts her hands on Maia's shoulders, turns her so that she's facing the mirror. "You could cut it," she says, holding Maia's hair back so that it looks like it just reaches her chin. "You have, like, amazing bones. It's all hidden. I mean, your hair is gorgeous, too. But you would look so good if you cut it off." She piles Maia's hair on top of her head, holds it there. "Or like a ponytail up here. You know? Like super messy. That could be cool."

"My mom would kill me if I cut it," Maia says.

"Dude, that's what moms do," Judy says. "Moms just freak out. When I still lived at home my mom was on my case all the time. She was like, 'Judy Marie, if I catch you smoking pot in my house *one more time* I will put you out on the *street*.' And then I moved out? And now she calls me all the time crying, all like 'Oh my god when are you coming over for *dinnnerrrrr*.' Just be like, 'Mom, *chill*.'"

"You don't know my mom."

"Her mom doesn't chill much," Cass agrees. "I'll cut your hair for you, though. If you want. You don't have to decide now."

"You should dye it," Judy says. "Red would look so good. You'd have to bleach it first. Like with your skin? It would be super Miki Berenyi."

Maia has no idea who Miki Berenyi is. She tries to imagine herself with red hair. With short hair. With any hair other than the hair she's always had, the glossy river of black that she usually keeps up but spills to the middle of her back when she takes it out of its bun.

"Do you want to buy all this stuff?" Judy asks.

"Not all of it," Maia says. "I don't have anywhere to keep it."

"Oh, *cool,*" Judy says, "you're, like, *disobeying.* Oh my god. That's so cute."

In the end, Maia buys tight black jeans, a band shirt ("New Order," Judy says, approvingly, "like seriously the best band *ever.*"), the black boots, and a soft and worn leather jacket that zips at an angle like a biker's. She buys red dye in a plastic container and a packet of bleach and a bottle of developer. She buys a charm bracelet like Judy's. The total is a hundred and fifty dollars, more than she's ever spent before in her life. Her parents opened a savings account for her when she was eight, and every month since then she's dutifully deposited her allowance. She never had a reason to spend money before she met Cass. "Do you want anything?" she asks Cass.

"Me?" Cass says, startled. "No, I'm good. Thanks." But Maia had seen her eyeing one of the sweaters, a wool pullover the color of storm clouds, and she adds it to her pile.

"This, too," she says.

Cass smiles. "You don't miss a thing, do you," she says. "Seriously, I'm fine. You don't have to."

"I want to."

"I'm not used to presents."

"All the more reason to get you one."

Cass shrugs, feigning indifference, but it's obvious beneath the facade she's pleased. "Thanks," she says, gruffly.

Judy starts to put Maia's purchases into a bag, but Maia stops her. "Can I change into this stuff?"

"Sure."

Maia puts the black jeans back on, laces up the boots, shrugs on the leather jacket over the New Order shirt. She puts her hair up like Judy suggested, in a messy ponytail on top of her head, and fastens the charm bracelet around her wrist. Judy gives her a bag for her old clothes, and she puts her khakis and loafers in with the hair dye. Cass is already wearing her new sweater.

"Wow," Judy says, "you really do look great."

"I know what I'm doing," Cass says.

"I'm sure I'll totally see you around. If you see Rusty, tell him I said hi?"

"Sure," Cass sighs.

They emerge from the dim shop into the sunny street. Maia is giddy with the freedom of her new clothes, her former self in the heavy plastic bag dangling from her wrist.

"Judy," Cass says. "God bless her. What a weirdo."

"Let's go get coffee or something," Maia says. "My treat."

"Come on, quit buying me shit. You buy me coffee all the time."

"I *want* to," Maia says. "Please. But you have to tell me who Rusty is."

Cass laughs. "I forgot why I never go in there. Just this guy I hung out with for a while. I stayed with him because he gave me drugs. And then he gave me the fucking clap."

"I've never had a boyfriend." Maia is not going to ask Cass what the clap is.

"Boyfriends are overrated."

"Oh."

Cass shoots her a sidelong glance. "You ever even kissed anybody, princess?"

"Yes," Maia says, embarrassed. She bites her lip. "I mean, just once. At a recital. This guy from Paris. He told me I was really good. At the piano!" she exclaims, catching Cass's smirk. "But I think he said it just so I would let him kiss me." Maia laughs. "In the janitor's closet. It was at some high school that had a big auditorium."

"Did you like it?"

"He was kind of a dick."

"They usually are," Cass says. "You are really good, though."

"I was a lot better than him," Maia says, and grins.

"I have no doubt."

Later, they make popcorn and watch MTV, a thing Maia has never done. "What do you mean, you've never seen MTV?" Cass says, horrified.

"I'm not really allowed," Maia says.

"Princess, you are *seventeen*."

"You met my mom."

"I did, yes." Cass shakes her head. Maia is astonished by the music videos, the men in tight pants moving against animated backdrops. A man eats cereal at a round table in the middle of the desert with a lady in a glittering red headscarf. A man in a white undershirt plays the flute in a tree. More men do a synchronized, hopping dance atop a sand dune. Now, dressed all in white, they carry a black box across the desert. The images are nonsensical, dreamlike.

"What is this?" Maia breathes; she is so agog Cass thinks she will reach out and pet the screen.

"It's rock music," Cass says, laughing. "Oh, girl. We gotta get you out of the house."

The video in the desert is over. Another comes on: someone pouring colored paint on a pretty lady lying on a beach, while men in suits sing on a wooden sailboat.

"I want you to cut my hair," Maia says. Cass pauses, a handful of popcorn halfway to her mouth, and looks at her thoughtfully.

"You don't have to."

"I want to."

"What about your mom?"

"Fuck my mom," Maia says, and a glorious thrill runs through her. "I want music video hair."

"Okay," Cass says. "Find me some scissors."

In Maia's bathroom, Cass combs out her hair, the black sheet of it falling around Maia's shoulders in rich waves. Each stroke of the brush soothes her. She looks at them in the mirror: Cass, raggedy and impish; her own smooth, solemn face with the black hair covering her like a coat of crows' wings.

"You sure about this?" Cass's reflection says to hers. "This is a lot of hair to grow back."

"I want to know who's underneath it."

"Fair enough," Cass says. "How short?"

Maia holds her hands level with her chin. "Short." She

closes her eyes, hears the crisp sound of the scissors opening, the shearing of them closing next to her ear. She can
feel her hair falling away from her head and drifting across
her body. The *shhkkk, sshhkkk* again, and again, and more
of her hair lands heavily on her shoulders, her bare feet.
Cass puts one hand to her chin, gently tilts her head one
way and then the other. "Look down," she says, and then,
"Look back up again." She rests one hand at the place where
Maia's neck curves into her shoulder, leaves it there, takes
it away. Maia can feel Cass's fingers running through her
hair, holding the strands to be cut next. When the noise of
the scissors stops for a moment, she feels Cass's cool palm
over her eyes. "Not yet," Cass says. "Let me make sure it's
even first." More snips. Her head feels so light she thinks it
is in danger of floating away altogether. Silence. "You can
look," Cass says.

Maia opens her eyes. The girl in the mirror is a stranger,
her sleek bob falling to either side from a ruler-straight
central part and ending sharply at her chin. The fine bones
of her face stand out in startling relief. The full curve of her
mouth crooks up at one corner in a disbelieving grin.

"Oh my god," Maia says. Behind her, Cass smiles,
pleased as a cat in cream. "It's perfect. How did you get it
so even?"

Cass lifts one shoulder, drops it. "There are a couple of
things I'm good at. You want to dye it?"

"I don't know," Maia says, and then, "Yeah."

"In for a penny, in for a pound," Cass says.

The dye takes forever. Cass makes Maia put on an old
shirt while she mixes lightener and developer in a bowl
Maia steals from the kitchen. The sharp chemical scald of

the bleach fills Maia's bathroom and makes them both cough. It burns even worse on Maia's scalp; Cass tells her she has to leave it on for at least forty-five minutes for it to strip the color out of her dark hair, and they watch more MTV, Maia's eyes watering from the sting and fumes. When Cass finally washes the bleach out of her hair she almost cries in relief. Cass lathers in the red dye, smearing Vaseline at Maia's hairline to keep the color from staining her skin, makes her watch more MTV, rinses the red out at last. The color stains the tub, the sink, the towels, the floor. Cass rubs her head gently with a towel, combs her fingers through Maia's hair. Maia stares at herself in the mirror.

If short-haired Maia was a stranger, this flame-haired creature is an alien. Maia turns her head from side to side, staring. The red is an unnatural, gorgeous blaze of color. Cass has transformed her into someone she had no idea was waiting inside her.

"People are going to look at you, now, princess," Cass says, watching Maia watch herself. "You better get used to it."

"I love it."

Cass wipes the back of her hand across her forehead in an exaggerated gesture of mock relief. "Good thing," she says. "No going back now. If your mom throws you out, you can stay with me. It's getting late; want to go to that show?"

Maia nods happily, though she can barely tear herself away from the mirror. She puts the New Order shirt and her new black jeans back on, laces up her new combat boots. Cass surveys the wreckage of the bathroom. "You want to clean up?"

"Fuck my mom," Maia repeats, gleeful.

Cass grins. "That's the spirit. I don't feel like walking. Can we steal your dad's car again?"

In the car, Cass roots around in her bag until she finds a scratched cassette tape, which she pops in the car's player. A surfy line of guitar comes through Maia's dad's old speakers, and Cass turns the volume up. The hook is poppy and sweet; a man's voice comes in, clear and almost as high as a girl's. Cass sings along happily.

"Why are they singing about caribou?"

"Ree-pent!" Cass yells with relish. "I don't know, it's the Pixies."

"Is that punk?"

"Sweet child of mine," Cass says, "I don't know what I'm going to do with you."

The show is at a falling-apart house in the old industrial neighborhood by the locks. The yard is a sea of teenagers dressed in black, smoking cigarettes and drinking out of bottles in paper bags. Cass laughs at Maia's huge eyes. "Nobody'll bite you," she says, patting Maia's hand on the gearshift. "Promise." Maia parks a block away, double-checks the locked doors. She follows a few steps behind Cass, pulling her shoulders up to her ears and hunching into herself. She wants to go home and crawl under her piano and never leave her house again.

These kids are terrifying. They're arrayed in rags, their hair standing up in spikes or ratted out in snarled manes. They have safety pins through their ears and hoops through their lips and chains around their necks and big black boots on their feet, and they stare at Cass and Maia as the girls walk by. Cass slows until Maia bumps into her and takes Maia's hand. "You're doing great, princess," she murmurs into Maia's ear, giving her hand a reassuring squeeze. "These fuckers've never seen a girl as pretty as you, is all."

"I think they hate me."

"No way. Their faces are all just frozen like that. Come on, let's find something to drink."

Cass drags her into the house. It's even more crowded inside, a mass of white kids in black clothes, drinking beer out of red plastic cups. Cass lets go of her hand and Maia shrinks back against a wall. The house is almost devoid of furniture. There's a wretched couch pushed against a wall, a collapsing shelf filled with dog-eared copies of *On the Road* and *Siddhartha*. "You wait here," Cass says. "I'm going to find the keg, okay? I'll be right back." Cass shoulders her way through the crowd. Maia bites her lip, hoping she doesn't look as terrified as she feels.

"You don't look like you're having a good time," someone says next to her. Okay, then. She does look as terrified as she feels. The speaker's a boy, tall and lanky, with dirty brown hair that falls in tangles down his back. He's wearing leather and spikes like the rest of them, but his eyes are kind.

"I'm not really—uh, I'm fine," she says.

"I'm Todd. You want a drink?"

"My friend went to get me one." He raises an eyebrow. "Oh. Sorry. Maia." He shakes her hand gravely, as if they're at a tea party, and takes a silver flask out of his pocket.

"You sure?"

"Oh, what the hell," Maia says, and takes the flask from

him. She unscrews the top and takes a gulp of whatever's inside. It burns going down and she coughs, laughing. "Holy shit!"

"Not a whisky drinker?"

"Not until now." A warm, buffering glow is already spreading through her. "I could get used to it, I bet."

"That's my kind of girl," he says, winking, and Maia realizes in astonishment that he is flirting with her. A *punk boy* is *flirting*. With *her*. What a day this is turning out to be.

"You ever hear these guys play before?"

"What?"

"The band," he says patiently. "Elephant Feticide?"

"Oh," she says. "No. Cass didn't tell me their name."

"You're here with Cass?"

"You know her?"

"Everybody knows Cass." He holds out his hand, and she realizes she is still clutching his flask.

"Sorry," she says, handing it back to him. "Can I ask you a question?"

"Shoot."

"Elephant Feticide? That's not, like—" She falters. "I mean, that's sort of a terrible name. No offense."

"It's not *my* band. My band is called Necronomicon."

"That's a mouthful."

"Part of the whole metal aesthetic," he says, and she can't tell if he's teasing her.

"Heavy," she agrees. "Heavy metal." He laughs, and she is delighted with herself.

"Ah, shit, girl," Cass says behind her, "I leave you alone for three minutes and you find yourself the biggest trouble in the room."

"Cass, Cass, Cass," Todd says, and scoops her up in a bear hug.

"My beer!" Cass cries, one hand aloft holding two plastic cups.

"Sorry," Todd says, releasing her. Cass hands one cup to Maia, who takes a cautious sip.

"She's never had a whole beer of her own," Cass explains.

"Hey," Maia protests.

"It's okay, he's good people."

Suddenly, a terrible noise like a trash compactor crushing a car full of cats screeches through the room. Maia jumps. "That's the band," Todd explains. She and Cass follow him into another room, where a sweat-covered, shirtless boy is banging furiously on a drum set and another shirtless boy is on his knees, howling passionately and extracting repetitive, dissonant chords from an electric guitar with vigorous enthusiasm. Maia winces and covers her ears with her hands. Around her, black-clad teenagers in various states of undress reel and crash into one another in a frenzied, violent dance that does not seem to correspond in any way to the music. An inebriated dancer slams into her and careens away, sending her beer slopping over the edge of her cup.

"Is it all like this?" Maia asks Cass.

"WHAT?" Cass shouts.

"IS IT ALL LIKE THIS?" Maia shouts back.

"IS ALL WHAT LIKE THIS?"

"ROCK MUSIC?"

Cass laughs so hard she doubles over, and Todd looks over at Maia, amused. Wheezing, Cass shakes her head. "COME ON, PRINCESS," she yells. "LET'S GO OUTSIDE."

In the yard, the din is considerably less, although the crowd is no smaller. They hunker under the eaves, unnoticed. Maia leans against the house and takes another delicate sip of her beer. Todd, she is pleased to note, has followed them outside. "You don't have to come out here," Maia says to them. "If you liked it."

Cass is still laughing. "Are you kidding? They're fucking terrible." She pulls her tobacco out of her pocket and rolls a cigarette.

"They are?"

"Pretty bad," Todd agrees.

Maia eyeballs Cass's cigarette and Cass catches her looking, passes it to her without comment. Maia takes the tiniest of drags and manages not to cough, though she hopes Todd can't see her eyes water in the dark as she gives it back to Cass. He offers Maia the flask again and she hands him her beer while she unscrews the stopper and takes a swig. The burn is no less but she expects it this time, and the warmth that follows it feels even better.

"I *like* whisky," she says.

"I like your hair," Todd says.

"Cass did it. Just today."

"It looks good. Really good."

"You know what," Cass says, "I'm going to go see if Felony is here, I need to ask her something." She leans in to kiss Maia on the cheek. "He thinks you're *cute,* you should *kiss him,*" she hisses in Maia's ear. "I'll find you again in a bit, okay? Don't leave without me," she adds in a normal voice.

"What do I do?" Maia says, panicked.

Cass looks at her and grins. "Don't drive away until I'm

in the car," she says, and then she's scampering off into the house. The noise has abated for the moment; perhaps the shirtless boys grew tired of their efforts and are resting.

"Well," Todd says.

"Well," she agrees.

"You go to school?"

"No, homeschooled. You?"

"Oh, school," he says. "We didn't really get along, me and school. I went to the community college for a bit, but it seemed better to just work. Travel a little."

"Where?"

"I went to Spain for a while. Met some people. I stayed in a squat in Amsterdam for a year." He tells her about the beaches in Spain while she drinks more of his whisky. The sun. Swimming naked in the sea.

"Why'd you ever come home?"

"Got my heart plumb broke," he says wistfully.

"I went to Barcelona," Maia says. "For a piano competition."

"Piano, huh? You must be good."

"I won."

He laughs. "You don't look like a pianist."

"I did until this afternoon. I'm trying out being a different person."

"Is that so," he says, looking down at her. He is much taller than she is. He reaches forward and tucks a piece of her hair behind one ear, his thumb gently stroking her cheek. "What kind of different person?"

"A braver one," she says, and kisses him. He smiles against her mouth and then kisses her back. He tastes like whisky and cigarettes and smells like sweat and leather and something else underneath, wild and musky. Kissing him is nothing like kissing Nicholas Bernière, mediocre pianist and practiced jerk, who'd jammed his tongue down her throat and covered the entire lower half of her face with his mouth. Todd's stubbled chin is scratchy but his mouth is soft, and there is a warmth spreading through her now that has nothing to do with the whisky. He puts both his hands in her hair and takes her earlobe gently between his teeth, and she shivers in delight.

"You're beautiful, braver girl," he says softly into the whorl of her ear, and a thrill goes through her all the way to her toes. No one's ever said it to her like that. She rests her forehead on his chest, drinking in the smell of him, and he kisses the top of her head. The band has started up again, with an even more awful noise; Maia would've thought such a feat impossible. "Not the classiest place for a first date," he says into her hair.

"I should find Cass," she says.

"It's early," he protests.

"I have parents," she says. "I mean, the kind that pay attention."

He takes her by the shoulders, holds her away from him, studying her face, and then he kisses her again. "I could throw you over my shoulder and carry you off," he offers.

She giggles. "You just met me."

"Some things do not require a long acquaintance, braver girl." He rummages around in his pocket and finds a pen, takes her hand. "Here," he says, writing on the back of her hand, "is my phone number. Do you make use of it." He gives her hand a little squeeze.

"Okay," she says, grinning like an idiot. It takes a force

of will to make herself let go of his hand. She turns around as she goes back into the house; he's still watching her. He gives her a little wave and she returns it, nearly walking into the door frame.

Cass is inside, talking animatedly to a girl with green and purple dreadlocks wearing a halter top made out of an old shirt. Maia catches her eye and makes a driving motion with her hands, and Cass comes over. "So soon?" she asks.

"At some point even my dad will notice I'm gone. But stay here, if you want."

"Nah," Cass says. "I see these people all the time."

"You want to sleep over?" Maia asks.

"Like a slumber party?"

Maia blushes. "Sorry, I guess that's sort of little kid–ish."

"No, it sounds fun. I'd love to."

Maia is quiet on the drive home. She can feel her tiny, claustrophobic world blowing wide open, all the possibility rushing in like a rising tide. The world is so much bigger than she had ever guessed; all these people in it, like Cass, like Todd, making their own decisions for themselves. She cannot imagine Cass ever doing anything she does not want to do, ever being told where to go or what to believe. Maia has been trapped for so long, surrounded by people who are as bound as she is—her father, Oscar. Who knows, maybe even her mother, stuck in a marriage she does not want, a house she cannot ever clean into a place she actually wants to be, a defective daughter she paid for and cannot return. Maia thought piano was her only path out; she'd never even imagined so many other roads existed.

"What are you thinking?" Cass asks, breaking the long silence.

"About today."

"Your first show," Cass says. "Sorry it was so terrible."

"It wasn't! I mean, the music was. But I—" Maia blushes so violently Cass can probably tell even in the dark car.

Cass chuckles. "He's cute."

"Yes."

"But trouble," Cass says. "Heartbreaker. All the girls love Todd. And Todd loves all the girls."

"Oh," Maia says. "I don't think I can see him again, anyway. My parents."

"It's not natural, caging a teenage girl like that."

"They'll never let me go out."

"Just tell them you're going anyway."

"I wish it was that easy," Maia says. "I don't even want to think about what will happen when my mom sees my hair."

"What are your parents going to do? They can't actually stop you from anything."

"I don't know," Maia says. How can she explain to Cass, a girl with no family, the power her mother has? It's a force that's almost physical. And if Maia went, where would she go? To Cass's? To Oscar's? Not likely. "It's complicated," she says.

"Fair enough."

"I'm going to audition. For this school. This music college in New York. If I get in, my parents will pay for it, for my life there. And they love me, and I guess I sort of owe it to them not to fuck up."

"You want to go?"

"It's the best school," Maia says.

"That's not what I asked you."

"I know." Maia bites her lip. "It's what I'm supposed to do."

"But do you want to do it?"

"I don't know if I know what I want."

"Hmmm," Cass says. "I guess that is complicated."

Maia makes a nest of blankets on the floor of her room, and Cass burrows in like a rabbit tunneling. "So clean," she says happily. "Everything smells good."

Maia gets under the covers and is about to turn out the light when there's a soft rap on her door. She freezes. "Maia? Can I come in?"

"*Shit,*" she hisses. There's no hiding Cass, or her own new hair. Even if her father didn't notice how long she was gone, or that she went out at all. "Okay," she calls. *In for a penny, in for a pound.* He opens the door and looks down at Cass. "Oh," he says. "Hello."

"This is Cass," Maia says.

"I didn't know you had a little friend over. Hello, Cass."

"Hello," Cass says. "Sir."

"I just wanted to say goodnight," her father says. "I haven't seen you all day."

"Goodnight, Dad." He crosses the room and Maia wants to pull the covers over her head. He bends over her, kisses her forehead. She can smell the whisky on his breath.

"Goodnight, sweetheart." Pause. "Is there something different about your hair?"

"Um, a little."

"Oh. It looks nice. Sleep tight."

"Sleep tight, Dad."

When the door is safely shut behind him Cass explodes into giggles. "Is there something different about your *hair*," she gasps. "Fucking *unreal*."

"Says my little friend."

"Oh, princess. I would not trade my life for yours for anything."

"I don't blame you," Maia says. "Goodnight. Sir."

"Goodnight. Dream about Todd."

Maia throws a pillow at her and is rewarded by the satisfying sound of it thwacking into Cass's head.

# NOW:
# BARRA DE
# NAVIDAD

Cass thinks sometimes about getting sober, but then she always thinks twice. She knows the story other people would tell about her: sad girl with a sad habit, sad vices to sidestep sad memories. If her life were a made-for-TV movie she'd repent at the end, yield up teary confessions on a couch in the office of a therapist who at last has made her see the error of her ways and cracked through her bitter shell to the caramel-soft girl beneath. Wrap with a softly lit shot of her shining face, a weepy monologue detailing the arc of her redemption, maybe a final scene of her walking slowly, bravely toward an anonymous group meeting for other girls like her, laying aside their differences to heal as an ensemble.

But there's no room in that sob story for the truth of Cass's own life. There are some things you don't get better from, some harms too deep to heal. There's the man in the black coat, the legions of the dead that follow him, more than enough for any ordinary person to live with; but the ghosts that haunt Cass are some of them as real as daylight. First the stepfathers, and then the street, which is not a kind place for anyone, let alone a girl. And even if Cass did wake up one day with her past a tidy package, a boxed-off set of old memories banned from seeping over into her daily life, there's more to it than that. More to it than forgetting, or giving back to herself what was taken from her in the moments when she's high enough to reclaim her own skin. What Cass loves is the freedom of speed jackhammering through her, the fractured seconds when anything is possible. What Cass loves even more than letting go is saying yes. Yes to every bad idea, to every drug, to every possible thing; yes to wide horizons, yes to euphoria, yes to the wants of the animal body. Yes to running wild in the night, yes to being monster more than girl, bare teeth and nails like claws and muscles like a wolf's. Nothing has ever made her feel as good as drugs, as good as drunk, not the magic Raven taught her, not her dreams of the dead, not even the promise of the man in the black coat lurking at the edges of the world she lives in, beckoning her over to the other side. She could get sober, but to get sober she'd have to give up what makes her live.

And now Cass is too high to think about anything except the vibration of the stars and the feel of the ocean breeze on her skin and the realization that she is never ever going to sleep again because there are too many things to do and it feels so good to be this alive and this awake and this young and they can go anywhere they want now and they can think anything they want and here they are in the world, little animals, little animals.

With every day that passes on the beach, Cass hates Jason more. He's fickle, tyrannical, prone to nightmares. He will only eat soft corn tortillas and cheese, turns his nose up at shrimp and shellfish pulled fresh out of the sea and sold in the village. He talks about himself incessantly. The more obnoxious he gets, the more Maia moons after him, asking anxiously if he is okay, what he needs, what she can get him, nursemaiding him through his days as if she's his nanny instead of his lover. Exasperated, Cass takes to swimming, or running on the beach, or going for long walks by herself; when she comes back, he's always drunk the lukewarm Coke she left in the car, looked through her and Maia's things in search of something to do or read or munch. If she leaves her alcohol anywhere he can find it, he drinks it; if she doesn't hide her drugs, he does them. It goes without saying that he doesn't have any money.

"Jesus," Cass yells one afternoon, when she catches him paging through her journal. He drops it like it's a scorpion. Maia's a ways down the beach, dozing.

"I'm sorry," he says quietly. His usual bravado is gone; he's almost sheepish.

"You are a *shit*," Cass says. "A fucking shit. And just

because my best friend has lost her mind don't think I have, too. I see right the fuck through you. Don't ever touch my shit again or I'll cut your dick off and feed it to you." His eyes widen in real fear, and Cass has to make a terrible face to keep from laughing.

"I know I'm a shit," he says unexpectedly. "I know. I'm sorry. I try—I try to be something else. You know, like a decent person. I get mixed up. I don't know how. I—" He falters.

Cass pushes her hands through her dirty hair. He's like a stray dog, bristled big to hide the staring ribs and mangy pelt and life of too many kicks. Jason might think he's special, but she's met a hundred boys like him.

"You're lucky Maia likes a project," she says curtly. "And I meant what I said about your dick."

Later that night he plays for them, as if in apology. They sit at the tideline under an upended bowl of stars, the night warm and luminous around them. Jason plays Johnny Cash and Bruce Springsteen, the Kinks, a song Cass doesn't recognize. "Who is this?" she says.

"The Vaselines," he says, looking out at the ocean. He cracks his knuckles, and then he plays them songs of his own. They are both like and unlike the songs his band played, each of them a little world that the three of them step into together. The loneliness, the ache, in Jason's voice is so raw that Cass cannot watch him play; it's like walking in on someone naked. Alone, he is even more compelling than he is with the band. The night beach around them drops away. Cass thinks of meadows and bumblebees, the sound of rain falling in the forest, the sun warm on her back, swimming naked in an alpine lake. The warm smell of pine and earth in the high passes of the mountains out on the peninsula. They built a fire earlier but the flames have died down to coals, and the night is close around them. Against her will Cass admits it: She can see this thing in Jason that Maia sees, this spark. She does not want to feed him or coddle him or ensure his safety or comfort, but even she is moved a little by his music. At the edge of the circle of Jason's voice she sees something shift in the darkness, lifts her head.

The man in the black coat is watching them, his pale face expressionless, his dead eyes flat and full of hunger. The red glitter of rubies at his throat, his white fingers curled into fists. "No," Cass says aloud, sitting up, "no, that's not right," and Jason, startled, falters on a chord, the jangling noise harsh and sudden.

"What's wrong?" he says.

Cass scrubs at her eyes with the heel of her palm, searches the darkness. Whatever it was that she saw, it's gone. "Nothing," she says. "I thought I saw something."

After their confrontation Jason is more gracious most days, offering to go into the village to buy more water or food, bringing back candy for her, or fruit, or woven bags from a roadside vendor. Cheap things—and who does he think he's kidding, he's bought them with Maia's money—but the sentiment is worth more than the gift itself. He's like a toddler, aggravating but without malice. No matter how much she resigns herself to him, though, she can't forgive him the worst offense of all: stealing Maia from her and transforming her into a near-zombie version of her former self. She takes on his opinions, his affectations, even his vocal tics. His drawling, sarcastic *"Yeaaaaah,"* his chortle, his peninsula hick's disdain for people who care about clothes or good food or money. Which is, of course, an easy spite to carry if it's someone else's money you're living on. But Maia won't hear a word against him, and Cass is on unstable ground, since she herself has been living off Maia's savings since they skipped town. He's divided and conquered them as efficiently as someone bringing a cleaver down on the ties that have bound them together in the last month. Wherever he goes, Maia's eyes follow him, adoring, her face turning after him like a leaf following the sun, until Cass has to look away. They will have to leave here, soon, drive north with what little they have left and figure out what comes next, and she has the sinking feeling the rest of the story will have Jason's name scribbled all over its pages.

He follows her into town one afternoon, scuffing his feet and whining, though she tries her best to dodge him. He's hungry but doesn't want shrimp, doesn't trust the roadside vendors—this though they've been eating from carts all week—thinks they probably have the kind of cheese he doesn't like, or flour tortillas instead of corn. "There's only one kind of cheese," Cass says, but he doesn't hear her. What does he expect, Monterey Jack to appear out of the ether like somebody abracadabraed it? Cass might be a witch, but she's no *I Dream of Jeannie.* The sun pounds down on their burnt shoulders. Jason's unpleasable, sulky, intolerable. They're standing in the middle of the dusty street, which is thankfully deserted; Jason makes her embarrassed to be white. "I don't want to go back to the beach without something to eat," he says.

"It's your own goddamn problem," Cass says, "if you won't eat anything that's here."

"I don't like anything that's here."

Cass forgets her resolve, what little forgiveness she's mustered, loses her temper with him altogether. "We should just fucking leave you behind," Cass snaps.

To her astonishment, his face goes as slack-jawed as if she's punched him.

"You can't," he says in a tiny voice. "You can't leave me behind." His eyes are full of despair. *You and I are more alike than I care for, little man,* she thinks. "You can't leave me," he says again. "You can't."

"Lucky you," she says, "it's not up to me." She turns her back on him, unable to look at the pathetic slouch of his shoulders any longer, and trudges back toward the beach. He waits for a moment and then runs after her.

"Promise me you won't," he says.

"Won't what," she says.

"Won't leave me."

She stops and faces him. "I'd leave you in a second," she says. "I can't stand you. But like I said, it's not up to me." She steels her face against the misery that crosses his.

"I told you I don't know how," he says. "To change."

"It would be nice if you learned."

"I never really had a mom."

Cass snorts. "You seem to have found the equivalent."

"I want you to like me," he says. "I love Maia. I do. I love her. I've never met a girl like her. I'm going to marry her."

"You're *what?*"

"That's what people do," he says, "when they love each other."

"Jesus, Jason, you sound like a kindergartener."

"Why are you like this?"

Cass shakes her head. "Give it a rest."

"She loves you. But I don't know how to even make you like me."

"You can't make me like you. That's not how it works. I have to want to like you."

"I'm trying really hard."

"You could've fooled me."

He shrinks back from her, wounded. "You're kind of a bitch, Cass."

She laughs. "Bingo, Jason," she says.

There's nothing she can do about him. He's like a canker. And now Maia's leaving her, the way Cass knew she would all along. The hurt of it is not her going. Cass is used to letting go of anything good. The hell of it's that Maia didn't quit Cass for her well-paved road to a good and meaningful life; she quit for this snively loser, this dirty-haired trainwreck of a boy-man. It's worse, infinitely worse. It's like he put something in her water. He has a kind of charisma, Cass will admit; the people here, improbably, love him, find his stumbling hacked-up Spanish adorable, his ineptness endearing. They, like Maia, will frequently attempt to feed him, clearly certain he is unable to do so on his own. It happened the whole drive down, too. Cashiers at gas stations, truck-stop waitresses, random mothers in parking lots. A forty-something woman in a business suit had come up to him in San Diego and handed him twenty dollars, apropos of nothing. Cass has seen it happen before with street punks like her, always white boys who were just the right mix of good-looking and vulnerable, dirt smudged along their pretty cheekbones so artfully it looked intentional. A legion of girls forever trying to nurse them back to health, fix them up, buy them food, give them one more chance. Jason's power to charm makes Cass want to cut his throat in his sleep. She has never let anyone take care of her. She has pride and her own wits, gets herself out of the trouble she gets into. She doesn't understand how boys like Jason can stand themselves. Easy for him to be the edgy artist with a diva's temper; Maia's just one of a long line of girls who'll fatten him up and cover his bills when he blows all his rent money on a new amp. Cass knows all about it. If Maia had ever been out in the world, she'd be able to see it, too.

She asks Maia about their money, one morning when Jason is swimming in the ocean, and Maia gets serious immediately. "We have to go home after this," she says. "I guess. I mean, I don't know where else to go. We're almost broke."

Cass thinks about this, pushing her bare toes through the sand. Home. Back to the squat. Maia could stay there, but would she want to? Does Cass even want to?

"We could try and get an apartment," Cass says, surprising herself. "Somewhere. Together."

"That takes even more money than gas."

"We could get jobs."

"Like this?" Maia waves a hand at herself, encompassing her dirty hair, shredded clothes.

"Sure," Cass says. "We can clean up a little. But plenty of places don't care. Restaurants, coffee shops. That kind of thing. Maybe a bar if we're lucky."

"We're not old enough to work in bars."

"We're old enough to lie."

"Right," Maia says. She is quiet for a while. Jason is a tiny dot, far away from them, a speck of black against the glittering sea. "I miss the piano."

"I'm sure," Cass says.

"I want to play like those boys play. Jason's band. I don't know how, though."

"Sure you do. You're really good."

"But not like that. They can just make things up. Play together. I mean, of course I'm a better musician than any of them. I don't think Jason can even read music. But the way they played—it's like they were talking to each other or something. Like this language I didn't even know about before. I want that."

"You could start a band," Cass says. "When we go home."

"When we go home."

"So we are. Going home."

"We could stay in LA." But Maia doesn't sound serious. Cass considers the idea, discards it. California is for weirdos and surf rats. The beach is nice, but it's no place like home. Does she want a real life, now? An apartment with Maia, a bed, a table, a bookshelf. Rent. A real stove. Things people have. Things people could lose.

"Do you want to go home?" Cass asks, tentative. "I mean, *home*."

"Seattle? I guess I sort of do."

"No, I mean home. To your parents."

Maia is surprised to realize that already her parents' house is the last place she thinks of when she thinks of home. Home for her now is just a smear of grey, the choppy water of the Sound, the green trees on the slopes of the mountains. "Jesus, no," she says. "I miss Oscar." She stops. "I called him," she says. "From Santa Cruz."

"I figured."

"He told me I was afraid of something. Something inside me."

"On the phone? That's kind of heavy."

"He's like that. Do you think I'm afraid?"

"Isn't everyone?"

"I don't know. I don't know what it is." Maia's face is so fierce Cass wants to hold her tight, sing her lullabies until her scowl eases and the tension seeps out of her shoulders. What demons could a spoonfed girl like Maia possibly have? And even if she does carry some burden Cass can't see, who doesn't live with darkness in the secret corners of their hearts?

Cass picks through the various things she could say. Maybe she hasn't given Maia enough credit, these long weeks, hasn't recognized that the pieces of Maia that look like her aren't pieces Cass made, but pieces that were there already. If anything, all she's done is given them the chance to shake themselves awake.

"We could call your parents. I mean, you could."

"Oscar said he'd tell them I was okay. Anyway, I stole their car."

"We stole the car."

"I'm not going to blame you for the car," Maia says. "That would be shitty."

"I didn't stop you. You don't want to call them just because of the car?"

"Maybe they won't say anything about the car. They never drive it. My mom has the BMW."

BMW. Cass almost laughs. *Oh, Maia.*

"We'll call them when we go north," Cass says. "From San Diego. You can tell them you're okay. See what happens."

"We can't keep going. We need money."

"Money helps," Cass agrees.

"A little house," Maia says, dreamy. "A little house for us, on a hill somewhere. It could be brick. A big room for the piano. And we could put patchwork curtains in the kitchen."

"I could grow herbs in the backyard," Cass says.

"And flowers. Lots of flowers. Dahlias."

"You could teach piano."

"We could start a band."

"I thought you wanted to be a real musician."

"I don't know. I thought I wanted that, too. It's the only thing I'm good for."

"That's not true," Cass says. "That's not even a little bit true."

"It's the only thing I'm good *at*."

"You don't know that. You've never tried to be good at anything else."

"I don't think that's how it works."

"Sure it is," Cass says. "Do you love it? Playing?"

"Yes. Of course," Maia says quickly, but then she pauses. "I don't know."

"Yes? Or you don't know?"

"I don't know if I really know what love is."

"Maia, are you really going to marry Jason?"

"Did he tell you he asked me?"

"Did you say yes?"

Maia raises her hands in a helpless gesture, drops them. "I know it's crazy."

"You met him *last week,* Maia."

"You're the one who's always telling me to loosen up."

"I didn't mean yoke your entire life to the first punk boy to come along and whisper sweet nothings in your ear."

"He needs me," Maia says. "He's just—he's lost. I know you don't like him, but you don't see him when we're together. When it's just the two of us."

"All seven days you've had, to get to know each other inside and out." *Who's lost,* Cass thinks, *him or you?* But she doesn't say it. Later, she'll wonder if it would've made a difference, if she had.

"I've always wanted to be the kind of person who could say yes to crazy things," Maia says. "I never even had the chance before now. It feels so good, you know? To just say fuck it. Fuck all of it. What's the worst that can happen? We'll fall out of love and it'll be over."

"Do you love him?"

Maia is quiet for a while. "I don't know. I think so. I think I could. Oscar told me so many times I don't know anything about love that I started to wonder if maybe I would never feel anything at all. I felt like that all the time until . . ." She trails off.

"Until what?" Cass prompts.

"Until I met you," Maia says quietly, not looking at her. "Everything changed when I met you."

Cass's heart is pounding so hard she's nearly dizzy with it. "I know what you mean," she manages, her tongue thick and stupid. Maia is still looking away. "Maia, I—"

She cannot get the words out; terror chokes her. All the times in her life she has been unafraid, and this skinny girl on a beach is what undoes her? It seems unfair. Maia turns to Cass at last, her brown eyes unfathomable, and Cass searches her serious face for some sign of what she herself feels reflected there, and then she thinks, *Fuck it, just jump,* and reaches forward to push Maia's hair out of her eyes, and when Maia does not move, does not say a thing, just keeps looking at her with those big dark eyes, Cass leans forward, every breathless inch a mile, and then she is kissing Maia, and Maia is kissing her back, and it is like how she imagined it and nothing like how she imagined it, Maia's soft mouth and her salt-scented skin and her hands in Cass's hair and Cass's hands against Maia's cheeks and down her shoulders and counting the notches of her ribs. *I am devouring,* Cass thinks, *I am devoured,* and Maia is whispering Cass's name against her mouth as she kisses her.

And then they hear shouting and Maia breaks away from her and Cass thinks *Oh no, oh no, oh never stop,* her heart frantic, her hands shaking, and she looks past Maia down the beach. Jason is running toward them, fucking Jason, his hands aloft, yelling. Maia licks her lips and straightens her shirt and looks up at Jason with a smile so fake Cass wants to slap it off her, and Jason is upon them, shouting "Look at this shell! You guys, look at this shell I found," so oblivious to everything, to everything, to everything. Cass blinks hard at the tears salting the corners of her eyes, moves away from Maia, looks away from them both.

"How nice for you," she says, and gets to her feet, and Maia does not stop her when she walks away.

# THEN

The day after Maia's first punk show they sleep through most of the morning. Maia has never slept in past nine in her life and when she wakes, sees the hands of the clock marking eleven, she is filled with a luxurious and slightly guilty glee. Hedonism suits her. Who knew. The door to her father's study is shut. She knocks softly. "Dad?" But there's no answer. She opens the door a crack and peeks in. Her father is passed out on his desk, his mouth open slightly. She assumes he's still breathing. If he isn't, she doesn't really want to know. She closes the door and goes downstairs to the kitchen.

She wanted to make Cass breakfast, but she's never even cracked an egg. So it's Cass who fixes them omelets filled with cheese and mushrooms and green onion. "You never cook before?" Cass asks her, stirring butter into the pan.

"I can make spaghetti. If the sauce comes out of a jar."

"Your mom cooks?"

"My dad does. If he isn't drin—if he feels like it. My mom's not really that domestic."

"Her house is sure clean."

"She pays people to do that."

"Huh," Cass says.

The omelet is one of the best things Maia's ever eaten. "Wow," she says. "You're good at a lot of things."

Cass smiles. "I only let you see my best side, princess."

Maia shovels omelet into her mouth as though it's her last meal.

"My mom used to drink a lot," Cass says casually.

"Yeah?"

"Yeah. I mean, she probably still does. I just don't live with her anymore."

"Is that why you ran away?"

"No." The expression on Cass's face tells Maia not to ask anything else. She picks up their plates and carries them to the sink.

"Don't tell me I have to teach you how to do the dishes, too," Cass says, laughing.

"Oh, come on," Maia says. "I'm not *that* helpless."

"If you say so, princess. Listen, I should probably go before your mom gets home, right?"

"I guess so."

"I had a really good time this weekend."

"Me, too," Maia says.

"I hope she doesn't kill you for the hair."

"It looks so good it'd be worth it."

"I don't know about that. It does look good, though. Go practice your piano, okay?"

"Okay," Maia says. Impulsively, she crosses the kitchen, throws her arms around Cass in a bear hug. Cass holds her tight.

"You want me to take you with me?" Her tone is light but she's not joking. Maia can feel the *yes* bubbling up in her, overriding common sense and her own cautious nature. But she's not ready. She's not Cass, with nothing to lose. Not yet.

"No," she says. "It's okay. Thank you."

"Thank *you*. I guess I'll see you on the Ave this week."

"That sounds good."

Cass kisses her cheek and then she's gone, leaving a faint whiff of patchouli in her wake. Maia washes the dishes, taking more time than she needs with each plate. She's finished and about to go to the piano when she hears a car door slam in the driveway and her heart sinks. She leans her head against the refrigerator. It isn't too late to run away. She could climb out the kitchen window, take off after Cass, hang out on the Ave until they see each other next. She could be a little nomad, too, with her new clothes in a pack on her back and nothing else to her name but her toothbrush and her new boots. She imagines trying to carry the piano out the window with her, and she's laughing when the front door opens and closes. Noises of her mother taking her shoes off, setting her heels neatly side by side. Her mother's stocking feet, padding across the hardwood floor. In for a penny, in for a pound.

"Hi," she calls out.

Her mother comes into the kitchen. "Hello, sweetheart," she says, her voice light and happy. Definitely a two-person conference, then. "How was your—" She stops short. "Please tell me that's a wig," her mother says. Her voice is cold. Maia takes a deep breath and faces her.

"I dyed my hair," she says.

"And cut it."

"And cut it."

"What in hell were you thinking?"

"I just wanted—I thought it might look nice."

"It looks awful. *You* look awful. Where was your father for all of this?"

"He was here."

"Of course he was." Her mother looks away with a pained expression, as though Maia is so ugly the sight of her cannot be borne. "I don't ask you for much," she says.

Maia licks her lips. "I know."

"Is it your mission to upset me? Can you not behave like a mature adult for once in your life?"

"I'm sorry," Maia mumbles.

"You are obviously not sorry, Maia. You are not sorry at all. You are trying to hurt me, and you've succeeded."

"I just thought it would look nice," Maia repeats. Against her will, tears are springing up in the corners of her eyes. She wipes at them furiously.

"Is something wrong?" It's her father, standing in the doorway. "I didn't know you were back."

"You allowed this."

"I allowed what?"

"This," her mother says, pointing at Maia. "You allowed her to deface herself. She looks awful. She can't audition looking like that. I don't even want her seen outside the house looking like that. It's an embarrassment."

"Oh," her father says, "Renee, I think you're overreacting a little. She looks nice. Unique. You look very unique," he says to Maia.

"I can't look at either one of you," her mother says. "I'll think about what to do with you later, Maia. I'm going to go lie down." She sweeps out of the kitchen, imperious. Her father sighs and runs his hands through his disheveled hair.

"Oh, sweetheart," he says. "I wish you wouldn't upset her."

"I didn't mean to."

"You know how she gets. It's important to her."

"What's important to her? Controlling my life?"

"Is that what you think?" her father says. "Of course not. She just wants you to be happy."

"She doesn't want me to be happy. She wants me to be perfect. She wants me to be something I'm not." Her father is staring at her, startled. "Never mind," she says. "I'm sorry. I have to go practice."

She doesn't see Cass again for a few days. The air in her house is icy and tense; her mother won't talk to her, which makes things easier, but the weight of the silence makes her want to scream. Go running through the rooms, slamming doors. Anything.

Oscar is happy enough with the other pieces he's chosen for her audition—the Chopin funeral march, Haydn's Sonata in C Major, Hob.XVI/50—which she has practiced so relentlessly that she dreams sometimes of a procession of ballet dancers pirouetting endlessly across a vast expanse to a surreal medley of the classical and the romantic. But the Ravel is proving to be her undoing. When she plays it for Oscar she can feel his eyes boring into her back, his mouth tightening. Her playing has gone suddenly inelegant, overly technical. In her hands, the piece clanks forward like an automaton. "Again," he says, "Again. Again. Again." She can't land it, can't nail it, can't make the music sing the way it should. In three days she is flying to New York to audition at the best music school in the country, and Oscar wants her to play this piece, and all she can think about is her hair.

"It will show your virtuosity," he says. "It is perfect for you."

"It's not going to show my virtuosity if I can't play it, Oscar."

"You will play it," he says serenely. "I know you. I do not give you things to do if I think you cannot do them."

His faith in her drives her to practice obsessively. Oscar hasn't commented on her hair; she wonders if he even noticed it. She wears the clothes her mother bought her, still, but she's swapped out the loafers for the combat boots, as though her head and her feet belong to someone else. Every time Maia's mother passes her in the house, she makes a tragic noise at the back of her throat. When Maia sees

Cass leaning against a wall on her walk home from Oscar's, her heart leaps in relief.

"Khakis and twinsets and combat boots." Cass laughs, giving her a hug. "You're teaching me all kinds of new things, princess."

"Shut up," Maia says. "I'm trying to keep a lot of people happy."

"Your mom?"

"Things aren't great."

"Sorry."

"It's not your fault. I wanted to." Maia buys them coffee and they sit on the sidewalk outside the coffee shop, smoking Cass's cigarettes, which Maia's slowly gotten used to, in companionable silence.

"I'm going to New York," Maia says. "For the audition I was telling you about. For that school."

"Are you nervous?"

"I'm supposed to play that piece I played for you, the first day you came over."

"That sounded really good."

"I keep fucking it up. I've never played it right, the whole way through. This part in the right hand. It's not supposed to be this hard. But I can't get it. I can't move my hands fast enough." Maia makes a fist and studies it. She's been practicing so much every day her hands ache even more than they usually do.

"What happens if you screw it up?"

"I don't get in."

Cass is thoughtful. "I'd be sad if you went to New York."

"You could come," Maia says. "Come with me."

"I've never been there. Maybe. That sounds kind of fun."

"That would be great."

"You ever done speed?" Cass asks.

"Are you kidding me? No."

"Take some with you. It'll make you play better."

"That seems like a bad idea."

"Balzac drank like thirty cups of coffee a day; worked for him."

"Bach wrote a cantata in praise of coffee," Maia says. "Coffee's not speed."

"It was just an idea."

Maia thinks about it. "Shit," she says, "why not. In for a penny, in for a pound." Cass reaches into her pocket. Maia laughs. "You just carry it around? Like for a rainy day or something?"

"You never know," Cass says. She taps a few pills out of a tiny plastic container and wraps them up in a cigarette paper. "Here. They won't make you crazy or anything. It's just dexies. Mash them up on a mirror or something and snort them." She laughs at Maia's expression. "You don't have to take them, princess. I don't want to ruin you."

"My life was just never this exciting before."

"Excitement can be overrated," Cass says. "Put those away before someone sees you. What, nobody ever hand you drugs on the street before?" Cass mock-snorts. "Preppies," she says.

Only her father flies with her to New York; her mother is too busy teaching, for which Maia is infinitely grateful. They fight about her hair up until the moment she leaves, her mother insisting she dye it black and Maia refusing. She has never fought with her mother about anything before in her life and the vehemence with which she defends herself startles both of them. Her father hides in his office until the moment it is time to leave for the airport.

When they get off the plane he straightens a little. Waiting for their suitcases, he taps his feet and whistles cheerily. He guides her from the baggage claim to the taxi stand with a surety that she's never seen in him, directs the taxi driver briskly, sits back in his seat with a new light in his eyes. Maia watches the buildings flash by, grow closer together. The cab lurches wildly from lane to lane, the driver muttering expletives as he cuts off other drivers and makes sudden turns. Maia clutches her armrest in terror, but her father looks about him with delight. They cross a bridge bigger than any bridge Maia's ever been on, heading toward the immense and glittering downtown of Manhattan, a place Maia has only ever seen in pictures, and it is not until this moment that she realizes all those pictures are of a thing that is real. The skyline is monstrous, alarming against a headache-grey sky teeming with clouds: a forest of grey towers rising out of the earth like stalagmites, the greatest mass of them concentrated in a spiny cluster at the south end of the massive island. And it is an island, something she never thought about; an island not like any other island she has known, adopted child as she is of the green and silent northwest. She has never seen so many buildings as tall as trees in one place. She can hear the Frank Sinatra song in her head. *New York, New York.* If all goes well for her tomorrow she could live here, as soon as the fall. "What bridge is this?" she asks, and her father says "Williamsburg," at the same time as the taxi driver. She nods as if this information means something to her and looks out the window again. "He should have just taken the tunnel," her father says under his breath.

The buildings flash by; the sun glitters on the river. Her father is sitting up straighter, craning his head around to look, pointing things out to her—"Over there, that's where we'll go to get Indian food—oh, and I'll take you to my favorite little coffee shop in the East Village, where I used to go—and I can show you the apartment I used to live in when I was in school—and the bar where I met your mother."

"Sure, Dad," she says, letting him prattle on. He points out landmarks—the Empire State Building, the Chrysler Building, Grand Central. "Times Square is over there," he says, pointing, "but only tourists go there, and we're not tourists. Oh, sweetheart, you're going to love it here."

"I haven't gotten in," she says.

"Of course you'll get in," he says absently, twisting around in his seat. "The Algonquin is over there, too—you know, the famous hotel, Dorothy Parker used to drink at the bar there, and all sorts of other people—they were called the Round Table." Maia wonders if Dorothy Parker is one of her father's New York friends.

"Cool," she says.

"Well, maybe you should see Times Square, just once. I suppose it's worth seeing. Of course no one ever *went* there, when we lived here. We only went to theater things in the Village. Marty"—Maia has never heard of Marty—"used to do the craziest stuff. Oh, you know, these performance art things, he would get all these models he knew to cover themselves in fake blood, and he'd roll around on the floor. He always said it was about capitalism. Linda"—

Maia has never heard of Linda—"was so jealous of the models, but after they had the baby she was the one who up and left him. For her guru, can you believe that?" Maia has never heard of a guru. "She lost her mind. Last I heard she was living in *Colorado*. We just had the best time, in those days. Little space down on the corner of Bowery and Second, we could barely fit all our friends in at once. You could hear all the street noise in there, too. I should have told your mother we'd stay longer. Three days isn't enough. We can go to the Museum of Natural History and see the dinosaurs. I used to love to go see the dinosaurs. And the Met. And I'll have to take you to Central Park. And you should really go to MoMA. We can see the Guggenheim, too, if you want." Her father has said more in the last ten minutes than he has in the last ten years.

"Sure," she says.

"You'll love it here," he says again. "You'll just love it. There's nowhere like it in the world."

"Yeah," she says, looking out at the sidewalks clotted with people, the looming buildings, the streets littered with trash. Bike messengers flash by, deliverymen riding fat-tired bikes laden down with bulging plastic bags, drivers honking, trucks belching exhaust. In the car next to their taxi, a man rolls down his window, sticks his head out, screams obscenities at a woman pushing a stroller who's trying to cross the street in front of him. Maia watches in horror as a cab drives over a pigeon, looks away quickly before she has to see the smeared, bloody mess. A homeless man in a wheelchair, his feet wrapped in dirty bandages, holds a Styrofoam cup in one hand and a tattered American flag in the other. He bangs the cup against his knee with an expression of resigned despair. No one hurrying past looks at him. The ominous sky glowers down at them, threatening downpour. A dirty cat stares sadly at the sidewalk in front of a corner store, a bloody sore where one of its ears should be, fur matted over its gaunt ribs. Even with the cab's windows rolled up against the cold, she can smell the cesspool stink of rotting garbage and worse.

"God, I miss it here," her father says dreamily.

Their hotel is very grand. Maia shrinks a little at the marble floor, the crystal chandelier. The ceiling is two stories high and the lobby is enormous, a vast expanse of spotless red carpet and polished cream stone. She feels exposed and awkward crossing it, pulls the cuffs of her jacket over her knuckles. Maia catches a glimpse of herself in the mirrored walls: frumpy, big-eyed as a bumpkin, disheveled, topped with a ludicrous mess of garish hair. In this city she's already nobody and not in a good way. The woman who checks them in has sleek shampoo-commercial hair and a fitted skirt that flatters her shapely calves, bats mascaraed eyelashes at her father and won't look at her. The woman's shade of lipstick is a tasteful, elegant red. Maia chews her own chapped lower lip and thinks of what Cass would do: throw her shoulders back, half-mast her eyelids, put up the corner of her mouth in the faintest of sneers. Scuff up the floors and track dirt all over the carpet with her boots, on purpose. *It's nice,* she can hear Cass say in her ear. *If bullshit is your kind of thing.* She laughs out loud, and the woman gives her a funny look.

Her room is across the hall from her father's. It has a view of the city, solid blocks of buildings spread out below her and bisected by broad avenues pulsing with traffic. Her father leaves her to shower for dinner. She takes the clothes she's brought out of her suitcase, spreads them across her bed: a black dress for her audition that in Seattle had seemed, if not glamorous, at least elegant, but here looks dumpy and poorly cut, its black the wrong sort of black, its fabric the wrong sort of fabric; her khakis, still pressed neatly; a sweater; two turtlenecks; and underneath them, tucked away like a secret, the soft grey thermal shirt she stole with Cass. The air in the hotel room has the canned taste of airplane, and when she tugs at the window she realizes it's sealed shut. No jumpers allowed.

But the water in the shower is hot and the towels are deep and soft, and it's the kind of hotel that has a terry-cloth bathrobe hanging on the back of the bathroom door. She looks at herself for a long time in the mirror, under the too-bright hotel bathroom lights that wash out her skin. Her eyes are tired and a little sad. Most of the dye has faded and now her hair is just bedraggled, the rough-cut ends a sickly, uneven pink. If she were Cass she would smoke in the no-smoking room, raid the hotel refrigerator, flip through all the channels, order a steak from room service. Would her dad notice the bill if she pillaged the wet bar? If he noticed, would he say anything? She opens the door, tallies up the tiny bottles of whiskey and gin. Nothing ventured, nothing gained: She gulps one down, not even caring what kind of alcohol it is, pictures Cass cheering her on. She tucks the empty bottle into the garbage under a pile of tissues, feeling pleasantly fuzzy. She brushes her teeth, puts on the stolen grey thermal and a pair of khakis, wishes she had brought her boots and Cass clothes. Her father knocks gently on the door as she's brushing her hair and she lets him in. "That's a nice shirt," he says.

"It's new," she says.

They ride the train together. The subway is terrifying, all light and noise and filth, the trains thundering along their tracks, too many people rushing this way and that and running directly into her and giving her terrible looks. She gets stuck in the turnstile and nearly cries in panic and humiliation. "Jesus, go back to Kansas," the man behind her snarls. Her father is happy as an otter, darting through the crowds, easily deciphering some arcane language of train numbers and lines. She runs after him, too proud to ask him to slow down. His dazed absentmindedness has fallen away, replaced by a sharpness and liveliness she's never seen in him before.

They come out of the train onto a busy street, cluttered with even more people. People hurrying back and forth, lovely people in lovely clothes, people on errands, people bustling, people shopping, people eating things as they walk quickly from one place to another. People yelling and waving their arms, people going in and out of apartments, people drinking in bars. There are more different kinds of people in a single block than in the entire city of Seattle: brown people, white people, tall people, short people, very beautiful people, funny-looking people, people speaking Spanish and French and English and Japanese and languages she doesn't recognize, old people, young people, people every sort of in-between. There's so much to take in her head hurts.

Her father leads her through a maze of streets at a breakneck pace. "Dad," she says, "where *are* we?" and he looks at her, surprised. "The East Village," he says, as if this is obvious. Why did she bother to ask? Whatever he says will mean nothing to her. There's an open space teeming with homeless people that she realizes belatedly is supposed to be a park; they walk past a man peeing nonchalantly against a garbage can next to a dispirited-looking patch of yellowed grass. Maia gapes, slowing, but her father doesn't even notice and she has to run again to catch up with him. At last he ducks into a tiny restaurant, only big enough to hold six tables. Most of one corner is taken up by an enormous statue of the Buddha with lit candles surrounding it and a little dish of tea at its feet. The warm, cozy room is quiet, a welcome relief from the chaos of the city outside its windows.

A smiling, grandfatherly man seats them, hands them dingy plastic menus, pours them tea. "Hello, hello," he says, half-singing the words. Maia is charmed. He winks at her and withdraws to the counter that separates the restaurant area from the kitchen. From this position he looks out over their heads, watching the street with bright eyes, humming to himself quietly.

"This is the best Vietnamese food in New York," her father says, beaming at her across the table. "You want me to order for you?"

"Okay," she says. "Sure."

The waiter has doubtless overheard this exchange; they'd have to whisper for him not to hear anything they say. He returns to their table, murmuring something to her.

"Sorry?" she says, "I couldn't hear you," and he repeats it, louder, and she still can't understand him, and he says it again, and then she realizes, to her absolute horror, that he is speaking to her in Vietnamese. Her stomach clenches. He stops, fumbles with his pad in consternation, realizes he's made an error.

"I'm sorry," she says, "I'm sorry, I'm not—I don't—" She makes a helpless gesture. Her father, ever the attempted gallant, nods emphatically.

"She's *adopted*," he says loudly.

"*Dad*," Maia says. "It's fine. It's not—"

But the waiter is mortified, apologizing over and over, and Maia is mortified. Her father is indignant, growing more so, and Maia has to put her hand over his hand and say "Dad, please stop" again, until he calms down. Her father points to some numbers on the menu. "NUMBER THIRTY-THREE," he says, still shouting, overenunciating his words. Maia winces. "NUM-BER THIR-TEE THREE. EX-TRA SPI-CY, and number thirty-six—do you want spicy, honey?—MAKE NUMBER THIR-TEE SIX EX-TRA SPI-CY." The waiter retreats, palpably relieved. Whatever moment Maia had had before, with her singing friend, is gone forever. She'd thought he'd liked her for no special reason, for her her-ness, and now she doesn't know what it was he saw, and she never will know, because her father ruined it and because no one has ever taught her the tongue she was born to, the language of a home she's never seen and probably never will. What would Cass do? *Dad. Fuck off.* But for all the things Cass knows, she'll never know what it's like to feel like this. Maia stares at her hands, her fingers knotted together on the table, her hands that look nothing like her father's. The father who isn't her father at all. Her real father could be dead. He could be in Vietnam, he could be here. For all she knows, he could be the waiter. It could have been so much worse, she knows this. It could have been anyone who got her, any cruel or terrible fate. Her father loves her as best he is able, and her mother—her mother wants her to succeed, at least. That is almost a kind of love. She is safe and warm and housed and fed and she is a brilliant pianist, and she is here in this city staying in an expensive hotel about to audition at one of the best music schools in the world. *Keep your head, girl,* Cass says in her gravelly voice. *I don't know how,* she says back. *Oh princess,* Cass says, *come on. You were born to survive, just like me. Somewhere in there is a girl whose name is trouble.*

"People shouldn't make assumptions like that," her father says, still huffy.

"It's fine," she says. "It was an easy mistake to make." Her father shakes his head.

"Tell me about the East Village," she says, and it's the right thing. He looks happier immediately.

"We used to have readings, at the bar down the street," he begins, and she lets him natter on. The readings, the nights on the town, the poetry, the people he knew, all of them living in terrible apartments full of roaches, subsisting on white rice and canned beans, the bodega that still sold grilled-cheese sandwiches for a dollar, riding the ferry to Staten Island for the lark of it, all of them working on their novels. The publishers' cocktail parties, witty conversation and free drinks and all of them stuffing themselves with hors d'oeuvres because it was almost the same as a free meal. Maia imagines a roomful of desperate clones of her father, rushing a white-draped banquet table, forks aloft, like something out of a horror movie. Her father had won prizes back then, for his short stories. He'd had a story in the *New Yorker*, been named to some list of bright young things coming up. He'd come close to actually being somebody, she knows, and to hear him tell it now fame was a thing he was destined for, him and all his bearded, white, bespectacled friends from good families, toiling away nobly in their garrets. Some of her father's friends did in fact go on to make something of themselves; sometimes when she's in a bookstore with her father, he'll touch a cover reverently, his face equal parts envy and awe. "Michael sold the book at last," he'll say, or, "Joseph. I knew he'd do it." Her father still wears blazers with leather patches at the elbows and shakes his head at reviews in the *New York Times*. "Nobody knows how to read anymore," he says, or, "Anybody can be a critic these days. It's a damn travesty."

"And then you met my mother," she says now, and the light goes out of his face like someone's slammed a door. She hadn't meant to be cruel, but the sight of his anguish makes her heart purr. Now they're almost even.

"And then I met your mother," he says, and right then their soup comes, rice noodles and chunks of meat swimming in broth, and it smells like heaven, and once they are eating neither one of them talks at all.

The next morning he walks her from their hotel to the school, buys her coffee and a croissant along the way. She's too nervous to eat and worries the butter will sully her fingers; she hands it back to him and says, "It's okay. I'm not hungry." She's clutching the music for the Ravel, though she knows the piece by heart. The pills Cass gave her are in her purse, folded into a napkin. She feels stupid in the black dress. Obvious. A hick. She has never been anywhere that made her feel so ugly so quickly.

The school is a big wedge of concrete and glass, rising out of a broad plaza like a Modernist tumor. Maia hates it on sight. There is a flat black reflecting pool, spotted with wishful pennies, out of which rises some sort of lumpy Cubist thing that is probably supposed to be a naked lady. Maia scowls.

"Do you want me to come in with you?" her father asks. He's fishing for a yes, she knows. It makes him feel good to be useful here, to be someplace where at last he is competent, where he knows what streets to take, how to ride the subway, where to find the right things to eat.

"It's okay," she says. "I'll meet you back at the hotel."

"You'll get lost."

"It's ten blocks. In a straight line."

"You might get turned around."

"Let me do this, Dad. On my own."

He looks down at her, owlish, his glasses slipping down his nose. She has thought, all her life, that she loved him, but what sits in her chest now feels more like pity, and she wonders if pity's what she's mistaken for love all along. Until now. Until Cass. He coughs.

"I—of course. I understand. I—you know your mother and I are so proud of you."

*Is that what you call it,* she thinks. "I know. Thanks, Dad."

"Call the hotel if you need anything. Anything."

"I will."

He puts an awkward hand on her shoulder, leaves it

there a second too long. She ducks from under his palm, crosses the plaza, and walks through the tall glass doors toward her fate.

A helpful security guard directs her to the second floor. In the bathroom she shuts herself in a stall, digs the pills out of her bag, a mirror, a pen. She grinds the pills into a powder with the end of the pen, hunched awkwardly over the mirror, paranoid she'll drop the whole operation into the toilet. She props the mirror on top of the toilet-paper dispenser, tugs a bill out of her wallet, rolls it into a little tube, almost knocks the mirror off the dispenser, curses under her breath. The bathroom door opens and she hears the *click-click* of heels. She snorts the powder off the mirror, coughs loudly, yanks at the toilet paper roll, makes a noisy production of blowing her nose, wonders if she's blown the drugs all back out again. She can imagine Cass laughing at her, hands on her thighs, doubled over. *Shut up,* she thinks, *you dick.* Cass would be better at it. Cass is better at everything, except for the one thing Maia is good at. Is it best to be extraordinary at a single thing or competent at all of them? She puts the mirror away, flushes the toilet, emerges from the stall wiping her nose. A woman about her mother's age with jet-black hair slicked into a bun—the heels—is applying lipstick in the bathroom mirror. Maia washes her hands and the woman looks her up and down. She's wearing a black dress that puts Maia's to shame; silk and cut on the bias, it fits her like it was made for her, skims elegantly over her lean, toned body. Maia sniffs.

"Sick?" the woman asks.

"I think I'm coming down with something." The paper towels are on the woman's far side and Maia doesn't want to reach across her. She wipes her wet hands on her dress. The woman's eyes widen a little and Maia wonders if she's done something untoward.

"A difficult day to be ill," she says. "You are auditioning?"

"Yeah."

"*Yes,*" she says, displeased. "You are the one playing Ravel."

"Yes," Maia says, chastised. She wrinkles her nose. *You'll feel the sparkle,* Cass said, and she can feel it now. Her vision's sharpening, the world around her blowing into a cloud of glitter. She can taste it at the back of her throat, that metallic tingle of her body coming alive. *Fuck this laminated old bitch,* she thinks. It's a thought she never would have had pre-Cass.

"The Romantics are not twentieth-century."

"What, you want me to play Boulez? Sorry to disappoint. I have to go," she says. "My audition is in a few minutes."

"I know," the woman says. "You are playing for me."

"Well then," Maia says. The speed is sparking through her and she is afraid of nothing. "I'll see you soon." She walks out with Cass's walk, her back straight, her head high.

The audition room is low-ceilinged and ugly. There are no windows. A short row of three metal chairs faces two pianos. Two of the chairs are full: an older man with almost salaciously exaggerated features—great white mane of hair, too-big lips, jowly chin, watery blue eyes behind black-rimmed glasses—and another woman, this one pinched-thin and angry-looking. Neither of them regard her with anything like friendliness or welcome. The woman from the bathroom stalks in, letting the door slam behind her. "This is Professor Brook," she says, indicating the white-haired man, "and Professor Hunter"—the woman. "And myself, you have already met. I am Professor Kaplan. The three of us will be judging your audition. You may begin whenever you are ready." She says *ready* as if she's skeptical such an event will ever come to pass. She folds herself into her chair, her chin high.

Maia crosses the room, sits at the piano, pulls her shoulders back in a little stretch. Whatever the stuff is that Cass has given her, it's good; she feels it glittering around her like a force field, her fingers twitchy, the breath in her lungs charged and magnetic. All the people who have sat before her, trembling and craven with fear, the room stinks of it, she can smell it, a cloud around her, but she's not afraid, not now, not now, not now and not ever again, imagining herself onstage, somewhere, anywhere, Carnegie Hall, why not, here she is, better than everyone everyone everyone. She doesn't have to be afraid because she is so good and she can feel the music in her chest, the chords waiting, ready for the motion of her hands that will bring the notes tumbling out of the place inside her where they wait, spilling out of her fingers, exploding into this shabby classroom with its flickering lights and patina of despair. How many people have failed before her, how many, a lot, she can see it, she can feel it, she can recognize it in the laminated bitch and the jowly man and the other one, they are waiting for her to fail, they are bored, they are expecting to see her collapse in front of them, fuck up the first measure, burst into tears. What does she look like to them, some fucking yokel, she's no yokel, she's better than anyone who has ever played for them in this room, and she is *alive,* alive alive alive alive alive. *I am going to blow you out of the fucking water, you twits,* she thinks. She takes a deep breath, flexes her fingers, brings her hand to the keys, and begins to play.

From the first note it is better than anything she has ever played before for anyone, for Oscar, for Cass, for the state governor, for her mother, for strangers, for auditions, for contests, it is better than every recording of this piece she has ever heard, it is her crossing over into the realm of the divine, the speed fireworking through her, her heart thundering, her teeth grinding, it's worth it, it's worth it, because she is playing like fucking god is moving through her, she is playing like a girl possessed. She is playing like she has never dreamed of playing in her life. She is the mermaid, she is the lover, she is Ravel dreaming over poetry in the dark, she is the keys, the strings vibrating, she is the wood of the hammers falling and the brass of the pedals and the charged atoms of the air whirling past her, she is the waves of sound, she is particles bright and living, she is shattering and coming together, she is breathing the music, she is transcendent, she is divine. She is outside of time, outside of her body, giving over to whatever force has taken hold of her, whatever moves through her now and draws her hands across the keys, she is flickering in and out of being, now human, now something else, now sound, now echo, she is breathing light, she is breathing light, coming through the first passage and into the second, and the right hand is perfect, perfect, the tremolo magnificent, her fingers sweeping through the glissando and reaching again for the chords. She hears a quick sharp intake of breath, one of them, which one she can't tell, she hopes it's the harpy. The music is an animal moving through her, a force, a tidal wave, an ocean, an earthquake. She is shaking with it. The siren song draws her down and down and down into the dark, in to the deep sweet ocean, into the palace of the undersea kingdom where kelp undulates softly on unseen currents, the light filtering faint and splintered from the world above, she is falling, falling, falling into all of it, falling in to drown, the man in the black coat waiting for her there as she knew he would be, his dead face alight with something nearly human, his hands reaching out to her, his voice in her head, her heart, her belly. *You play like Orpheus himself, child, come play for us in the long night,* and she thinks *I can't, you know that, I can't, this is my world, this one.* His face fills with sorrow and she brings her hands down for the last soft, watery notes, the quiet at the end of the storm, and tilts forward into the piano, breathing hard, her whole body thrumming, back in the audition room again, and she knows she has won.

The room is dead silent. She lifts her chin, takes a deep breath, plays the Haydn briskly and without flaw, the speed making her fingers move with an unnatural precision. She gets a little grandiose in the opening passage of the Funeral March, which suddenly strikes her as a little pompous—who wants to go to a *funeral*—but comes back to herself for the delicate melody of the following section, imagining Oscar gazing out the window with a faintly wistful expression, as is his wont whenever he listens to her play Chopin. Then the stately, lumbering chords again, why not be a little silly, she's the best thing these people will see in their entire careers and she knows it, they will be talking about what just happened in this room for the rest of their lives, about her, about how she is *better than everyone.* Her breath is hot and fast in her throat. She is elated, trying hard not to grin in triumph. When she is done she waits a moment, her head bowed almost primly, and then she stands and looks at them for the first time. The harpy's mouth is open a little and the jowler rubs at his chest distractedly with one immense, hairy paw. The pinched woman has lost a little of her sharpness, leans back in her seat with an expression that Maia can only describe as dazed. "Thank you," Maia says politely, and then she walks out of the room without waiting for them to reply.

She's halfway down the hall when she hears a sharp "Wait!" It's the harpy, clip-clopping toward her. *How does she walk in those heels?* Maia wonders. She stands there, her heart still racing, until the harpy's caught up with her.

"Who taught you to play like that? Not Oscar."

"You know Oscar?" Maia asks, startled.

"Knew. He taught here, a long time ago."

"Oscar taught *here*? He never said anything."

"No," the harpy says. "He wouldn't." A flicker of distaste crosses her face.

"I love Oscar," Maia says. "Oscar taught me everything I know."

"Other people will teach you more."

"Like who? You?" The harpy raises an eyebrow but says nothing. "That's how it works, right? You sink your teeth into whatever young talent you think will carry your name to the stars? You can't do it yourself anymore so you want me to make your name for you? Does anyone even know who you are? Does anyone fucking care? Because I don't. I don't care about any of this. I don't care about you. I don't care about coming here. I thought I did. I thought this was what I wanted. I don't give a *shit*." The words are huge and thrilling, coming from somewhere at her core, getting bigger and bigger and faster and faster. The harpy is staring at her in shock. "You and my mother and my father and all your fucking plans for me, you can go *fuck* yourselves. I don't want to sit here and listen to some dried-up old bitch tell me how to live my life. You don't care about the piano. All you care about is making sure your name goes on the goddamn program. I want to fucking make *art*." Maia wheels around without waiting for the harpy to answer, imagines Cass a stadium of one giving her a standing ovation as she half-runs down the hall. The euphoria lasts all of a few seconds before it dissipates into a cloud of dread. *What the fuck,* she thinks, *did I just do?*

Outside, she leans on the building, her heart pounding. The speed is betraying her; she's just jittery now, her fingers twitching, her pulse too fast. There's a pay phone across the street. She crosses to it, finds a stray handful of quarters in her bag, drops them in, dials Oscar's number. He answers on the fifth ring. She's never been so glad to hear his " *'Allo?*"

"Oscar."

"Maia!" he says, delighted. "*Chérie!* But why are you calling? Aren't you in your audition now?"

"I just finished."

"And?"

"Oscar, I—I've never played like that."

He's cautious. "This is good?"

"Oh my god, Oscar, it was like—it was like someone else was playing me. It was beyond good. It was the best I've ever played in my life. I wish you could have seen."

"Ah," he says, with a long sigh. "I wish this also, my dear, but it is the curse of the teacher to have his pupil outgrow him. You will be a wonderful pianist, my dear, and I shall beg you not to forget me when you have got your first contract with Deutsche Grammophon and a nice touring program, hmm?"

"Oh, Oscar," she says. "Of course I'm not going to forget you. But Oscar—I said some things—I—" She falters. *I called the head of the department a dried-up old bitch.* "I'm not sure if coming here is the right thing for me to do."

He is quiet for a long time. "This school will make your career. You will meet everyone who is important."

"But I don't think that's what I want."

"You are too young to know what you want."

"That's not true," she says, stung.

"Young people have grand ideas, always," he says. "It is the job of their teacher to corral them, do you see? You will get in, and you must understand that this is a great privilege. You have worked so terribly hard, harder than any pupil I have ever taught, and you are tremendously gifted, Maia—I do not say this unless it is true. You are the most gifted student I have seen in many, many years. Since I was a student myself. You want to throw this all away because you have a strange mood at the audition? Absolutely not, *chérie,* I won't allow it. I won't allow you to be so foolish."

"You didn't like it here. You never even told me you taught here."

"Kaplan. That bitch," he says, without rancor. "I was better than her, you know. She always hated me for it."

"Then maybe you can understand why I wouldn't want to—"

"No," he says, cutting her off. "I cannot. Myself, I have

made a terrible mistake. I have ruined my life. And for what? For nothing. For an illusion. It doesn't last. What lasts is a career. A life of art. You have a chance at this and I will not allow you to toss it aside. Do you hear me? I will not."

"I thought you of all people would understand."

"I of all people? I of all people do not understand. You are being foolish, you are a child who knows nothing of the world. You do not leave your house except to come to my house. I am telling you that if you make this mistake you will never forgive yourself. You will be a ruin. It will be over for you."

"Oscar, why didn't you tell me you taught here?"

"Because it was another life," he says. "That Oscar, I do not even know him. He is a stranger to me."

"You can't make the past go away by pretending it didn't happen."

"You are quite young, my dear, to be lecturing me on the uses and nature of the past, and I will thank you to cease at once."

"I sort of told them—I told that woman to—I wasn't polite."

"Then you will apologize."

"I will *not*," she says, horrified.

"My dear, I know she is not a nice woman. Believe me, I know this quite well. But she is in charge there, god help them, and it is in her hands your fate rests, god help you. When someone has got quite a lot of say over what will happen for you in the future, you must be polite to this person. You mustn't make enemies, my little one. You are not a man."

"Oscar."

"Do you think it does not make a difference? It is very American of you, to pretend there is no difference. It will end your career, if people find you difficult. It has ended mine, and I am not a woman. It will end yours even more quickly. You will write her a—how do you say? an absent apology?"

"Abject."

"Yes, thank you. An abject apology. You will grovel. You will offer to lick her shoes clean with your little pink tongue, if it is necessary, is that clear to you? She will like this. It is her greatest passion, to be correct and magnanimous. You will tell her you have seen the error of your ways. When she is satisfied you have got no pride left you will get in, and you will go. Do you understand?"

"I—" she begins, and then she thinks, *I what*. Oscar has nothing left, no hope, no future. Oscar has nothing but her, and she is throwing his dreams for her back in his face. All these people, living through her, and now that for the first time she is beginning to live for herself, she is also coming to see that it will not end well for any of them. But she cannot bear to break his heart. "I understand," she says.

"I will see you in a few days, my dear, and we will not speak of this tantrum, and when you receive your acceptance letter we shall have a little party, don't you think? A recital."

"Sure," she says. "Okay. Sorry. I was being silly."

"Yes. You are young," he says. "Young people are always silly. It is why they must trust their betters. *Bisous, chérie.*"

"*Bisous.*"

She hangs up the phone, stares dully at the receiver. More than anything she wants Cass. *I wonder what it would be like,* she thinks, *for someone to actually see me. To look at me and see what I am. What I want. Who I can be.* She puts her hands in the pockets of her coat and thinks about what she is going to tell her father.

# NOW:
# BARRA DE
# NAVIDAD

Cass is fuzzy-drunk on some terrifying cheap liquor Jason dug up, sitting at the edge of the water and smoking the absolute last of the weed. She doesn't know much about tequila, but she's pretty sure it's not supposed to taste like paint thinner. They've seen no other white people, the entire time they've spent on the beach; it's the wrong time of year, and other Americans—*tourists*, they'd all concurred with contempt, the one thing the three of them can manage to agree on—prefer the beach towns to the north and south, replete with luxurious resorts.

She doesn't have her candles or her herbs but she has her cards, and she's laying them out on a scrap of cloth on the sand, over and over. The Chariot. The Empress. The Six of Swords. "I need help," she says. The Lovers. The Hanged Man. "I can't keep going. I need help." The Magician. The Fool. The Lovers. Death.

The Magician.

Something changes in the air. She looks up and he's there, standing a little ways down the beach, looking at her. She didn't see him come. He is tall, and so thin it is almost painful to look at him, and dressed, despite the fact that they are on the beach in Mexico, in a long black coat and close-cut black trousers and a black shirt that flows loose and soft like silk. *White* is not the word for him; he is so pale he fluoresces. He has stepped out of the dark and into her waking life, but that's not possible, so he must be someone else.

"Hi," Cass says. "Did you—are you—you're American?"

*No.* His voice is so deep she feels it in her bones rather than hears it. It echoes through her, turns her blood cold. *You know what I am, child.* She looks down the beach. Maia and Jason are nowhere in sight. *Ah, shit,* she thinks. The luck of Cass: she's the kind of girl who will meet a tourist-ing serial killer on beach vacation. Or a ghost. Whatever the fuck he is. He is not the man from her dreams; he cannot be. Nothing Raven told her ever prepared her for anything like this. When the people in your head are standing in front of you, cool as you please, the hot white afternoon sun on your face, the heat haze making you stupid. She could swear he's smiling, but his death's-head mask is impassive, the cold black eyes regarding her as though she's an insect pinned on a corkboard. *I had forgotten what it was like, to feel the sun on my back.* He holds his pale hands toward the paler sun, palms facing upward, stands there still as a crow on a wire. His black coat does not move in the faint breeze coming off the water. *Come with me, Cassandra. I have something to show you.* He holds his hand out to her and, not knowing what else to do, she stands and takes it, and the sun winks out.

They are standing in the apartment from her dreams. Beyond the wall of glass, a dark sea heaves against a darker sky. The candles in the chandeliers burn with an eerie greenish light that does little to dissipate the gloom. The room is deathly cold and Cass shivers in her tattered shorts and T-shirt. "What is this place?"

*You know where you are, Cassandra. You know what I am.*

"No," she says, looking around her. There's a wall behind her she hadn't noticed before, windowless and lined with oil paintings. Cass thinks at first they are landscapes, but when she gets closer she sees they are populated with figures. She walks down the line. In one, a man rolls a boulder up a hill, his face contorted in agony. In another, a woman stands on a parapet, her face grief-stricken, her skin an ashen grey that makes her look as though she is made of stone. There are dozens of paintings, and Cass looks at every one, as the man in the black coat waits behind her.

When she gets to the last, she pauses. It looks newer than the others, somehow; the style is more modern. It's a study of a man on a grassy lawn, a big house behind him, all angles and windows. He's looking at something outside the frame of the painting, his face sad. Behind him, half-obscured, the figure of a woman in a white dress, her features hidden. "This is Jason," Cass says slowly. "This painting is of Jason."

*You know what I am,* he says again. *You know what I want.* She chews the edge of her thumb. Does the man who's haunted her dreams since she was a little girl really want *Jason?* Whiner and narcissist, inept cook and hapless navigator, a boy who could not take care of himself if he were given ten thousand dollars and a road map to the adult world? His music is good, but despite the other night on the beach, it's nothing special. Cass cocks her head, considering. Maybe there's some secret side to Jason that she's too spiteful to see. Maybe Maia's right about him; maybe he really is worthy of her love. She's having a hard time believing it, but if this skeleton in a fancy suit is bent on collecting Maia's boyfriend for his nocturnal freak show, Cass isn't going to argue. The gods always want boys for their special projects; girls only ever go crazy or die. Or betray.

"You want me to, like, get him for you?" she asks. "Doesn't he have to make his own deal with the devil?"

The man in the black coat shrugs, one shoulder rising to his ear and dropping again, his eyes never leaving her face. In every fairy tale Cass has ever been told the witch is a trickster, the gods turn traitor. Fickle as toddlers and as cruel. If he is from the dark palace that haunts her dreams, if he has crossed that black and undulating river, he is not on her side, whatever story he tells. But she thinks, then, of her life restored, her Maia brought back to her, unhitched from the stringy-haired monster that has insinuated himself into their friendship like a cancer. She knows all those old stories, too, musicians selling their souls at the crossroads, signing away on the dotted line. Jason wants to be famous, and the man in her dreams wants Jason, and if he really is what she dreams of, there is nothing he cannot do. She looks down at the floor. "You can have him," she says. "But he doesn't like me. You'll have to talk to him yourself."

*It is you I have come to, Cassandra. You whom I have followed here. You who led me to what it is I seek. And you are, after all this time, what I expected to find.*

"What the fuck is *that* supposed to mean," she says. His eyes are so dark she cannot tell where the pupil ends and the iris begins, and behind them there is nothingness. A dead white plain, a black palace with a thousand doors.

*You are not a fool, child,* he says. He reaches into his black coat and pulls out something round and red and tosses it to her, and she raises her hand instinctively to catch it, her eyes following its rosy arc, and when she looks again he is gone. She blinks, once, twice, and she is on the beach again, the hot sun on her face, shaking her head to clear away the cobwebs of the dreaming world. There is nothing to suggest she was talking to anyone other than herself, save what she holds in her hands: a pomegranate, sweet-scented and heavy, cool against her palms. "No fucking way," Cass says, and starts to laugh. "No *way.*" Whatever he is, he has a sense of humor.

Her bottle is empty and the joint is dust. The sunlight glitters on the water. Cass takes her shirt off and puts it over her head, stretches out on the sand, and falls backward into sleep.

When she wakes up, the sun has tracked most of the way across the sky and is sinking into a gold-purple blaze at the edge of the world. She has to think about where she is for a while before she gets up. The pomegranate is still real, next to her on the beach. Her belly is tender, the beginning of what will most likely be a nasty burn. She picks up the fruit and it's cool in her hands, despite having sat out on the beach while she slept.

Jason and Maia are asleep in their cabana. The lowering sun falls across Jason's stubbled cheeks in strips. His mouth is slack, his face as innocent as a child's. One hand is tucked beneath his chin, the other outflung, as though he's reaching for something far away. Maia's curled up against him, her head on his bony chest, the tangle of her bleached hair spilling across his faded shirt. Cass stands looking at them, the two of them a locked door she cannot pass through, a barred gate with DO NOT ENTER writ large across its iron bars. She is overcome by the childish impulse to throw a handful of sand at Jason's head, curls her fingers tighter around the fruit instead. Maia murmurs, her eyelids flickering open. "Hey, you," she says, her voice raspy with sleep.

"Hey," Cass says. "I got us something." She holds up the fruit and Maia's eyes widen.

"Far *out*," she says, sitting up. "Where on earth did you find that? I didn't even know they grew around here."

"Got it from some guy," Cass says, and sits next to Maia, stretching out her legs. The cabana is cool and dim and tilting slightly. "I'm sort of drunk," Cass adds.

Jason opens his eyes, shading out the sun with one hand.

"What is that?" he asks. Maia takes his hand and brings it to her mouth, bites his knuckle gently.

"Pomegranate," Cass says.

"I don't know what that is."

"It's good. Try some." She takes out her knife, cuts through the thin red skin to reveal the nest of ruby seeds.

"How do you eat it?"

"Like this." She mimes dropping the gemlike fruit into her mouth, pretends to chew. He laps what she's given him up from his hand. Red juice stains his palm. He swallows and she hears a chord on the wind, faint and far away. She waits for gods, demons, a celestial host. Nothing happens. The waves crash against the beach, the sunlight falls in slats, Jason looks at her with his ice-blue eyes. *He's all yours,* she thinks. *Take him quick and don't let him come back.*

"That's good," he says.

"Here," Maia says, "you have to try this," and takes a red seed between her fingers. "Open your mouth." Jason parts his lips. Maia puts her fingers in his mouth and pinches the seed between them and the tangy juice fills his mouth as the seed bursts and he laughs.

"Do it again."

She does, and opens her own mouth. "My turn." They have gone to some world of their own, their eyes on each other, their lips bright with pomegranate. Cass cannot look away from them. The air has gone still, the ocean soundless, the sun dim. Time stops. Cass can feel the deep slow pulse of the earth, the blood moving in her veins, the breath stopped in her lungs. Maia swallows. Cass closes her eyes. A sound, then, like a great bell tolling, somewhere in the deep. Her skin goes cold.

And then the moment passes and the sky undims itself and the breeze flutters in off the ocean, and the waves murmur against the beach, and Maia and Jason are looking at each other, dreamy-eyed as lovers in a tragedy, just before the knives and poison bring down the curtain. "You want some, Cass?" Maia asks, holding out a blood-colored handful of seeds.

"What the hell," Cass says, and opens her mouth wide.

When she tells the story years from now she will tell it untrue. "That week was the best week of my life," she'll say. Sun on the beach, sand, blue water. At night, more stars than she's ever seen in her short life. Maia: tanned dark and laughing, legs long in her cutoff shorts. Cass will tell it how she wishes it had happened, the three of them kin, Jason a sweet-natured Puck to her and Maia's Castor and Pollux. As if with her lying mouth she can remake the truth of what she did.

They go home. It's time. Nothing seems to have changed. Cass watches closely for traces of demons, signs Jason is spending sleepless nights wandering the paths of Hell. He looks tired, but not in any new sort of way. *I imagined that whole weird-ass thing,* Cass thinks. Cass's own dreams are blurry, aimless; sometimes when she wakes her muscles ache unreasonably, as if she's walked a long way, but if the man in the black coat comes to her again she does not remember when she wakes. Whatever is keeping him from her, she's grateful. She ran out of Raven's herbs a long time ago.

The three of them pile in the car, doing the best they can to brush sand from its seats, from themselves. They are tan and salt-skinned, beachy-haired as mermaids. Cass drives. Jason sleeps in the backseat. The miles flash by in a sunny blur. Maia calls Oscar from a gas station in San Diego while Cass pockets beef jerky, peanut butter crackers, packages of gum. Snacks that will litter the car, unopened, for the rest of the drive home. When Maia gets back in the car her face is still.

"How'd it go," Cass says.

"I got in," Maia says.

"Got in?"

"To that school I auditioned for."

"You gonna go?"

Maia starts to laugh, her shoulders shaking, laughs so hard she has to rest her head on the steering wheel, and then the laughter turns to harsh, choking sobs, and she's crying, crying her sweet heart out while Jason snores away. Cass touches her shoulder, rubs gentle circles.

"Hey," she says. "Hey. Princess. Hey." But the knotted muscles in Maia's back don't loosen, and it's a long time before she raises her head and wipes her nose with the back of one wrist.

"No," she says, as if nothing has happened. "I don't think I will."

Maia and Jason get married in a twenty-four-hour roadside chapel in LA, with Cass their only witness and a hung-over Elvis impersonator officiating. They'd splurged on a hotel room to celebrate; that afternoon, Maia and Cass had left Jason there, gone to find Maia a dress. They'd found a Salvation Army on Ventura Boulevard and flipped through racks of ridiculous, puffy dresses—"I'm not going to the *prom*," Maia said, laughing. Finally she found a white silk slip, edged in lace. She tried it on for Cass, came out of the dressing room twirling and barefoot. The slip was luminous against her clear skin, burnished deep brown by weeks of sun. Her eyes were bright, long legs bare, long graceful hands poised like a dancer's. She was so beautiful Cass turned her face away, feeling her own heart splinter in her chest. "How do I look?" Maia asked, grinning. Fury pulsed through Cass's heart, wild and sudden as a flash flood.

"Don't do this," Cass said. Maia's smile flickered and died.

"I want to be happy," she said softly.

"You think marrying the first dirty rocker to bowl you over is going to do that?"

"Cass. Don't."

Cass shook her head. "It's your goddamn funeral, princess." The hurt on Maia's face was worse than anything Cass had ever seen. Cass left Maia there, in the white slip, her brown eyes filling with tears, walked straight out of the Salvation Army into the blinding afternoon sun, walked into a liquor store and back out again with a stolen bottle of bourbon thumping gently against her thigh. She drank it all in an alley and threw most of it up again when she was finished, and then she slid down against the stucco wall and buried her head in her arms and cried until there was nothing left in her. When she was done she walked back to the Salvation Army. They were just flipping the Open sign to Closed. Cass pounded on the door until an exasperated-looking woman let her in. "It's an emergency," she said. "My friend's getting married." The woman studied Cass, scowling, but whatever desperate thing she saw in Cass's face made her relent.

"Hurry up," she said.

"Thank you." Cass bought a bouquet of fake roses and a hat covered in silk ribbons. She sat outside on the sidewalk, pulled the ribbons off the hat and the roses off their plastic stems, knotted the ribbon around the roses, piecing them together into a crown. She walked back to the shabby hotel, knocked softly. Maia flung the door open. Jason was asleep on the bed, oblivious to the tiny drama playing out around him.

"I'm sorry," Cass said, and gave her the flower crown.

Maia said nothing, the headdress clutched in one hand, her brown eyes wide and pleading, and Cass took her free hand, curled it into a fist, brought it to her heart. "I'm not much of a flower girl," she said.

"You can be my best man," Maia said, and she finally smiled. She held Cass and Jason's hands both, on the drive to the chapel.

The Elvis impersonator looks like Cass feels, and she's surprised he makes it through the brief ceremony without vomiting or passing out; but then, she's surprised she does, too. She wears her dirty cutoffs, her spiked dog collar, and a Misfits shirt she's stolen from Jason. Afterward they order Chinese takeout in their hotel room. They have to call six places before they find one that's still open and willing to deliver. Cass pulls the covers over her head and falls asleep before she has to listen to Maia and Jason having sex in the next bed.

In Big Sur they spend the night again in the campground where Maia nearly took a header off the cliff. The stars are thick as paint in the night sky and the ocean roars beneath them. Maia walks to the brink again. Cass follows her and they stand together for a long time, looking out at the heaving wine-dark sea.

"Can I ask you something?" Cass asks.

"Sure."

"Were you going to jump? That night?"

Maia is quiet. "No," she says. "I don't think so. I thought I—" She pauses, her brows drawn together. "I can't remember," she says. "I think I thought there was somewhere to go at the bottom. Someone I wanted to see. It's hazy."

"I'm not going to let you jump," Cass says.

"I know." Maia looks over the edge of the cliff. "It's not really that far, anyway. I'd just break my legs."

"Then I'd carry you home."

"Let's just save ourselves both the extra trouble. Cass?"

"Hmm?"

"Do you believe in ghosts?"

"Yes," Cass says simply.

"I never used to," Maia says.

"Until?"

"Nothing," Maia says. "It's nothing. Just a dream I had."

They haven't eaten in a while, but Cass pocketed another bottle at the last grocery store before the road wound up into the hills, and they pass it around that night until one by one they drift into sleep. Cass dreams of the bone forest, the black river. The skeleton man is at her side and together they are looking for something, although Cass does not know what it is they seek. *You will know when you find it,* he says to her. *You have always known you were not like other people.* He is walking faster and faster and soon she has to run to keep up with him, and then he is drawing ahead, his black silhouette disappearing into the dark wood. The white trees shimmer sinister against the velvet blackness between them. She is running alone down a dirt path, crying *Maia! Maia! Maia!*

Cass starts awake. The sky is edged pale, the stars fading out as the sun rises. The broad silvery mass of the ocean stretches out to the edge of the world. Her head hurts and she's freezing and her hair is soaked with dew. Next to her, Maia and Jason are curled into the scant comfort of each other; Jason's fingers are knotted in the tangle of Maia's hair. Asleep, Maia's face has none of its new wariness; she looks as young as a child. "I'm sorry," Cass says aloud, but to whom she is apologizing, for what, she cannot say. She drifts back into an uneasy and dreamless sleep until Maia shakes her awake gently a few hours later, and they get back in the car and keep driving.

They take turns at the wheel and drive straight through for the next fourteen hours. Cass has always thought the most disorienting part of any journey is not the trip out, but the road home. After everywhere they've been, Cass and Maia, it's unnerving to see the familiar lights of Seattle on the horizon. None of them has talked about what would happen when they actually got here, as though they can stave off the inevitable by refusing to discuss it. Maia's driving as they cross the city limits, her hands so tight on the wheel her knuckles are white. Cass wants to reach forward from the backseat, put one hand on her shoulder.

"I guess you can just drop me off at the house," she says instead. She'd told no one she was leaving, and she's told no one she's coming home, but there's always a place for her somewhere, there. She can sleep on the floor if some other miscreant's stolen her bed. She's not picky. Maia bites her lip.

"Maybe I can stay there, too," she says. "Until we figure something out." Where Jason lives exactly has never been clear, but he certainly doesn't have a place of his own.

"Find a phone," Jason says. Maia pulls off at the next exit, drives them to a gas station. Cass is beginning to feel as though she's spent her entire life in gas-station parking lots. Jason is on the phone a long time, gesticulating with one arm. Cass can't make out his expression in the dark. When he gets back in the car he seems triumphant.

"We can stay with Percy and Byron," he says. He's grinning like a banshee.

"What's up, baby?" Maia asks. Cass flinches at the "baby."

"They want us to make a record," he says.

"Who does?"

"Some big-shot producer. Got our demo, says it's the best thing he's heard in years."

"Are you serious?" Maia's elated. "That's amazing!"

"I guess that means your band didn't break up with you," Cass says sourly. Jason turns his radiant face to her.

"I told you," he says. "They need me. They know that. We're going to be rich."

"I doubt that," Cass mutters, but he ignores her. His eyes are distant.

"I knew it would happen," he says. "I knew it would happen just like this. I've waited for this my whole life." He touches Maia's cheek. "It's happening just the way I wanted it. You're my good-luck charm. Let's go home."

Cass directs them to her house. Maia gets out of the car to hug her tight. "Thank you," she says.

"For what?"

"For everything. For taking me with you."

"You took me with you."

"We took each other." Her skin smells sweet. Cass holds her tighter, buries her face in Maia's hair.

"I love you." But she shapes the words without speaking them, mouthing them into Maia's tangles like a benediction. *I love you. I love you.* They will leave her here and drive away together, and she will never see Maia again, and she had thought she knew what it was like to weather hurt but any wound she's borne before this one was nothing like pain at all. The mess in her chest now is so real she can feel it, a monster knitted together out of barbed wire and broken glass.

"I want to get a house with you," Maia says. "When we have a little money. Can we?"

*With Jason? Not fucking likely,* Cass thinks. "Yes," she says aloud. "That sounds really good."

"Patchwork curtains."

"Patchwork curtains," Cass agrees.

"I'll see you soon."

"Sure." Maia lets her go. Cass does not watch them drive away.

The house is candlelit and noisy. Cass had been hoping to slink unnoticed to some corner, curl up and lick her wounds in peace, but there's a seated circle of whooping black-clad trouble in what once was a living room when this was a house for real people.

"Hot fucking damn!" Felony yells, her eyes wide. "Where the fuck did you go, bitch?"

"Road trip," Cass says.

"Road trip my ass," Mayhem says, grinning. "You got your knickers in a twist and ran off with that little rich girl."

"Something like that." Cass drops her bag by the door. "Let's talk about something else."

"We're playing spin the bottle!" Felony bellows in glee. Cass sees now that there's an empty fifth of Potter's at the center of their circle. "I already got seven minutes in the closet with Chainsaw, but that fucker wouldn't put out." She pouts across the circle at Chainsaw, who shoots her a look of unadulterated terror.

Cass laughs, suddenly gladder to see these people, her people, than she's ever been in her life. "Aren't those two separate games?"

"We make our own rules," Mayhem says. "Come on. Sit down." Cass tucks herself in among her own tribe, and they shift to make room for her. Mayhem slings an arm around her shoulders. "Don't you run off like that without telling us again," she says, kissing Cass's cheek.

"Yes, Mom," Cass says, trying to hide her smile. "Somebody give me a drink."

Byron, Jason's drummer, and Percy, the bassist, live in one half of a shabby duplex in the Central District. The patchy front lawn is scattered with cigarette butts and empty beer cans. Their battered van is parked in the street. Byron lets them in, giving Jason a dirty look and ignoring Maia altogether. Inside, grubby carpet covers the floor. Curtainless windows stare out into the backyard, where a watery streetlight illuminates a tragic-looking tree leaning toward a chain-link fence as though it is trying to escape. A burn-scarred coffee table sports a collection of overflowing ashtrays, and the room stinks of old smoke and stale beer. Maia's heart sinks, and for the first time it occurs to her to wonder what she's gotten herself into. "Maybe I should stay with Cass," she says, though she has no idea if it would be any better there. *Poor little rich girl, all alone in the world,* she thinks, imagining Cass rolling her eyes. She misses Oscar with a sudden, awful pang.

"You're welcome wherever I'm welcome," Jason says.

"You don't seem very welcome."

"They're just being assholes." She follows Jason into the kitchen, where Percy is staring at an unboiling pot of water, a package of ramen clutched in his left hand. Jason opens the fridge, takes out a couple of beers without asking, tosses one to Maia.

"Shit, man," Percy says, though whether this is approbation or a general commentary on the state of the universe, Maia can't tell. "You got back just in time. They want us to start recording on Friday."

"What day is it now?" Jason asks, taking a long swallow of his beer.

"Tuesday. Wednesday?"

"Wednesday," Byron says, coming into the kitchen. "Hey," he says to Maia, as though seeing her for the first time.

"Hi," she says shyly.

"We got married," Jason tells them.

"What?" Percy drops his ramen. Maia curls her toes inside her boots.

"Sorry we missed it," Byron says sourly. Maia shrinks back against the refrigerator. He looks her over and something in his expression softens. "Hey," he says again, "come on. You must be tired after all that driving, huh?"

She nods.

"We don't have anything fancy, but the couch pulls out. You want to crash out?"

"Are you tired?" she asks Jason.

"We have a lot to talk about. You go ahead and sleep," he says dismissively. Maia pulls her shoulders up to her ears and looks at the floor. Jason kisses the top of her head and then turns to Percy. "We need to practice, like, all day tomorrow, then," he says, and Percy nods, and they begin an intense, earnest discussion of which songs should go on their soon-to-be album, as if Jason has not spent the last two weeks with her, swimming in the wide salt ocean and promising her the rest of his life.

"Come on," Byron says, touching her shoulder. "We'll be up all night talking about music. You'll be bored out of your mind." She follows him back into the other room, lost as a duckling.

"I know a lot about music," she whispers, but he doesn't hear her, and she doesn't bother to repeat it. He helps her pull out the couch into a bed. "No sheets," he says apologetically, "but let me find you a blanket." He disappears and returns with a grimy sleeping bag, which Maia takes gingerly.

"He's like that with everyone," Byron says.

"What?"

"Jason. We put up with it, you know, for the band. But he can be a real asshole. Don't let it get to you."

"I guess it's working out for you," she says. "The record deal."

He shakes his head. "He always said we would do it, you know? Me and Percy, we only half-believed him."

"Are you getting paid a lot?"

"Nah. It'll probably turn out to be nothing. They're flying us down and paying for studio time. They'll get some songs on the air. That's a big deal, I guess. But you can't let that stuff go to your head. People get fucked over by record companies all the time. Or they put out an album and no one ever listens to it. Or they record an album and the record company never puts it out at all. It's what you get for bowing down to the man," he says sadly. "I've seen it, like, a million times. No good comes of capitulation to the mechanisms of capital."

As far as she can tell, Byron is all of nineteen or twenty, and has not lived long enough to see much of anything a million times, but he seems adamant in his world-weariness. "Well," she says. "Congratulations."

"You, too, newlywed. Looks like we're both stuck with him now." He pats her shoulder awkwardly. "See you in the morning."

"Thanks," she says. He leaves her in the living room. She curls up on the pullout bed, trying not to let any part of the sleeping bag touch her exposed skin, and buries her face in the crook of her elbow. She can hear the rise and fall of their voices in the kitchen as she cries herself to sleep.

Later, Jason wakes her out of her fitful slumber, sliding into the bed behind her and nuzzling the back of her neck. "You awake still?"

"Mmmm." She rolls over, burying her face in his chest, and he puts his arms around her.

"You're the most beautiful girl in the world," he murmurs into her hair. His hands move lower, slide up under her shirt to cup her breasts. She lies still as a doll as he fits himself inside her, kissing her eyelids, her cheeks, her mouth. "I love you," he says, "I love you."

"I love you, too," she replies, but all through the depths of her she feels nothing, nothing at all.

In the morning the boys load their equipment into the van and drive away, like sailors abandoning her to a widow's walk. "See you," Byron says. Jason gives her a hasty kiss, but he's focused on his guitar, the drum kit, the amps, loading the equipment according to some precise system known only to him. "Don't put that there!" he barks at Percy, who rolls his eyes.

When they are gone Maia goes back into the house. It was too much to hope, obviously, that they would have a piano. She could call Oscar. She could call her parents. Neither of those options holds any particular appeal. Instead she methodically washes and dries the dirty dishes in the kitchen; from what she can tell, every dish they own. When that's done she scrubs the dirty counters and sponges grease spatters off the cabinets. She unearths a filthy mop in the hall closet, rinses it out as best she can, fills the sink with clean soapy water and mops the kitchen floor. She rinses the mop out again and puts it neatly back in the closet, pokes around until she finds a battered vacuum cleaner serving double duty as a coatrack under a pile of old flannel shirts and thermal underwear. She empties the living-room ashtrays, opens the windows wide to let in the clean, rain-scented air, drags the couch cushions out to the front porch where she thumps the dust out of them. She picks up the beer cans scattered about the living room, dusts off the television, and vacuums the carpet. The vacuum cleaner belches dust and emits a faintly alarming odor of burning hair, but it seems to suck up the worst of the carpet's extra coat of grime.

She is afraid of what she will find in the bathroom, but it's a little better than some of the punk houses she's been in in the last few weeks. There's a nearly full bottle of bleach scrub, perhaps purchased in more ambitious times, under the sink. The floor is piled with a collection of wet towels, which she kicks out into the hall, and the toilet is a horror. The bathtub is ringed with dirt, the sink coated with a thick spackle of toothpaste stains and hair. She sighs and gets to work. It takes a long time, but when she is done the bathroom is, if not clean, at least no longer a place that might scar for life an unsuspecting visitor.

In the hallway, a rickety flight of wooden steps leads down into an abyss that proves to be a basement. A rusty chain dangles from a single bulb overhead; when she tugs it, the bulb's feeble light illuminates an astonishing collection of rusted bicycles, skateboards in various states of decay, battered old guitars, blown amps, camping equipment, and, improbably, a brand-new set of skis. Maia crows aloud in triumph when she sees what she's looking for: covered in lint and crusted, spilled detergent, but unmistakably a washer and dryer.

She drags the dirty bathroom towels downstairs, stuffs them in the washer, and adds most of the contents of her own bag—a sad little collection of ragged cutoffs and T-shirts, a few pairs of underwear, her dirty socks, the New Order shirt she bought with Cass. There is just enough detergent left in the bottle for a single load. She starts the washer—Cass would be so proud—and goes upstairs to find something to eat.

When the laundry is done she showers in the newly clean shower, dries off with a towel warm from the dryer—which she hangs tidily on the bathroom's lone hook—and puts on clean clothes. It's late in the afternoon and there is nothing left for her to do. In the living room, she picks up the phone and dials her parents' number. Her father picks up. At his soft, familiar "Hello?" she feels a strange mix of love and relief and anger that pinches at her ribs with a sharp twang.

"Dad," she says.

"*Maia*. Where are you?"

"I'm in Seattle."

"You're coming home."

"I don't—I can't. Not yet." *Not ever, now,* she thinks, but she's not ready to tell him that yet. "I have to figure out some things first."

"Your mother and I are—we are—we're distraught, Maia. I don't understand how you can do this to us. After everything we've done for you. We love you."

*That's not love*, she wants to scream at him, *that's not love, you might have bought me but you don't own me. I am a person, a person, a person, and I am not your child.* "I'm sorry," she says instead.

He sighs heavily. "Can we see you? Will you give us that? Can't you at least meet us for dinner? I can't believe you're in Seattle and you won't even see us. Your mother called the police. You have to come home, you know. Where are you staying?"

"I'm staying with—with a friend."

"I don't understand how you can put us through this."

"Let's meet for dinner. Tonight?"

"Will you come here?"

"Can we meet somewhere else? I just—" She falters.

"I'll make a reservation at that seafood restaurant on First," he says. "Meet us there at seven. Do you have a way to get there? Should we pick you up?"

"Well," she says, trying not to laugh, "I do still have the car."

"Of course." He doesn't think it's funny. "See you in a few hours." He hangs up.

She doesn't have a key to the house. She writes Jason a note: *Out for a bit. Back later tonight,* and leaves it on the kitchen counter. She has nothing to wear to a seafood restaurant requiring reservations, but at least her clothes are clean.

She drives to Cass's house, hoping she can find it again, and is pleased when she sees the ramshackle, lopsided mess of it where she remembers. No one answers her knock, but the front door is unlocked, and she steps inside. "Hello?"

A sleepy-eyed girl emerges, squinting, from a hallway that must lead to whatever passes here for bedrooms. "Who the hell are you?"

"Is Cass here?" The girl's eyes widen.

"Oh, I heard all about *you*. Cass!" she bellows. "Your little princess is here!" Maia winces.

"Thanks," she says.

Cass stumbles into the living room, yawning, and gives Maia a big grin. "Never thought I'd see you again."

"Don't be stupid."

"Where's your *husband?*" She pronounces it *huzz-binn.*

"Cass. Come on. Please." The girl who called Cass is watching this exchange with interest. Cass clicks her tongue against her teeth. "Can we go somewhere?" Maia asks.

Cass shrugs, suddenly sullen. "Let me get my hoodie."

Maia drives them to Gas Works Park. Cass follows her to the grass slope that ends in the still grey water of the lake. Old, rusted factory works loom overhead against the gloomy sky. The air is chilly and damp; a goose honks at her irritably and poops on the grass in a defiant sort of way. *Welcome home,* Maia thinks.

Cass is quiet, pulling out her tobacco and rolling two cigarettes. They smoke in silence. Maia watches a sailboat move past, headed for the harbor.

"I'm going to see my parents tonight," she says.

"You moving back home?"

"No way."

"They wouldn't let you?"

"I can't even imagine living there now."

"You don't have to keep running away," Cass says.

"It's not that."

"Are you sure?"

"I don't know," Maia admits. "I don't think so. I changed a lot."

"It's only been a month, princess."

"But you know what it's like. When everything changes. Even if it happens overnight. Like you can't imagine being the person you were before ever again."

"Yes," Cass says. "I know all about that. What about the piano?"

"I don't know," Maia says again. "I don't want to be—I don't want what they wanted for me."

"Do you know what you want for yourself?"

"No."

"Is that why you married Jason?"

"Is that why you're mad at me?"

Cass narrows her grey eyes into a squint. "Oh, princess," she says. "Yes. No. I don't know, either. Do you love him?"

"Not the way I love you," Maia says. Cass flinches.

"No," she says quietly. "Apparently not."

"Can we be friends again?"

"We were never not friends."

"You know what I mean." She puts her head on Cass's shoulder. Cass stiffens, then relents, gathers Maia up in a hug, rests her chin on the top of Maia's head.

"We can be friends again," she says.

*I just want to be happy,* Maia thinks. *I just want to be dumb and happy and without dreams. I want to stop thinking.* "'The fault is not in our stars, but in ourselves,'" she says.

"I don't know about that," Cass says.

They sit in the wet grass and hold each other, and both of them find they have nothing else to say.

Her father has chosen a restaurant with white cloth table-cloths and white cloth napkins and too many forks. They are already waiting for her when she walks in the polished glass doors. Across the restaurant, big windows overlook the Sound. Seagulls flap awkwardly in the breeze off the water, honking at one another in continual outrage. Her mother is in pearls, a neat suit cut to fit her body and highlight the graceful curve of her waist. Her father is drunk. Her mother looks her up and down, disgust registering clearly on her face, and then kisses her stiffly on the cheek.

"You look nice," her father says. Whether he is being polite or is so loaded he genuinely believes what he is saying is hard to say.

A waiter shows them to a table by the window, brings a basket of sourdough bread. When she was little, she used to pull the soft part of the bread out first and then cover the tangy crust with butter. Maia's mother pushes the bread basket to the edge of the table. Maia can't remember the last time she ate a real meal. Mexico? She ate a package of ramen, today, in Jason's kitchen. Before that, she has no idea. She reaches across her mother for a piece of bread, gnaws at it. The silence is excruciating.

"So," her mother says at last. "Were you going to tell us where you were?"

"Renee," her father says. "Let's start with something a little less—why don't you tell her about the end of your semester?" Her mother shoots her father a look of such withering contempt that even Maia cringes.

"It's fine," she says. "I drove down the coast."

"In our car," her mother says.

"In your car," she agrees.

"It's really my car," her father says.

"It's *our* car," her mother snaps. He wilts.

"Something to drink?" The waiter is back.

"Manhattan," her father says immediately.

"Make that two," her mother says.

"Three," Maia says. She waits for the waiter to challenge her, but he is looking at her mother, who raises an eyebrow.

"Three Manhattans," says the waiter, rather uncertainly, and vanishes again.

"Looks like she learned *something* from you," her mother says coolly to her father. Flustered, he looks down at the tablecloth. "And what did you do *down the coast,* Maia?"

"I got married," Maia blurts. Her parents stare at her in total silence. Across the restaurant, a small child begins to scream. As its mother attempts to shush it, its desperate cries increase in volume and passion.

"Please tell me you're joking," her mother says. Maia shrugs. Her mother pushes her chair back from the table. "Excuse me," she says. "I believe I will go freshen up in the powder room."

"Don't want *potty,*" the child howls. "Don't, don't, *don't.*"

Her father clears his throat. "Married," he says. "I—my goodness. Will he follow you to school, then?" The waiter returns with their drinks, looks around for her mother.

"You know what?" Maia says to him. "Why don't you just give me hers."

*So much for that,* she thinks, on the drive back to Percy and Byron's. The rest of the dinner had been, predictably, a disaster—"After everything we've done for you," her mother repeated, "after everything we've given you, you do this to us"—but she had survived it. They had even told her to take the car, which was more than she'd dared hope for. She feels, if not the elated and glorious sense of freedom she'd felt in the first wild, magical days on the road with Cass, at least a sense of relief. Now they know what she is.

Her father had pressed a wad of bills into her hand at the end of the meal, when her mother was in the bathroom again, hugging her close. "I don't understand what you're doing, sweetheart," he said. "Just let me know when you're ready to come back. We can mail in your acceptance letter for you. I'm sure they'll understand." He still thinks she is going to New York.

And, she realizes, she still can. Jason has a record deal. Maybe he won't need her anymore. Cass could come with her. There's no reason they couldn't have their apartment with the patchwork curtains across the country, instead of here. Her mother will never forgive her, but her father has barely even noticed the extent to which she's wronged them. He was the one who told her to keep the car. A new life away from Oscar and his failed dreams, her mother's suffocating presence, her father's tragic circle around the drain. The idea has more appeal than she'd been willing to admit, when she and Cass were still driving. When it seemed like everything was going to work out and the whole world was waiting for them. She'll be eighteen in a few weeks. Old enough to go to war.

The lights are on at Percy and Byron's, the front door unlocked. She lets herself in. They're drinking champagne in the living room, listening to records. Jason turns to her as she comes in, his eyes alight. He runs for her and picks her up and twirls her around, kisses her sloppily. "You'll spill your champagne," she says, laughing against his mouth.

"Too late, too late," he says happily, "here, here." He finds a chipped mug, fills it, hands it to her. "Cheers," he says.

"What are we toasting?" she asks, raising her mug to clink against his, and then Percy's and Byron's.

"The album," Jason says. "Our album. Come into the studio with us tomorrow."

"Me?"

"Play with us. On a couple of tracks. There's a piano at the space. If it sounds good, we'll record it. These guys have money like you wouldn't believe, they can afford to pay for the extra time."

She looks over at Percy and Byron, who are not meeting her eyes. "I don't know."

"I do," he says, picking her up again. Her champagne sloshes over the rim of her mug. "I do."

"Okay, okay," she says. "If you want. I'll play with you."

They drink their champagne. He doesn't ask her where she's been, and she is too tired to tell him. He's so excited he's bouncing around the room, jumping up to change the record every three minutes, pouring more champagne, running to the kitchen and back, bringing beer, whisky, ice, more glasses, a tub of ice cream, spoons. No one has said anything about how clean the house is, and she wonders if she's offended them. After Percy and Byron stumble off to bed Jason pulls out the couch bed and undresses her slowly. She moves to turn the light off and he touches her hand. "No," he says. "I want to see you." She tries to be quiet, mindful of his bandmates in their rooms, but she can't help herself. When he is intent like this, so focused on her, his clear eyes boring into hers, it feels so good. Like being seen at last, like finding her way home. Here, in her own body, finally, she is full. "I love you," he says in her ear, "I love you, don't ever leave me. Promise you'll never leave me."

"I promise," she says.

"Never."

"Never."

"Not for anyone."

"Jason. I promise." He tugs her hair back until she has to look him in the eyes. Sweaty skin to sweaty skin, under the now-clean sleeping bag she washed this afternoon. She can smell herself on him.

"Promise," he says. "Anywhere I go, you'll come with me."

"I promise," she says again. "I promise."

"Not for her."

"Not for who?" she asks, but she knows. He closes his eyes, rests his cheek on her shoulder, and she curls one arm around him.

"Everybody leaves me," he says into her neck. She can feel the damp weight of his tears on her skin. "Everybody. I'm going to make the best album in the world. And it won't make anyone stay."

"I'm here," she says. "I'm here. I promise. I won't go anywhere. I'm here." Long after he falls asleep at last, she lies awake, looking out into the dark with unseeing eyes.

The next morning she gets in the van with them. Percy and Byron still aren't speaking to her, and she knows without having to ask that they think bringing her along is a terrible idea. She wonders what they think of her; some "Chopsticks"-playing parlor trickster whose greatest accomplishment is banging out "Happy Birthday" from memory at some all-girl slumber party? She stares out the window, wondering if she'll ever find another world besides Oscar's where anyone takes her seriously. If this is what it is to be a girl, she's no longer sorry she's missed out.

The studio is a low one-story triangular brown building,

windowless and grubby, up by the canal. Maia eyes it dubiously, unimpressed. The door is unlocked and Jason walks in without hesitating. Inside, it's dark, and Maia has a brief impression of a vast and cavernous space, far bigger than is possible for the tiny building to contain. She can hear water running somewhere, and the faint movement of a breeze. But someone flips a light switch and they are in an ordinary building, cleaner than she would have expected from the outside. White walls are covered with framed show posters. She recognizes a sound booth, and the recording room. Against one wall of the main room is an old upright piano that's seen better days.

And then Maia sees him: the man from her dreams. Not possible, but still real. He is so thin there is nothing to him but skin and bone, but dressed elegantly in a well-cut black suit and a long black coat that looks almost like a cape. He looks up at Maia through the glass of the sound booth window, and even from here she can tell that his eyes are so black there is no difference between where the pupil stops and the iris begins. They look at each other for a long time. There is something so beautiful about him that her breath catches in her throat. Next to him, Jason looks like a child. She touches Byron's arm as he carries a guitar past her. "Who's that?" she asks, tilting her head toward the booth.

"That guy? Producer. Why?"

"Just curious."

"He doesn't really talk," Byron says. She nods and lets him go.

Jason's all business: directing Percy and Byron, setting up equipment, fiddling with knobs and dials. Awkward and aware of the producer's eyes following her, she wanders over to the piano. The notes are tinny and stifled; it wasn't a particularly good piano when it was new, and it's probably thirty years old at least. Its sound is a far cry from what she's used to, but it's at least in tune. She runs a few scales. It's the first time she's played in weeks and her whole body opens up. She plays the first chords of the Ravel, but it feels like a travesty on this piano, and so she plays Chopin instead, the Nocturne in D-flat Major, imagining Oscar sitting behind her, murmuring, *It does not do to be fussy with Chopin.* Chopin makes her think of homesickness, a kind of lostness, though Oscar despises that kind of sentimentality and scoffed at her when she told him so. But yearning, at least, is something she understands.

She plays now for the last weeks, the mystery of where she is going, the mess she's made of her own life. She plays for Jason, for herself, for Cass, the last chords moving up the keyboard as light and sorrowful as leaves falling, her hands coming to rest on the final notes, her heart easing a little. She shakes her head, coming back to herself. When she turns around the band is standing behind her, watching her. The producer has opened the door of the sound booth and is leaning against the frame. She meets his flat black gaze.

"Man, that was really beautiful," Byron says, his voice catching. Maia smiles to herself at the thought of these scruffy, sullen boys, with their dirty flannel shirts and their metal records, made maudlin by Chopin. *That'll teach you,* she thinks. She cannot look away from the producer.

"I told you," Jason says, his voice tinged with triumph. She wonders why it was that Jason was so set on her coming here. She'd told him, of course, that she played, but he's never heard her, has no idea how good she is. She'd never have suggested herself that she come, though it's what she told Cass she wanted. To play like them. To be part of something, of making something, larger than herself. To create instead of just repeat, instead of just transmit. Here's her chance, now, but the actual possibility of it, the reality of it, fills her with a cold terror.

They start with a song she knows. Jason gave her their four-song demo tape when they first met, and she's listened to it a hundred times by now. "I wrote all these songs for you before I met you," he'd said, and he'd been so serious that it hadn't even seemed a corny thing to say. They play the song once through without her, and she listens carefully for the ways the melody fits together with the bass, the places where there is room for her. But though she can identify the chords, the notes—if they asked her to, she could transcribe the whole song—she cannot see her way in. Its parts are knitted together with a bond she can't unravel, and the weave of it has no place for the delicate threads of her. *I can't just make stuff up,* she thinks, panicking. *I don't know how, I've never done it, I never should have said yes to this*—and the sound of her own fear fills her head, until there is no music left in her at all.

"Now this time, you come in," Jason says.

"I don't think I can," she says.

"Just try it," Byron says. "You can just play with the melody for now if that's easier."

Maia shakes her head but puts her hands on the keys. "Okay," she says, her voice tiny. They begin the song again. She waits. Here. No. Here. No. Here. Her sweaty hands freeze on the keys. *I can't do this. I can't do this. I don't make things. I don't know how. I don't know how.* The injustice of it: She is a better musician than any of them, than all three of them put together. They finish playing. She will not look at them, refuses to see whatever it is that's in their eyes. Pity or disappointment or contempt. *Why did you do this to me?* she thinks at Jason, furious. *Why did you think this was a good idea?*

"We'll start again," Byron says. "Just come in whenever you're ready." They play through a third time and she sits at the keyboard, her hands frozen into claws. She considers playing the Chopin again, over them, to drown them out with what she knows. They finish, begin again. When they start to play the song for the fifth time she pushes the bench away from the keyboard and walks out the front door.

She sits on the sidewalk for a long time and cries. Wishes for Cass, for Oscar, for her car so she could at least get out of here. She hears soft footsteps behind her. *Jason,* she thinks. *What on earth am I going to say to him?* But it's the producer.

"I'm sorry," she says.

His voice is so low it's almost as though she hears it inside her.

*There is no need to be sorry. I know what you are capable of. I have been listening to you for a long time.* He squats on his haunches next to her, the movement graceful. He reaches out with one bony finger, traces the salt trails across her cheek. His touch is cool. She closes her eyes. He strokes the side of her cheek, his fingers lingering at the corner of her mouth before returning to the curve of her cheekbone, the touch lulling her into a haze. *So beautiful.* he says. *So few among you are this beautiful, I had forgotten. I had forgotten.* His fingers come to rest at her mouth, his thumb tracing the line of her bottom lip. A slow warmth spreads through her.

"I had a dream about you."

*Did you?* His tone is neutral, maybe a little bemused. *Do you like this band?*

"I married the singer."

*I could lend them a bright future. Do you wish such a thing?*

"I don't know what you mean."

*All the riches of this earth can be yours, child, and the world below. Would you follow him anywhere?*

"Jason? I promised him," she says, a little dazed. It is as if he can see into the heart of her, this stranger from her dreams. He cups her chin with his hand and looks into her eyes.

*Would you follow me instead?*

"I said no," she says. "You know I can't. You know."

He smiles. *I will see you again,* he says. He stands slowly, taking his hand away, and she wants to cry out in protest, but though her mouth opens no sound comes out. She cannot move her head as he walks away. Her muscles have gone liquid, her body soft and unresponsive, the whole of her molten. She brings one hand to the corner of her mouth, feeling the icy burn of his touch, as though he has branded her. When she is able at last to stand she climbs shakily to her feet, opens the door of the van and crawls inside, curls up on the backseat and falls asleep immediately. She dreams of a dark forest full of dead white trees, a black palace standing in the middle of an empty plain, the producer's hands moving slowly across her body with deliberate grace.

His mouth at her throat, his voice in her head, the soft coat wrapping around her, and then darkness.

She wakes up on the drive back to the house. Someone has put a blanket over her. They're talking in low, elated voices. "That last take, man," Jason says. "That was fucking perfect. That was *perfect*."

"This album is going to be something," Byron agrees.

"It's going to make us famous," Jason says. "It's going to make us famous."

"Too bad about Maia." Byron.

"She's fine," Jason says.

"She's really good," Byron says.

"She can't play for shit with other people," Percy says.

"I don't want to hear it, man," Jason says.

She sits up, pulling the blanket around her shoulders. It smells of cigarette smoke and boy, and she thinks all the way back to that first night on the beach, the five of them. What if she'd just fallen asleep, instead of going down the beach with Jason? What if in the morning they had all gone their separate ways, and none of this had happened? Where would she be now? Her cheek still hurts where the producer touched her. She wants Cass, desperately. *She can't play for shit with other people.*

"Hey, babe," Jason says. "You awake?"

"Yeah," she says.

"Just in time to celebrate, then," he says.

No one brings up what happened at the piano with her directly. For that small mercy, she's grateful. They stop at a liquor store. She looks out the van window at the rain-streaked parking lot. It'll be fall again soon. If she wants to go to New York, she has to decide. Her mouth feels swollen, bee-stung. She licks her lips as if she can taste his skin there. She thinks of the pomegranate Cass fed her on the beach in Mexico, the sweet-sour tang of the bloody seeds, bursting with juice in her mouth. The sharpness of it on her tongue like a promise. *I will see you again.* "Please," she says aloud. The air around her stirs; a brush of something against her face, soft and dry, like wings. The heat at the heart of her throbs.

The boys come running out of the liquor store, whooping and kicking their heels. They pile into the van, opening the first bottle before they even get the door closed, passing it around. At the house, Maia touches Jason's shoulder before he goes inside. "I'm going to go see Cass," she says.

"Bring her over here," he says magnanimously. Maia knows their enmity is mutual. But he's kingly now, triumphant. They are already talking about music videos, shooting in LA. She wonders what the producer said to them while she was asleep, to make them so certain.

"Sure," she says.

In the car on the way to Cass's she listens to the tape Cass played for her on the way to the beach, that first night with Jason. The singer's rich, unearthly keen fills the car. A candle flickers at the front window of Cass's house. Maia knocks and lets herself in. Cass is sitting on the floor, a tarot spread laid out in front of her, a pint bottle of whiskey at her side. She raises her head. "I was going to go out," she says, "but I had a feeling you might come."

"You need a phone," Maia says, stealing a sip of Cass's bourbon.

"We need a lot of things."

"Come back to the house with me?"

Cass narrows her eyes. "I don't think Jason will be that happy to see me."

"He told me to invite you."

"He did?"

"They recorded their album today. I think he's feeling generous."

"You're really selling me on the idea now," Cass says, but she's smiling. "Come here. Have a cigarette with me first."

Maia sits cross-legged on the floor, her knee overlapping Cass's thigh. She rubs one hand up the length of Cass's broad back as Cass rolls two cigarettes, lights them, hands her one.

"I tried to play with them today," Maia says.

"When they were recording? How'd that go?"

"I couldn't do it. They played the same song over and over again and I couldn't do it. I couldn't even play a fucking chord."

"You've never tried playing with other people before," Cass says. "Don't be so hard on yourself."

"There was this other guy there. The producer. He made me feel better about it, I guess. I ran out of the studio, Cass. It was really bad. But he came outside and—" *And touched me*, Maia thinks. *He touched me, and I can't stop thinking about it, and I might be going crazy.* "He had these eyes. Like, all the way black. You know what's weird? I think I dreamed about him."

Cass freezes under her hand. "What do you mean, you dreamed about him?"

"Before. When I used to play that Ravel piece, the one I played for you? I fell asleep one night at the piano when I was practicing and dreamed about this guy who told me he'd been listening to me. And then today, in the studio, I felt this . . ." Maia trails off.

"You felt what?"

"I don't know," Maia says. "Is he someone you know?"

"No."

"Are you not telling me something?"

"No," Cass says again. "No, it's nothing. It's nothing."

Maia is silent for a while. "I haven't gotten my period since I met Jason."

"Oh, baby. That's not good."

"No," Maia says.

"What are you going to do about it?"

"I don't know."

"You're probably just late."

"Probably."

"If you're not," Cass says. "Whatever you need. I'll go to the doctor with you."

"Have you ever—you know. Done that?"

"Sure," Cass says. "It's not that bad. It's over really fast. The doctor was kind of a jerk. But the nurse held my hand."

"It might be kind of cool, to have a kid," Maia says. "I could have a girl."

Cass laughs. "I don't think you get to pick."

"I know. But if it was a girl, we could raise her together. We'd make her so cool. You could tell her what music to listen to and I could teach her to play the piano. She would be so brave. She'd do whatever she wanted with her life."

"Maia. Or you could just do that yourself. With your *own* life. You're seventeen."

"Almost eighteen."

"You don't need to live your dreams through someone else."

"I know," Maia says.

"Do you?"

"Sure," Maia says, looking down at her lap. "But it's Jason's. If it's a baby. It's his baby."

"It's not a baby," Cass says, "and if it were, it's yours."

Maia pushes one finger against the floorboards. Cass wants desperately to brush her hair out of her eyes, kiss the place where the line of her neck meets her shoulder. She looks away instead. "Jason's not like other boys," Maia says. "He's fragile." Cass shakes her head. "You're strong," Maia says. "He's not strong. I think having something to take care of—I think it would change him. Be good for him."

"That's a terrible reason to have a kid."

"Better than whatever reason my parents had me," Maia says. "Since it turned out they didn't want me."

"You don't know that that's true, Maia. You don't know anything about them or why they gave you up. If you have a baby now, it'll change everything."

"Maybe that's what I need."

"You're already strong."

"Not like you," Maia says quietly.

Cass sighs. "Come on," she says, standing up. "I feel like getting drunker. Let's go back to Jason's."

"Cass? I love you."

"I love you too, princess." Cass pulls Maia to her feet and pushes her toward the door, avoiding her eyes. "Come on."

# THEN

What Maia does tell her father, in the end, is only slightly less than the truth: that she aced her audition, which she did. He's so pleased he hums in the taxi on the way to dinner. This time, they eat at an Italian restaurant with real tablecloths and cloth napkins, and no one tries to talk to her in a language she does not know. She pokes at her linguine with her fork, takes sips of the glass of wine her father ordered for her. Something her mother never would have done. She wonders what else would happen, if she spent more time with her father alone. The last couple days have suggested there's a whole person hiding somewhere inside him, a stranger who blossoms when he's on his own soil. He is chattering to her about where she will live in New York, how he will come visit her, how her whole life is about to begin. She's coming down off the speed and the crash is dulling her senses, leaving her leaden and depressed, but her father doesn't notice. She excuses herself to go to the bathroom and locks herself in the low-lit marble-tiled room. It's tasteful, a wicker basket of real towels next to the sink. She splashes her face with water and stares at herself in the mirror for a long time. When she gets back to the table her father is regaling the waiter with tales of his genius daughter, the pianist. The waiter is doing his best to appear interested.

"Dad, stop," she says, sitting down, and the waiter, seeing his chance, murmurs something and flees. She lets her father talk for the rest of the dinner, in the taxi back to the hotel, in the elevator up to their rooms, and when at last she shuts the door on him that night he is still talking, still telling a story that has nothing to do with her. That night she dreams she is walking with Cass along an oily black river that winds through a forest of white-barked and leafless trees, both of them looking for something that is just out of reach. But what it is they seek, she cannot say.

Back home, she goes through the motions of her life as if nothing has changed, but something irrevocable has shifted inside her. A month passes, and then another. She practices, goes to Oscar's, reads her geometry textbooks in her room. Her roots grow in. She wears the grey shirt she stole in front of her mother, and her mother says nothing. She starts wearing the New Order shirt, the torn jeans. More clothes she gets with Cass. Tattered cutoffs with black tights. A sweatshirt with holes where her thumbs poke through. Still her mother says nothing, her silence a war of attrition that Maia, too, can keep fighting. Her house is becoming more unbearable by the day.

"June," Cass says one afternoon. Maia took her father's car without asking again—being treated as though she's invisible does have some advantages—and they drove to Gas Works Park, where they're watching a spittle-streaked, shrieking toddler lunge after some geese with a handful of bread. Cass leans back in the grass.

"Watch out for goose shit," Maia says.

"Already checked. Summer makes me stir-crazy."

"Me, too."

"You ever even been anywhere?"

"Europe."

"Europe, of course," Cass says in a fake posh accent. Maia hits her on the shoulder. "But I mean, like, *traveling*."

"I've traveled lots."

"You've gotten on a plane and come back. It's not the same thing if you go just to go."

"Go where?"

Cass shrugs. "Anywhere. Hop rails, hitch. Just put some stuff in a bag and say goodbye to your life for a while. When I've been back here for too long, I get restless. I go traveling every summer."

Maia thinks of Cass leaving her and is overwhelmed by an unexpected sense of panic. Cass is her only friend, and now her best friend; the thought of losing her is as awful as cutting off one of her limbs.

"I'd miss you," she says. "A lot."

"I'd miss you, too," Cass says, taking her hand.

"What if I went with you?"

Cass looks up, surprised. "Why would you want to do that? You have a whole life here."

"So do you."

"But you have to practice every day. Get ready for your future. All that stuff."

"I'm sick of my future."

"Don't say that."

"I am," Maia says. "I'm sick of it. I've never done anything I wanted, anything for myself, until I met you. I'm going crazy from it. That show you took me to—I know that was no big deal, for you. You do that stuff all the time. But all those people—"

"Todd," Cass interrupts, smirking.

"Todd," Maia agrees, her cheeks red. "But all of them. All your friends. You just do whatever you want."

"You only see the good side, Maia," Cass says. "You don't see the hard parts. You don't see us in winter, sleeping in two sweaters and a coat and four pairs of socks because there's no heat in the house."

"It sounds like camping."

"It's not like camping when it's every day of your life."

"I want to try it," Maia says. "I want to try something. Anything. I want to go out in the world and forget who I'm supposed to be for a while."

Cass props herself up on her elbows. "Todd has a car," she says.

"*I* have a car."

"Your dad has a car."

"He won't miss it."

Cass looks at her. "Are you serious?"

"I'm totally serious."

"What about the piano?"

"It's not like we'd leave forever. Just a couple of weeks."

"We could drive to California and back. I know a lot of people on the way down. We could sleep on the beach."

"Let's do it."

"You *are* serious."

"I'm always serious."

"That," Cass says, "is definitely not true."

"I have some money," Maia says. "A thousand dollars."

Cass whistles. "Even better," she says. "With that kind of money, we could flee the country."

"When should we leave?"

"Monday," Cass says. "Road trips should always start on a Monday." They grin at each other, elated.

"That's in three days."

"Yes."

"What do I need to bring?"

"Yourself," Cass says. "A sleeping bag."

"That stuff you gave me. For New York. Can you bring more of that?"

Cass laughs. "Baby girl, I'll bring you a fucking pharmacy, you ask with those big eyes like that."

"Just the two of us."

"Just the two of us," Cass agrees.

For the next three days her secret burns in her like a coal, until she is sure her parents will feel its heat radiating out from her skin. The promise of the open road, Cass at her side, gives her the fortitude to weather the bleak silence of her house. She buys a military rucksack at a thrift store and fills it with the clothes she's bought with Cass, her new-old shirts, her worn-through jeans, her cutoffs. These clothes are like soft skin against her own skin, not stiff and unyielding like the clothes her mother dresses her in. These clothes have their own histories already, their stories tangling with hers when she puts them on. In these clothes, she feels at home. On Sunday night she kisses her father in his study: haze of bourbon, his pipe in its ashtray, the pile of dog-eared manuscript pages. The sight of her father's book makes her sad. "You're a good girl," he says, patting her shoulder. *Keep thinking that, Dad,* she could say, but she doesn't.

"Goodnight."

"Goodnight, sweetheart."

Her mother is in the kitchen, wiping the spotless counters one last time. Her golden hair hangs down her back in soft waves. "Goodnight, Mom," Maia says, and her mother turns, surprised. For a moment, the wall comes down.

"You haven't said goodnight to me since you were a little girl."

"Feeling sentimental, I guess. Have a good class tomorrow."

"Thank you."

"Things have been weird," Maia says. Her mother stiffens.

"That's one word for what you've done."

"It's not about you."

"I find that hard to believe."

"You would." Maia bites back the rest of what she's almost said. There's no point in it. Her mother is what she is, will never be another thing, more giving or less harsh. Her mother is not her mother at all, not body or bone or blood. In the world she was first born into these people would have been strangers thousands of miles away, and she would be growing up in a country far from here. *Mother* is just a word like any other, ordinary until you make it mean something. She knows she is being unfair; this woman has done, to her credit, the best she knows how to do.

"Sorry," she says. "Goodnight. Mom."

"Goodnight." She leaves her mother in the kitchen, sponge moving in smooth circles across the counter's gleaming surface.

The morning is so easy it's as though she was born to start running. Her mother leaves for the college; her father shuts himself away. The car keys are in the drawer in the kitchen. She writes them a note. *Please don't worry about me. I need to think about some things. I promise I'm safe. Sorry I took your car, Dad.* She checks everything one last time. Toothbrush, Ravel sheet music, underwear, socks. Sleeping bag. When she gets down to it there's little she wants to bring. She writes a postcard to Oscar—*I'll come home. Don't be mad. I love you*—stamps it, tucks it in the pocket of her bag to mail later.

"Goodbye," she says to the lifeless house. She won't miss it, she realizes, looking around her. She won't miss anything save the piano, and that she can always come back to. The front door shuts behind her, and she is free.

# NOW:
# SEATTLE

Maia puts the Ravel in her bag and goes to see Oscar a week after Jason records his album. She does not tell him she's coming; instead, she shows up at his front door, at the same time as her lesson used to be, knocks as she always did. When he opens the door he does not seem surprised to see her.

"It took you a long time," he says. "To come see me."

"I'm sorry."

"Come inside."

She follows him through the house to the piano room, her heart leaping at the sight of the Steinway. *This,* she thinks, *this is what I am missing.* She crosses the room and touches it, reverently.

"It can be yours again," he says behind her. "This life, it was so bad? Come back, child. Come back to me. Tell me you will go to school in the fall."

"I'm pregnant," she says.

He sighs. "You are joking."

"No."

"You can have this taken care of."

"I don't want to."

"You are ruining your life."

"Maybe," she says. "But it's my life to ruin."

"Why," he says. "Why are you doing this? Your whole life is in front of you, Maia. Your career. Go to New York. Forget about this summer. Forget whatever foolishness you have been captured by these last months."

"I'm broken, Oscar. Something in me is broken. You saw it all along."

He comes to stand next to her and puts his hand on the piano and looks at it with a love that is so naked Maia almost steps away from him. "I know what it is like," he says. "There was a time when I was young when I was like you also, always searching, always unhappy with myself, and I made a mistake, and it undid me. I cannot watch you do the same thing."

"I'm not making a mistake. It's what I want."

He dismisses her with a wave of his hand. "You are seventeen years old. Forgive me, Maia, but you are too young and too stupid to have any idea what you want. It will be years before you know anything about yourself, and by then, if you do this, it will have been done, and you will be like me, looking back on all your life with nothing but regret. Do you know what I was? I was a great pianist, Maia. I could have been a Horowitz or a Rubinstein, everyone around me knew this, I knew this. I was teaching a little in the conservatory, you understand, but it would not have been for much longer."

"What happened?"

"I fell in love," he says. "I fell in love with one of my students. I was young. He was younger. We were careless, I was found out. It was a terrible, terrible scandal. His father threatened to sue the school—he was tremendously wealthy, you understand, a major donor. All very well for the Greeks, but this is a newer time." He sighs. "The young man was not—he was not courageous, I think is how you say it. The father threatened to disinherit him. So the boy said that it was I who had seduced him and it looked bad, you see, as I was his teacher. Martha Kaplan was not the head of the department then, of course, but she disliked me, as I was quite a lot better than she was, and so she was most pleased to encourage him. It was the ruin of me, this foolishness, and when it became public the boy never spoke to me again. I had thrown away my life for him, and he would not even see me."

"What happened to him?"

Oscar laughs. "He went into the stock market. He was not an especially good pianist; it was not his musicianship that I loved. The father had always been mistrustful of the arts. An entire field of homosexuals and destitutes." He touches the piano again. "My other students rallied for me, but it was no use. It was kind of them. They stole for me this piano."

"They stole a *Steinway*?"

"Well, you know, they were fond of me. I think it was quite a project for them."

"Didn't the school notice?"

"Oh, of course, I am sure. But it was already such a nasty business, and they did not wish to have any more questions asked. I am only telling you this because I regret it every day of my life, Maia. It is a great joy to me, you must understand, to have taught you all these years, but I had a real life, the beginning of a real career. I would have been great, this is not a doubt. Now instead it is you who will be great. I will not allow this foolishness. You will go to the doctor and have this thing taken care of, and you will leave me here, sad old man that I am, and go to New York, and have a fine destiny ahead of you, have I made myself clear?"

"Oscar," Maia says. "I'm not you."

"Young people think they are all different from one another," Oscar says quietly, "and in this they are always quite incorrect."

"I'm sorry," she whispers. "Oscar, I—"

"Do not talk," he says. "Let us not ruin our afternoon with any more talking. Play for me."

"What do you want me to play?"

"Play me the Ravel."

She sits at his magnificent piano, the piano she knows as well as if it were her own. The tenor of it, the weight of the keys, the movement of its pedals under her feet. She knows its moods, the way its tone shifts a little in the winter no matter how dry Oscar keeps the room, the way it opens up again in the summer, like an animal breathing in. She hasn't played the Ravel for weeks, but it doesn't matter. She plays now for Oscar the way she played at her audition for those stone-faced Gorgons wishing her failure. Everything she has learned about loss this summer, about wanting, pours out of her and into the keys. Instead of the mermaid she thinks of the producer, his black eyes watching her, the producer in a palace with tall windows that look out over the sea, the producer calling her name, calling her down. *I will see you again.* The notes washing out of her like waves breaking against the shore, light sparkling across the breakers. Like a ghost she enters the music, her own self washed clear, dissolving away until she is nothing but motes of light, kelp moving in the slow deep currents, the silver wink of a fish glinting. She plays knowing the truth of the fate she's spun for herself: She could never have played like this if she had not learned what she learned when she left; but in leaving, she's undone her own future, taken away the chance she had to make this music her life.

After the final chords fade away from the still room, she raises her head and sees that Oscar's eyes are wet. "You are better than I ever was," he says. "You are better than I ever was, and you are throwing it away in front of me."

"I'm sorry, Oscar."

He shakes his head. "I would like you to leave now."

"Oscar—"

"Please," he says. "Please, Maia. Go."

She leaves the sheet music on his piano and walks through his house alone without saying goodbye.

The producer throws them a party the night the record releases. Jason is so nervous he gets drunk at eleven in the morning. Byron and Percy are beside themselves with anxiety. Maia is confident that if she stays in the house with them all day she will lose her mind. *I will see you again. Tonight.* Tonight she will see him again. She presses her hand to her chest, as if the flutter there were visible. "Come on," she says, "let's go to the park."

"It's cold," Jason moos. "It's *raining.*"

"We'll go to the zoo, then."

"Let's just go get breakfast," Byron says.

"Fine," Maia says.

"You go," Jason says. "I'll stay here. In case someone calls."

Maia refrains from pointing out that the phone's been shut off for a week, since none of them has money to pay the bill. "Okay, baby," she says, kissing him. "We'll be back soon."

"In time for the party."

"It's not even noon yet."

"But you'll come back."

"We'll come back."

Maia and Byron and Percy pile into Maia's car. They don't see Cass, with her hood pulled up against the rain, trudging down the sidewalk to the house, Cass climbing the steps to the front porch and knocking. Jason opens the door.

"Hi," Cass says. "I came by to see Maia."

"She just left. Did she know you were coming?"

"No," Cass says. "Do you know where she went?"

"She left me," Jason says disconsolately.

"Jason, are you *drunk*?"

"You can come inside." Shaking her head, she follows him into the living room. Jason and Maia are still sleeping on the pullout bed; they haven't bothered to put it away this morning. Cass tugs off her wet sweatshirt and hangs it over a chair, perches on the edge of the bed.

"Well," she says. Jason slumps down next to her and puts his head in his hands. "Did she actually leave you? Or did she just go somewhere?"

"They all left me," he says, his voice muffled.

"You *are* drunk."

"You know what we have in common?" he says, raising his head to look her in the eye. "We both love her. And she's going to leave both of us."

Cass can't tell if he's baiting her. *Oh, fuck you, pretty boy,* she thinks, but if he is trying to make her angry she refuses to let him, and if he isn't, then he is genuinely sad. She feels sorry for him, as much as it pains her to admit it. And he's not wrong. His clear blue eyes are pleading. He's lost weight he can't afford in the last weeks, and his cheekbones are startling, his collarbone as stark and graceful as a girl's.

"I know," she says.

"This record," he says. "This record is going to make us rich. He promised."

"Who promised?"

"The producer."

Cass swallows. "Maia told me about him. What else did he promise you?"

"The whole world," Jason says. "Above and below. He said he would make me famous. He said within a year the whole world would know my name. He said I'd never have to think about anyone leaving me again, because everyone would love me, everyone, and Maia would follow me anywhere, and I'd have more money than I ever dreamed of."

"Is that what you want?" Cass asks cautiously. *Did I do this?* she thinks. *Did I do this? Or did you? What the hell does he want with a walking tragedy like you?*

"I don't want her to leave me."

"She won't leave you," Cass says. "If she were going to leave you, she'd have done it by now."

"Everyone leaves me," he says. "Everyone."

"What is it, anyway," Cass asks, sick to death of him, "that she sees in you?"

"Something she doesn't see in you, I guess," he says. She raises her hand to hit him and he snatches her wrist and holds it there, staring her down, and she's surprised by the strength in his skinny arms.

"Go to hell," she says.

"I'll take her with me," he says, "and there's nothing you can do about it, it's me who has her, not you." She pulls her arm free of his grip and slaps him for real, hard, and he grabs her wrist again. She hits him once more with her free hand and he grabs that one, too, their eyes locked on each other, Cass breathing hard. "Fuck you, Cass," he says, "I won," and he pulls her in and kisses her, his mouth as mean as a bruise. She knees him in the gut, but halfheartedly, the blow not even knocking the wind out of him, and kisses him back, his hands still vice-gripped around her wrists. He pulls her down on top of him. *I hate you,* she thinks, *I hate you,* but whether it's Jason she hates, or herself, she can't say. She lets him let go of her wrists long enough take off her shirt and push her back on the bed, raises her hips so he can undo her jeans. His body is bony and his breath smells like whisky. He pins her wrists above her head and holds her down and fucks her, and Cass looks over his shoulder at the asbestos-popcorned ceiling and thinks about birds and the ocean and Maia's hands on the piano, in her beige house, all those months ago. "I'm sorry," he says in her ear when he comes. "I'm sorry. Please don't listen to me. I'm sorry." She puts her face in the curve of his neck and inhales. He needs a shower.

"Put your clothes on," she says. "They might come back." She leaves him, goes into the bathroom to wash her face and between her legs. All the towels are dirty. She stares at herself in the mirror. She does not feel guilt, or remorse, or elation. She does not feel anything at all. Inside the bone cage of her ribs her heart sits like a dead thing, unmoving. She touches the Cass in the mirror, fingers meeting fingers in the glass. "You ruin everything," she says softly.

She waits with Jason for Maia to come home. They watch television in silence, a PBS documentary about the savannah. "They're going to shut off the electricity soon," Jason remarks, as a static-fuzzed lion takes down a baby wilde-beest, the rest of the herd stampeding.

"Guess you better get famous quick, then," Cass says.

When Maia comes in the door at last she is flushed with happiness, her brown skin rosy. "Cass!" she cries, running across the room and tackling her. Cass lets Maia take her down without resisting.

"I came to help you get ready," Cass says. Maia sits on her, gazing down at her solemnly.

"Do you know how to do makeup?" she asks. "I got eyeliner. But I don't know how to put it on, really."

"Do I know how to do makeup," Cass says. "Girl, please." Maia clambers off her and kisses Jason.

"Hey, baby," she says. He draws her closer to him, kisses her back greedily. Cass looks away.

"You came back," he says.

"Of course I came back. Come on, the car is coming for us at seven. It's already four. Cass and I have to get ready."

"I'm not dressing up," Jason snarls.

"It's your party," Maia says.

"Then they'll take us as we are."

"Okay," Maia says, soothing him. "Okay, baby. Whatever you want."

"They're sending a car?" Cass says.

Byron laughs from across the room, where he's trying to get another channel to come in on the television. "They haven't paid us a fucking cent, man," he says. "They told us our whole advance went to recording and we have to wait for royalties. But they're sending us a fucking limousine."

"Don't even want the party," Percy mutters. He's holding the television antenna while Byron fiddles with the dial. "They could just pay the electric bill for us instead."

"It'll be fun," Maia says placidly. "Come on, Cass. Anybody need the bathroom before we take it over?"

Cass sits on the toilet seat while Maia showers, humming to herself. *I fucked your husband. Your husband and I fucked.* She tries the thought on like a new coat. Who has husbands? The only husbands she has encountered thus far were the stepfathers, and they never did anybody any favors. "We didn't do anything for your birthday."

"I know," Maia says. "I've known you for a year now, isn't that crazy?"

"It seems like longer."

"And like no time at all at the same time." Maia shuts off the water. Cass passes her the cleanest of the towels. "This house is disgusting," Maia says ruefully.

"Maybe this record really will make a lot of money."

"That would be nice." She pulls open the curtain, the towel wrapped around her hair. Her long brown body is still lean, her belly flat. If Jason's kid is kicking around in there, Cass can't tell. This creature, this Maia, unselfconscious, wise beyond her years, is a completely different person than the cocooned princess who found Cass in the street all those months ago. Here's Maia, utterly transformed, and yet Cass is the same hardscrabble traitor she's always been. *I fucked your husband.* Maybe now she's just worse.

"You look so sad," Maia says, kissing the top of her head.

"It's nothing," Cass says.

"Are you sure?"

"Get dressed and I'll do your eyeliner."

Maia leaves the towel on her head and walks naked into the living room to find her clothes, and Cass trails after her just to see the expression on Byron's and Percy's faces. She's not disappointed. Back in the bathroom, Maia puts on her dress. It's the white slip she married Jason in. Cass helped her dye her hair again a few days ago, and it flares a brilliant red against her brown skin. She perches on the edge of the sink as Cass draws swooping cat's eyes with black liquid liner. "I stole it," Maia says proudly.

"Sssh," Cass says. "Don't move or I'll fuck it up."

When she's done she surveys her handiwork. "You look beautiful," Cass says, her voice catching.

"Now you."

"I'm not coming."

"Cass. You have to. Are you kidding me? You can't leave me. Please come."

Cass thinks of an entire excruciating night spent at Jason's side, sighs. Probably there will be free food, at least.

"Anything for you," Cass says.

"Thank you. Cass—" She stops. "If this does—if this record really does sell. You know. If things change. Nothing will change for us. For you and me."

"Of course not," Cass says, and maybe she even believes it.

"I love you, Cass."

"I love you, too. You can buy a really nice piano, at least." Maia's eyes get soft, and Cass wonders if she's hurt her. "I'm sorry," she says, "I didn't mean to bring it up."

"I'd be in New York right now."

"Are you—do you wish you were?"

"No," Maia says. She chews her thumb, an unconscious echo of Cass's habit. "No," she says again.

It's Maia, now, who dresses Cass, in a soft, short velvet-and-lace dress that hangs loosely. "I look like an idiot," Cass says crossly, but Byron and Percy whistle appreciatively.

"No," Byron says, "you look like a girl. It's a refreshing change." Cass throws the television remote at him. Maia insists on doing Cass's eyeliner, but she makes such a mess of it—one eye hopelessly crooked, the other with a jagged black spike where Maia's hand slipped—that Cass washes it off and does it herself. Jason's shaken out of his sulk and opened another bottle of whisky. He's still unwashed, his dirty hair falling in his eyes until Cass wants to yank it out of his head, but Byron has put on a clean flannel shirt for the occasion. They wait in the living room for the limo, passing around the whisky and fidgeting. Someone has put the bed away. Maia sits on the couch, one arm around Jason's shoulders. She's put on a moth-eaten fake fur coat that somehow makes her look even more queenly. Jason kisses her cheek and whispers something in her ear. Byron paces in tighter and tighter circles. Percy sits at the other end of the couch, gnawing at his knuckles. Only Maia, serene and lovely in her white slip, displays no sign of nervousness. Her face is flushed, her expression expectant, as though she is waiting for something she's been promised. *We're just kids,* Cass thinks, looking at all of them. *God help us, we're just kids.*

The party is in a penthouse apartment on the top floor of an old hotel building downtown. The building is old-fashioned, with stately marble columns and oak paneling, but the apartment is a sleek and modern expanse of open space, with floor-to-ceiling windows installed so cleverly that they look like a seamless expanse of glass. It seems familiar, for some reason Cass can't pinpoint, and then she realizes in shock that it is the apartment she dreamed about on the beach in Mexico. The city glitters below them. Beyond it is the dark sweep of the Sound, the ragged edge of black mountains against the star-speckled, moon-less sky.

The apartment is packed. "Jesus," Byron mutters, shrink-ing back against Cass as she follows him in. She pats his shoulder. *Who* are *these people?* she wonders, these tall and long-limbed people, elegant and beautifully dressed. The four of them look homeless in comparison. Jason lifts his chin defiantly.

But among these people, Maia shines like a star, comes into her own. She is radiant, her back straight, her head high. She shrugs the fur coat off her shoulders, and a man is already at her side to take it from her with a little bow; she acknowledges him with a regal tilt of her chin. She searches the room, and then her eyes light up. "He's here," she says.

*He* is the man in the black coat. "No," Cass says, but it is him, here, real, the skeleton's face and skeleton's hands, the well-cut black suit, the dead black eyes. He is smiling. Jason stands up straighter next to her. The skeleton man walks toward them, toward Cass and Jason, toward Cass and the boy she sold him, the boy who sold himself, and Cass opens her mouth to say something, anything, and then he walks past the both of them, past Percy, past Byron, leaving Cass and Jason with their mouths agape in shock. The man in the black coat holds out his hands to Maia and she takes them, her lips parted, her face turned up to his. And Cass thinks of the painting in the apartment in her dream, the painting of Jason, the girl in the white dress at the edge of the frame, as though she is following him; and

Cass understands in an instant what it is she has lost. The man in the black coat kisses Maia softly on the forehead, looks over her shoulder at Cass, and smiles.

*Welcome, Cassandra,* he says. *I believe we have a friend in common.*

# THEN

The sun is so bright for their leaving it feels like an omen. They drive west, west toward the ocean, through miles of deep green woods, silent trees looming overhead. They stop in a roadside diner in a run-down logging town in the late morning and eat pancakes and drink watery black coffee that the cheery waitress keeps refilling. "You girls from around here?" she asks, knowing they'll say no. The diner has an old photo booth in the back near the bathrooms, and they squeeze in together on its plastic bench, pull shut the faded red velvet drapes, and feed it quarters. Frames one and two, they can't think of anything funny to do and just grin maniacally at the mirror in front of them; frame three, they flip off the camera in unison; frame four, Maia turns to Cass and kisses her impulsively on the mouth, then pulls away quickly after the flash, blushing. Cass looks down at her lap. They wait for the strip of pictures, laugh at themselves in the quartered line of images. Maia tucks the photos in her bag.

They keep driving, windows down, sun pouring in all over them like honey. At last they see the green-and-white signs: OCEAN BEACHES. Maia parks the car in a gravel lot by the side of the narrow highway. They can hear the distant roar of breakers.

They walk on a wet trail through the woods, ridges of mud rising around puddles that wink patches of blue sky and leafy green back at them. The earth smells rich and heavy and clean. Birds call at them from the high branches; a squirrel, enraged, scolds them and then darts away. Maia flexes her fingers, thinks of the ache of constant practice leaving her bones, her muscles loosening in the warm weeks ahead. She breathes in deep and holds out her arms, twirling. "Look at us," she says.

"Look at that," Cass says, and points at the slice of blue-grey ahead through the trees. "That's the Pacific." Cass takes off running and Maia follows her, and they crash along the trail and come out at the shoreline, scramble over driftwood, sunbleached logs as big around as boulders, and then they are sprinting flat out across the stretch of fine grey sand to the ocean's edge. At last, rolling out at their feet all the way to the horizon, the heaving blue mass of it.

They are alone on the beach. The sun's high and hot in the sky. Gulls call at them, wheeling on the wind. They could be the only girls left in the world, the two of them, their futures in front of them like a bright ribbon unspooling.

Maia laughs with her mouth open wide, her head thrown back. Bleached hair, blue sky. Cass pulls her shirt off, strips down to her underwear; after a second, Maia does the same. "Oh," Maia says, and Cass says, "What?" and Maia says, "Towels, we forgot towels," and Cass says, "Princess, we have the sun, and we will dry ourselves as god intended instead," and Maia laughs again. When they get back to the car, they'll roll all the windows down, let the salt breeze in to move across their skins as they head south. The two of them, alone in all the world together. Running not away, but toward. "Are you ready?" Cass asks.

"Yes," Maia says. "Yes. Let's go." Cass takes the first step toward the water, and Maia takes her hand.

# ACKNOWLEDGMENTS

Thank you: As always, my parents and my extended family, particularly my tireless publicists Aunts Mo and Bernie. Cristina Moracho, the best life partner a Petlet could wish for. Justin Messina, sweetheart and dreamboat, who patiently endured an endless barrage of questions on the nature and habits of classical musicians. Melanie Sanders, amazing friend and equally amazing copyeditor. Friends, cheerleaders, treasures: Hal Sedgwick, Bryan Reedy, Meg Clark, Nathan Bransford, Tahereh Mafi, Mikki

Halpin, Kat Howard, Bojan Louis, Neesha Meminger, Kate Zambreno. Brianne Johnson, miracle of agents. Sara Goodman, unicorn among editors. The truly magnificent WORD bookstore in Brooklyn, especially Jenn Northington, Molly Templeton, and Buffy Night. Everyone at St. Martin's who's worked so hard on my books: Jessica Preeg, Sarah Goldstein, Stephanie Davis, Anne Marie Tallberg, Anna Gorovoy, Rafal Gibek, and Olga Grlic. I'm indebted to the inimitable, much-missed Charles Rosen, whose work I had the delight of discovering while writing *Dirty Wings*, and to whom Oscar owes his insistence on detective stories. And thank you, dear reader, from the bottom of my heart.

READ ON FOR

A SNEAK PEEK OF

# ABOUT A GIRL

COMING SOON FROM
ST. MARTIN'S GRIFFIN

In her dream they are sitting at the kitchen table in the apartment she grew up in, the morning light slanting in through the windows and making patterns on the floorboards. The smell of bread baking and the coffee brewing in its ancient percolator. Tangle of vines tumbling from houseplants, patchwork curtains, the jars of herbs in their neat rows on the shelves. Outside, the summer, waiting for them to go out into it. History rising unbidden from the depths, old stories surfacing again in bright scraps. Dandelions and the smell of apples. Blackberries on the vine. Sudden knife of memory: the two of them in the park by the canal, guitar music, sun on their shoulders, the low hum of bees. Then, bare trunks white as bone, clacking in a hot, breezeless dark. The black river surging, thick and viscous as oil, past her bare, bloody feet. The girl across the table lights a cigarette; slow inhale, slow exhale.

"Where have you been?" she asks, and the girl across the table shrugs. Her perfect face unlined, her hair longer now, a glossy black, her brown skin as smooth as if the years between the past and the present have fallen away to leave them in some place between that is neither that time nor this one. White sleeveless dress; the line of her collarbone, sharp as the edge of a mirror. The years she has spent in hell have left her unmarked but all the laughter has gone out of her. Her brown eyes are inscrutable. The cigarette burns, forgotten, between the knuckles of her first and second fingers.

"Here and there."

"Come back."

"Babycakes. You know I can't. I brought you something."

"What kind of something?"

The girl smiles, then, at last, that heart-stopper of a grin that's hers and hers alone. Wise and wry and sharp. Stubs out the cigarette directly on the table: smell of scorched wood, a spreading black mark. "A surprise. You'll like it." She pushes her chair away from the table, stands, yawns. "I have to leave," she says.

"Don't."

"You know how much I love you." Not now or ever just *I love you*, not ever anything easy, or clear.

"Not enough to stay."

The girl reaches forward, touches her mouth with two fingers, takes them away. "You know it's not about that. You look so happy. It's good to see you. But I have to go." Turning, walking away, the way she did the last time. Not looking back.

In her wake, the smell of burning: the hot white scorch of her absence, searing itself into the world over and over again.

When she wakes up it takes her a while to come back to herself. Where she is now: her apartment in the city with its cool green walls. Through the window she can see the trees, winter-stripped of their foliage, branches stark against a murky grey sky. The dream is still real under her skin. She stumbles out of bed, pulls on a sweatshirt, wool socks to stave off the chill of the floor, wanders out of her bedroom into the living room. Raoul is perched on the couch, a mug of coffee in his hand and one on the coffee table waiting for her.

"I heard something," he says. "At the front door."

"No one rang the buzzer."

"No," he says.

"You didn't look?"

He shakes his head.

"I dreamed about her," she says.

"So did I."

She sighs, walks to the front door, opens it, looks around. Nothing. The hall is still and cool, their neighbors' doors shut tightly. No ghosts, no long-gone girls. And then she hears a rustle at her feet and looks down at the doorstep, and there it is, straight out of the Old Testament. A baby, its eyes closed tight, wrapped in a grey blanket, fast asleep on the *Aliens*-themed welcome mat Raoul bought her when they moved in.

"Oh for fuck's sake," she says resignedly. "That crazy bitch."

Raoul comes up behind her, puts his chin on her shoulder, looks down, starts to laugh. "Good thing we rented a three-bedroom," he says.

# THE BLACK
## SEA

Today is my eighteenth birthday and the beginning of the rest of my life, which I have already ruined; but before I explain how I got there I will have to explain to you how I got here, which is, as you might expect, a little complicated. If you will excuse me for a moment, someone has just come into the bookstore—and no, we do not carry the latest craze in diet cookbooks, and thus she has departed again, leaving me in peace upon my stool at the cash register, where I shall detail the particulars that have led me to this moment of crisis.

In 1969, the Caltech physicist Murray Gell-Mann—theorist and namer of the quark, bird-watcher, and famed perfectionist—was awarded the Nobel Prize for his contributions to the field of particle physics. When he won he commented, referencing the ostensibly more modest remark by Isaac Newton that if he had seen farther than others it was because he stood on the shoulders of giants, that if he, Murray Gell-Mann, was better able to view the horizon, it was because he was surrounded by dwarfs. (Newton himself was referring rather unkindly to his detested rival Robert Hooke, who was in fact a person of uncommonly small stature, so it's possible Gell-Mann was making an elaborate joke.) While I am more inclined to a certain degree of humility, I find myself not unsympathetic to his position, as I myself am considered very precocious. For good reason. Some people might say insufferable, but I do not truck with fools. ("What you're doing is good," Murray Gell-Mann told his colleague Sheldon Glashow, "but people will be very stupid about it." Glashow went on to win the Nobel Prize himself.) Excuse me, if you will, someone has come in enquiring after *Lolita* for a summer high-school reading assignment—well, of course we have *Lolita*, although I don't really know if that's the sort of book high-school teachers are equipped to teach—no, it's not that it's dirty exactly, it's just—yes, I did see the movie, I saw them both—twelve dollars, thanks—cards, sure. Visa is fine. Okay, goodbye, enjoy your summer. There is nothing that makes me so glad to have escaped high school as teenagers.

My name is Atalanta, and I am going to be an astronomer, if one's inclination is toward the romantic and non-specific; more accurately, I am most likely going to be a theoretical particle physicist investigating the nature of dark matter, although I am aware that I am only seventeen and this may change slightly by the time I have obtained my doctorate and subsequent research fellowships, particularly considering the highly competitive nature of the field—which is not, of course, to say that I am not equipped to address its rigors, only that I prefer to do work that has not been done already, the better to make my mark upon the cosmos. I live in an apartment in a neighborhood of Brooklyn that has only recently become relatively wealthy, with my Aunt Beast, who is not my aunt, but my mother's childhood best friend; my uncle Raoul, who is not my uncle, but my aunt's childhood best friend; Henri, who presumably was once someone's best friend, but is now more notably my uncle's husband; and Dorian Gray, who is technically Raoul's cat but I am privately certain likes me best. Atalanta is a ridiculous name, which is why most people call me Tally, including Aunt Beast, who picked it. My situation would be confusing to the average person, but this is New York, where unorthodox familial arrangements are par for the course. In my graduating class there was a girl who was the literal bastard child of a literal Luxembourgian duke; a boy whose father was a movie director so famous the entire family traveled with a bodyguard; a lesser Culkin; and a girl whose mother had made her fortune as a cocaine dealer before successfully transitioning to a career as a full-time socialite and home decorator; and I didn't even go to private school. My household of two gay not-dads and sometimes-gay not-mom doesn't even rate a raised eyebrow.

My biological mother ran off right after I was born, which is unfortunate, but I've had some time to accustom myself to her untimely departure. In fact, she ran off before I was born, and then ran back again briefly to deliver me to the household I now inhabit, and then ran off again, but as I was too small for these technicalities to have any effect on me at the time, for all intents and purposes it is easiest to say simply that she ran away. I have gathered she was something of a flibbertigibbet and a woman of ill repute, although Aunt Beast is not so unkind as to say so outright. I can only imagine she was dreadfully irresponsible on top of her flightiness, as I think it extremely poor form to cast off the fruit of one's womb as though it is little more than a bundle of dirty laundry. No doubt this abandonment has left me with lingering psychological issues, but I prefer to eschew the realm of the emotional for that of the empirical. My mother left me on Aunt Beast's doorstep, which is a good origin story, as far as they go. Aunt Beast is not a beast at all, but she did read me *A Wrinkle in Time* at an impressionable age, and I have since refused to call her anything else, even though I am now a few hours short of eighteen and a fine scientist and high-school graduate who has secured a full scholarship to an excellent university you have certainly heard of in order to absorb the finer points of astrophysics.

I do not technically need my job; my grandfather, in addition to being quite famous, was also quite rich, and if I had wanted to, I could have got into his considerable estate, which slumbers quietly in a trust, increasing itself exponentially every year. But Aunt Beast is adamant about not touching any of his money, and we live off the now-tidy sums she makes selling her paintings to museums and ancient and embittered Upper East Siders fossilized in their own wealth. Raoul teaches English to young hooligans, and Henri, who was once a tremendously good dancer, and a principal in one of the best companies in New York, retired over a decade ago, his body shot and his knees ground to dust, and became a massage therapist. I am terrified of my grandfather's money and would prefer not to touch it at all. New York does not teach one to think highly of the wealthy, a class of persons so inept they are incapable of even the most basic of tasks, including cleaning their own homes, doing their own laundry, raising their own children, and riding the subway. Money cannot buy me much of anything that interests me other than a very fine education, which I have already managed for myself, and an orbiting telescope of my very own; but even my grandfather's money is not quite enough to construct a personal satellite or particle accelerator, and so I see no use for it.

I am told my mother was a great beauty. The only evidence I have of this fact is an old Polaroid of Aunt Beast and my mother when they were teenagers, taken in the garden of my grandmother's old house in the city where they'd grown up, that Aunt Beast had framed and hung over the couch in our living room. It's summer; you can tell because of the backdrop of swimming-pool-blue sky and jumble of wildflowers. My mother is laughing, her chin tilted up; her sharp cheekbones cut the light and send clear-edged panes of shadow across her face. Her skin is a few shades darker than mine and her hair, straight as my own, is bleached white where mine falls down my back in a waterfall of coal. She is indeed beautiful by any objective measure, not that it has done any of us any good. Aunt Beast is in her shadow, dressed in the same black clothes she still wears, her habitual sullenness battling a reluctant smile. You can't quite make out the color of my mother's eyes but Aunt Beast says they were brown, in contrast to the blue of my own, which I have apparently inherited from my grandfather. My father is a mystery, not in the sense that he is mysterious, but in the sense that I have no idea who he is at all. From what I have heard of my mother, it is not unlikely that she had no idea herself.

I myself am not a great beauty, so it is lucky I am preternaturally clever, else I would have no assets whatsoever to recommend me. My person is overly bony; I have the ungainly locomotion of a giraffe; and while my face is not unattractive, it is certainly not the sort of countenance that causes strangers to remark on its loveliness. My nose is somewhat beaklike. My skin, at least, is quite smooth and a pleasing shade of brown, but not even a white person ever got cast as the lead of a romantic comedy because they had nice skin; additionally, white people are not subject to the regular and displeasing lines of enquiry my skin occasions ("What are you? No, I mean where are you from? No, I mean where are you *really* from? No, I mean where are your *parents* from?"), which has nothing to do, obviously, with my attractiveness, and everything to do with the troglodytic nature of my interrogators, but I find these interviews inconvenient nonetheless. My eyes are striking, but they are not enough to distinguish me. The apparatus of popular culture would have one believe that one's success with the opposite sex is irreparably hampered by a disinterest in, and lack of, conventional attractiveness, but

I am pleased to report that this is not always the case. In fact, I have had sex twice: the first time, when I was fifteen, at science camp, with one of the graduate-student counselors. It was not a memorable experience. The second: after prom, my junior year, with a date Aunt Beast had dug up for me somewhere (double-date with Shane; awkward, beery-breathed post-dance groping on the couch of Shane's date's absent parents; actual moment of entry so hasty and uninspired I was uncertain for several moments as to whether I was having sex at all; the next day, he sent me *flowers* at *school*, which I threw away immediately) and whom I elected not to contact subsequent to this occasion. I had thought, in the spirit of scientific enquiry, that I would repeat the experiment, in order to ascertain whether my own results would more closely match the ecstatic testimony of novelists and poets upon a second trial, but I am sorry to report they did not.

And as for Shane, I don't know if there is any point in telling you about him, since I don't know if I will ever—oh, I am being melodramatic, and also getting ahead of myself. I have known Shane for so long that his name is as much a part of me as my own. As a small child, I'd opened the door to our apartment, alarmed by the thumping and cursing of the movers, and caught a brief, tantalizing glimpse of a pig-tailed, overalled urchin of about my age being towed along behind a set of parents entreating the movers to handle their belongings with something resembling care.

"They have a girl in there," I announced to Henri, "I think I should be friends with her," and so Henri baked cookies and sent me out to bear them to our new neighbors. Shane answered the door and we ate all the cookies on the spot, and Shane and I have been best friends ever since. I was there when he told his mom he was a boy, and she cried and then said, "Well, it's not like you ever wore dresses anyway, and you know your father and I will always love you"; I was there when Shane grew boobs, and assisted him in assessing the most efficient and low-cost mechanism for concealing them; I was there the first day of our freshman year, when Aaron Liechty, senior, hulking sociopath, and national fencing star (this is New York; only the automotive high school, last refuge of miscreants, has a football team), cornered the both of us in the hallway and sneered, "I don't know what to call you, a little faggot or a little bitch," and Shane said, cool as you please, "You can call me sir," and punched Aaron Liechty square in his freckle-smattered nose. Blood geysered forth, brighter even than the flaming red of Aaron Liechty's hair, Aaron reeled away moaning, and from that point onward, Shane was a high-school legend and folk hero. Only I knew the truth: that Shane had never hit anyone before in his life, that breaking Aaron Liechty's nose was a stroke of sheer luck, and that afterward he had dragged me into the girls' bathroom, where we'd locked ourselves in a stall and he'd cried into my shirt for ten minutes. Excuse me—yes, it's very cool in here, thank you—yes, awfully hot for this time of year—no, I only read the first one and thought it was sort of badly done—yes, children seem very excited about them—no, I don't have a problem with *wizards*, I just prefer *science* fiction, and I think the rules of magic in her worldbuilding are a little arbitrary, it's clear she's just making things up as she goes along, and why is it always a *boy* wizard, anyway, it's clear the little girl is significantly more intelligent, why is he the one who gets to be special—well, okay, there's a Barnes and Noble in Manhattan, I'm sure no one will argue with you there.

Shane and I had not excelled in high school so much as we had endured it; he, like me, is a genius, but his gifts lean in the direction of being able to play guitar riffs back perfectly after hearing them only once, unknotting the tangle of chords and distortion and knitting the resultant bits back together again in flawless replicas of whatever he just listened to—and, of course, of writing his own songs, a skill that seems as elusive and astonishing to me as the ability to, say, walk cross-country on stilts. I have always been a lot smarter than people around me are comfortable with, and unskilled at concealing it, and had an unfortunate penchant for reading science-fiction novels in public long after the point where such a deeply identifying quirk was forgivable. My peers were disinterested in the finer points of celestial mechanics and I, once I thought about it at any length, was disinterested in my peers. Only Shane—and thank god I'd had him, boon companion, co-conspirator, confidant, and literally my only friend—would let me ramble on ad nauseam about Messier objects and telescope apertures, and only he never made me feel odd or untoward for my outsize and grandiose ambitions, my unwavering passion for Robert Silverberg, and my penchant for quoting particle physicists in moments of great strife or transcendent happiness. I had the sense sometimes that even my teachers were frightened of me, or at the very least had no idea what to do with me. And really I think it was only Shane's friendship that insulated me from any more terrible and pervasive horrors than being the person no one wanted to sit next to in AP Calculus; people were afraid of me, but they all liked Shane, and I suppose imagined that even such an easily ostracized specimen of humanity as myself must have had some redeeming qualities if he was willing to put up with my company. People gave me a wide berth, but they left me alone.

I do not blame Aunt Beast or Raoul for failing to educate me in the delicate task of disguising myself enough to make other people understand how to talk to me; Aunt Beast barely graduated high school, and although I have never asked Raoul about it I do not imagine growing up a poet and homosexual is a particularly thrilling experience for teens of any era or clime. I am an only child—so far as I know, anyway—and never had friends my own age, save Shane, even as a very small child, instead spending my evenings in the company of Aunt Beast, Raoul, and Henri's witty, funny, brilliant friends, who treated me as though I were a person in my own right with opinions of interest. Which, in fact, I was. Aunt Beast and Raoul had raised me with a kind of fearless self-possession that, I soon realized, was not considered seemly in a girl, and I had never been able to help being smarter than the vast majority of the persons who surrounded me. The prospect of college was the only thing, sometimes, that got me through the sheer unending drudgery of adolescence.

Shane has no plans of going to college, preferring to eschew the hallowed halls of higher education for the chance to make a career as a rock musician, and if anyone I know is capable of this feat it is indeed he. Shane is forever trying to get me to listen to better music. He was, anyway, before—oh, *god*. I am not accustomed to this sort of—

anyway. I really *have* ruined everything—but I can't—oh, *god*. He has a vast and catholic palate, his tastes ranging from obscure Nigerian jazz to obsessively collected seven-inches from long-forgotten eighties punk bands to sleepy, potheady dub. He likes a lot of the same old stuff that Aunt Beast and Raoul listen to, distortion-heavy rock music with guitar riffs like a wash of noise; he likes hip-hop; he likes, although he would never admit to it in public, hair metal, a clandestine passion he also shares with Raoul, to the extent that they sometimes swap records with as much furtive-ness and stealth as if they are conducting a drug deal. His record collection takes up an entire wall of his room and is sorted alphabetically and by genre, and if you let him he will discourse extensively about stereo equipment with the obsessive focus of a birder ticking off the legion of rare species he had spotted. I am prone to frequent bouts of insomnia, and sometimes I will call him late at night and ask him about different kinds of speakers, and drift off to sleep at last with the murmur of his voice in my ear. I used to do that, anyway.

This benign state of affairs continued, to the great sat-isfaction of all parties, until quite recently, when Shane's presence began without much warning to have a decidedly untoward effect upon me—where last summer I would have thought nothing of lounging about in my underwear, dozing in his bed in the hazy June heat and watching him play Super Mario Brothers on his old Nintendo, or practice the guitar, brows knitted together in concentration, thick dark hair falling over his high forehead, now the elegant line of his neck and the soft slope of his shoulders, his back rounded—his mother is forever trying to get him to sit up straight—the gentle curve of his belly, summoned forth in me a terrible and all-pervasive nervousness that sent me pacing around his room until he snapped, with irritation, that I should calm down or leave. I could no longer look at the gentle curve of his mouth without imagining it on my own, no longer punch him in the shoulder without wishing he would retaliate in turn by pinning me to the ground and ravishing me, no longer grab carelessly at his hand without willing the electricity I now felt at his touch to spark an answering flare of light. All of this might have been bearable had my passions been gentle, but they were most emphatically no such thing; the dissatisfaction of my prior forays into the field notwithstanding, sex with my best friend now seemed the only possible resolution to the terrible forces that raged within me, and I was utterly unable to think about anything else—electrons, stars, planetary orbits, the grocery list—in his presence. Watching the dirty parts of movies with him was excruciating; I could be unexpectedly rendered speechless if the two of us wandered past a couple making out in the park; when he hugged me goodbye, careless and oblivious, I had to will myself not to lick his skin. His long, lovely hands, bitten-nailed, working the Nintendo controller's joystick or moving up and down the neck of the guitar, would come to my mind unbidden later, in the humming air-conditioned dark of my own room. I would think of those hands actively engaged in doing deeply unchaste things to my person, and bring myself nightly to new heights of lust before becoming overcome with terror that he could somehow see through walls and blankets and the thick pane of my skull to observe the pornographic spectacle of my thoughts, and then I would desperately attempt to turn my imagination to other, less salacious imagery. I told myself at first that I was coming down with something, that I had been watching too much television and my formidable mind was going soft as a result, or that I had been reading too much Shakespeare and too little Wheeler (although Wheeler himself is prone to exuberantly poetic fits of exegesis and is perhaps not the best party to consult when besieged by unwanted passions), but finally even I had to admit that my feelings for my best friend in all the world had abruptly leapt the track from the blissfully platonic to the mundanely carnal. Oh, hold on. Can I help you find anything? The red book that was on the third shelf down? Or the fourth one? No, I don't know what book that would—well, how long ago? A *month*? I really couldn't tell you—oh, you mean that stupid fake economist who writes for the *Times*—well, you can't argue that his data is questionable—yes, it's over there. Fourteen ninety-nine. Do you need a bag? No? Okay, have a nice day.

Shane had girlfriends, in high school—not many, and none serious, and none remotely threatening to the near-umbilical bond that united us, like those jars of twinned fetuses joined at hip or shoulder and bobbing in a formaldehyde brine that you saw in old anatomical books. I'd never been jealous because none of them ever really registered, a short lineup of pretty, bland-faced girls with shiny hair who were not as smart as I was, did not know every sentence Shane would speak before it left his mouth, and were not invited to the womblike environs of our respective apartments, where we regularly holed up on his or my couch watching old slasher movies and eating microwave popcorn by the bagful, Shane occasionally and unsuccessfully trying to beguile me into smoking pot out of a soda can with a hole punched in its side.

And every morning thus far, since we graduated (me with a 4.0, Shane by the skin of his teeth) and launched ourselves into the last summer before the rest of our lives begin, I have told myself upon waking, firmly and with conviction, that I would spare myself the torture and stay home, go into work on my days off and dust the bookshelves, insist Raoul accompany me to a museum, take up oil painting—anything but open the door of my apartment and walk, with bated breath, down the hall to his. Every afternoon I abandoned my resolve and capered, aquiver with frantic anticipation, to his door, imagining that that day would be the day he would at last fling it open, take me in his arms, and kiss me until both our knees buckled; every day, instead, I curled up in a state of frenzied anguish in his bed while he, oblivious, lit another joint. As June wore on I stayed over later and later, hoping against hope that my patient, enduring presence in his house would suddenly evoke in him the same terrible passions that had taken hold of me and he would be seized by the overwhelming urge, as I was, to bring our friendship out of the phenomenological world and into the sublime; but the forceful (and admittedly silent) messages I beamed at him continuously went entirely unheeded—and some part of me, the last bit of my brain still operating under the auspices of reason, was relieved. Because, of course, if Shane and I did actually consummate this entirely monopolar passion, we would no longer be best friends; we would be something else, and I was—I am, clearly, but again I am getting ahead of myself—entirely unprepared to navigate whatever it was we would become. Will become. May not become, now. When not distracted by lust, I existed in a more or less constant state of seething rage—I was furious with him for making me feel something that was outside of my control and even more furious with him for not, at the very least, reciprocating it; I was furious with myself for having feelings; and I was furious with biology in general, for wiring me so faultily— adolescence had been bad enough, without its sending a wrecking ball careening through the perfectly satisfying equilibrium I had enjoyed up until the moment oxytocin went riotous in my brain, turned me into a dithering idiot, and ruined the last summer I would have with my favorite person in all the world. (*And yet*, singsonged that hormone-maddened frontal lobe, *what if he feels the same way too; you could spend the whole summer kissing, just think.* He didn't feel the same way, obviously, or we would have been kissing already, but for the first time in my life, reason could not vanquish my feelings, delusional as they were.)

This dreadful torment continued until a fateful after-noon a week ago. "I got something you have to hear," he said—me, freshly showered, hair brushed, even a dab of Aunt Beast's vanilla oil at my wrists and throat, as close to pretty as I could make myself; him, stoned and oblivious ("Something smells like cookies," he'd said, confused, when he hugged me hello)—both of us sprawled on his floor, gaz-ing vacantly at the ceiling (his stupor drug-induced, mine a paralysis of lust). He sat up suddenly, as if abruptly re-membering something important, and fiddled with a pile of cassettes next to his record player. (*Turntable*, he always corrected me.) "Unbelievable," he said, "this album is un-believable. I finally tracked it down. Hold on." He selected the cassette he'd been looking for, extracted it reverently from its plastic case, and inserted it gently in the tape deck. Soft click of the play button, a rustling hiss of static, and then, low and sweet, a honeyed drift of chords on an acoustic guitar, and a man began to sing. The sound quality was terrible but the voice that came out of Shane's speakers was like something out of another world, deep and pain-soaked and full of yearning, and despite the recording I could tell that what I was listening to was something extraordinary. We listened to the entire tape without speaking: one bittersweet, yearning song fading into another, weaving together a rich and gorgeous and strange tapestry that carried me out of my body and its perilous wants into some other, more transcendent place of loss and hope and waiting. At last the final, aching chord faded and I sat in stunned silence, slowly coming back to my body, the messy familiarity of Shane's room, the feel of cool air moving across my human skin. My heart was pounding as hard as if I'd just gone running with Aunt Beast. "Holy shit," I said.

"Jack Blake," Shane said reverently. "He was the real deal."